# "ALL OF THESE MEN MUST DIE!"

*Filled with the seething power of three Kushite deities of war, I strolled toward the ship of my enemies. My senses were so acute, so heightened by the forces of the Neteru raging within me, that those I passed seemed to move slowly, trapped by limitations of time that no longer confined me.*

*I climbed the plank and stepped aboard, where two hapless warriors attempted to bar my way, demanding identification and a statement of my business. Casting off my robe, I seized two darts and flicked them, then walked on as the men writhed upon the deck, clawing at the missiles buried in their throats.*

*Looking across the ship, I spied Kho-An-Sa. With his customary pompous air, he barked at his sailors as they prepared to get underway. Suddenly shouts went up as the dying men were discovered, then Kho-An-Sa turned my way. At first a look of surprise came over him, followed by that dreaded smile that I despised so much.*

For Robert Compton Adé:

Quashie!

Rod.

5/6/05

SHADES OF MEMNON II

## Memnonian Man

I'm searching high and low
Searching for myself
I've looked around the world
For the legends left
This desert is so cold
On a moonless night
I'll shift the sands of time
Til' the broad daylight
They say your history
Is your dignity
Each one wants one
To keep the children free
Memnonian Man
From the Original Land
Son of the Sun
Memnonian Man
- *Brother G*

# SHADES OF MEMNON
## BOOK TWO
### "RA FORCE RISING"

## BROTHER G

## SHADES OF MEMNON II

# SHADES OF MEMNON II

# SHADES OF MEMNON
THE AFRICAN HERO OF THE TROJAN WAR AND THE KEYS TO ANCIENT WORLD CIVILIZATION
## BOOK TWO
# "RA FORCE RISING"

Copyright © 2001 by Gregory L. Walker (Brother G)

Published by Seker Nefer Press, a division of  Seker Nefer Group. www.memnonlegend.com.

First Printing 2000.

This novel is a work of historical fantasy fiction based
on the legends and myths of the great African hero Memnon.

Book cover artist credit: Derrell Spicey
Book cover design: Courtney Jolliff / Direct Effect and the Ancestors
Bang Masta D and Brother G photo credit: DaShan Thomas/Crimson Studios
Library of Congress Cataloging-in-Publication Data:
Walker, Gregory Lyle
Shades Of Memnon: The African Hero Of The Trojan
War And The Keys To Ancient World Civilization
ISBN 0-9662374-2-0 (Original 2000 Softcover Edition)
1, Mythology. 2, Historical Fantasy Fiction.
3, African Studies. 4, Martial Arts. 5, Spirituality.
I Title
Library of Congress Catalog Card Number: 00-192740

# BANG MASTA D AND BROTHER G

Brother G (Gregory L. Walker) is a Chicago based journalist, poet, historian and author. While working part-time for the Associated Press, Brother G spent 10 years conducting research for the African Legends genre, writing "Shades Of Memnon," and developing contacts in archeology, anthropology and linguistics worldwide. Dedicated to making Ancient History accessible to all, Brother G teamed with hiphop genius Bang Masta D, who wrote, produced and performs the Shades of Memnon hip hop soundtrack.

*Dark like the shade of no other*
*Dark like the shade of my Pa*
*and my mother*
*Dark like the shade of my sister*
*and my brother*
*Dark like the shade of his color*
*The shade of Memnon . . .*

## SHADES OF MEMNON II

### Acknowledgments:

I would like to thank my ancestor, Her Ab Mung Sa, for his and the rest of the Shepsu's continued support.

Thanks also to my dear one Montreece Webber, who maintains the website and laid out this book. Thanks to Derrell Spicey who threw down on the cover art once more, Donino Hill who rocked the interior art again and Bang Masta D who keeps laying down Memnonian lyrics. Other family and friends: Thank you greatly. We shall rule the world soon!

*Three the Memnonian way:  Derrell Spicey, Bang Masta D and Brother G*

SHADES OF MEMNON II

# INTRODUCTION

In Shades Of Memnon Book I you witnessed the re-introduction of the Memnon tradition, once the world's most <u>widely known heroic lore.</u> This is a bold statement and since the publication of the first book I have been challenged about the standing of Memnon as a world figure in ancient history.

I introduced the concept of "Epicology," the study of an epic tradition through historical scholarship and mythography, in an effort to bolster my position that Memnon is the foremost heroic figure in world history. I consider it a shame that this legendary figure has not been included in popular culture and an even bigger shame that some people have exhibited suspicious disbelief simply because they have never heard of Memnon. So in this second book I have decided to take the Epicological study further by including an astonishing scholarly essay by my mentor Dr. Clyde Ahmed Winters.

Dr. Winters is an anthropological linguist, a true genius of our times who needs to be more widely known. He has taught Afrocentric studies and comparative linguistics on both the secondary and college level. As the author of over 110 articles on Afro-Asian Studies, Dr. Winters is presently working on the reconstruction of Paleo-African, the Proto-language of African languages. He helped start, along with the renowned Ivan Van Sertima, the influential book series "The Journal of African Civilizations."

Dr. Winters began publishing internationally due to the constricting "Egypt centered" nature of African centered scholarship in America. He acknowledges the greatness of ancient Kamit and the need for Kamitic studies, but having traced world civilization through his "Proto-Saharan thesis" sees an equal need for the study of these civilizations also.

The "Proto-Saharan thesis" states that there were tremendous African civilizations in the Sahara before it dried up. They left due to desertification, settling in the Americas, Europe and Asia. This is where the Memnon tradition comes in. Memnon was said to be affiliated with Ethiopians where the sun sets, where the sun rises and also along the Nile Valley by the ancient writers. I found Dr. Winters "Proto-Saharan thesis" to be the key to unlocking the mystery of these statements about Memnon, revealing him to be an Epicological figure who actually represents these Proto-Saharan people. The great admiration given to

Memnon represents the standing of those the Greeks called "Blameless Ethiopians"- the mighty Kushites originally from the African Sahara. The Greeks say that all civilization came from them and ancient writings from India say they ruled the world for thousands of years. But these are legends, just one half of the Epicological process. The other half consists of hard archeology, anthropology and linguistics. This I leave to Dr. Clyde Ahmed Winters in his eye opening essay "Memnonia." Enjoy.
**Brother G- 2000**

SHADES OF MEMNON II

# SHADES OF MEMNON II

# BOOK II
## CONTENTS

SHADES OF MEMNON II

## "MEMNONIA" BY DERRELL SPICEY
*Depicting Memnon in Ancient Greece, Egypt, Iran, and Mexico*

# MEMNONIA
## by Clyde A. Winters

In <u>Shades of Memnon</u> you will be reading about the ancient Xi or Kushite people of ancient times. These Blacks who founded the historic civilizations in Mesopotamia, China and the Americas came from the Proto-Sahara [1]. Six thousand years ago in the highlands of the Sahara these people developed a unique culture, which included writing, black-and-red ware and a highly developed boat technology. At this time numerous waterways stretched up into the Saharan highlands. Many of these waterways emptied into the Mediterranean and Indian Ocean [2].

Africans created the most ancient civilizations of the world. These early civilizations were usually called Kushite cultures. The Black/Africoid people of these cultures lived in an area extending from Nubia in the south to Persia (Iran) in the North. The Kushites were the first people to civilize Arabia before Muhammad; Canaan before the Jews/Hebrews; Mesopotamia before Assyrians; and Elam and India before the Indo-European speaking Aryans.

In ancient times the Sudan was called Kush, and modern Ethiopia Punt, much of Mesopotamia and the Indus Valley was called *Puntiya* and *Kushiya*. We thusly had a Kush in Africa, and a Kush in Asia.

The GRECO-ROMAN WRITERS made it clear that the Kushites lived in the Sudan and Asia. Homer alluded to the two Kushite empires, when he wrote: "A race divided, whom the sloping rays; the rising and the setting sun surveys". Herodotus claimed that he derived this information from the Egyptians.

Archaeologists call the first Kushite people the A-Group. The area where the A-Group originally came from was called *Qes, Qushana*. The Egyptian term for these people was *K'sh,* and *K'shi*. The Hebrews called them Kush. In the cuneiform inscriptions the Sudanese were called Kushiya. In the Abyssinian Ethiopic inscriptions of King Aezana, the Kushites were called *Kashi* or *Kasu*.

A major ethnic group among the Kushites was the Manding and Dravidian-speaking people. The Manding call themselves *Si* people. They were the founders of the Xia civilization in China where they were called *Xi* (Shi); and in Olmec civilization of Mexico, who also called themselves *Xi* (Shi).

# SHADES OF MEMNON II

In Sumerian inscriptions the Kushites were called *Meluha=Kasi* (Kush). This term referred to the Africans in the area of Nubia and northeast Africa.

The ancestors of the Kushites lived in the Sahara, and are therefore called Proto-Saharans[3]. The Proto-Saharans originated in the Mountains of the Moon area. From here they migrated through Nubia and the Sudan to settle in the Highland areas. At this time the Sahara was much wetter. This period of African history is called the Aqualithic.

The Kushites were known in antiquity as great seamen. They used their sewn boats to settle West Africa, North Africa, Europe and Asia. The French linguist Lacouperie wrote, "Their activity in trade, their boldness in seafaring expeditions and the extensive spread of civilization, which followed their efforts, have won them a lasting fame." According to the Indian book **Matsya**, the world belonged to the Kushites for 7,000 years.

The Greek historian Herodotus said the Ethiopians were "the tallest most beautiful and long-lived of the human races". And the Greek poet Homer described them as "the most just of men; the favorites of the gods."

The Roman author, Diodorus claimed that Egyptian civilization came from Nubia, the modern name for the country called Kush. The Egyptians recognized their origins in the interior of Kush, by erecting altars to Kush in Memphis, Thebes and Meroe under the name of "Khons", the god of the sky to the Ethiopians; Hercules to the Egyptians.

### *Ta-Seti*

The Meroitic Sudan influenced much of Egypt's ancient history. According to Egyptian documents the Meroitic Sudan or Kush was a prosperous country which traded with Egypt as early as 4,000 BC. From this area the Egyptians learned the twelve hieroglyphs that were used to make their alphabet. Here we also find the animals and plants represented in the hieroglyphs.

The first empire of Nubia was Nwb. By 3300 BC, the Nubians/ Kushites had established the first monarchy in human history. Artifacts found in the Qustul tombs near the Egyptian-Sudanese border show various symbols of Nubian royalty later used by the Egyptians.

On a stone incense burner from Qustul, we find a palace facade, a crowned king sitting on a throne in a boat, a royal standard stood before the King and hovering above him, the falcon god Horus. The rulers of Upper Egypt wore the crown on this King. Many scholars believe that this ancient civilization of Nubia was called *Ta-Seti*. The people were called *"Steu"* bowmen.

The name Ta-Seti is engraved on the plaque of Hor Aha, from Abydos in Egypt, and the Gebel Sheikh Suleiman inscriptions and sealing from Nubia.

These inscriptions in Ta-Seti hieroglyphs from Qustul are important because they show that 5300 years ago, 200 years before the rise of Egypt that the first monarchy on earth appeared in Nubia, just as the Egyptians, Greeks and Romans had claimed. The Ta-Seti had the same funeral customs, pottery, musical instruments and related artifacts. The major pottery used by these people was the Red and Black ware, which the Kushites later took with them to Asia.

The A-group culture founded civilization in Nubia. We know about the A-Group based on their pottery styles. The early A-Group (IA) is typified by black topped ware (pottery). The Middle A-Group (IB) is characterized by wavy handled jars. The creators of the Qustul tombs represent Late A-Group remains.

The Qustul incense burner indicates kingship, wealth and royalty in Nubia. The A-Group Cemetery L had tombs that equaled or exceeded Egyptian tombs of the First Dynasty of Egypt. The A-Group cemeteries extend from Kubaniyya in the North, to Malik en-Nasir in the Second Cataract to the South.

There is considerable evidence of royalty among the A-Group. The links between Egyptian government and A-Group civilization include l) the pharaoh figure, 2) Horus (the Falcon God), 3) the palace facade, and 4) the sacred bark (boat).

The glyphic evidence of A-Group government includes the Faras seal, the Sarras West seal and the Siali sealing. The Faras seal indicates royalty due to its depiction of the palace facade and sacrifice. The Sarras West seal shows a bark (boat), a man holding a staff or harpoon near the stern, and stepped throne. The Siali sealing has an archaic falcon perched on a palace facade, Horus the falcon seats atop a "serekh", while a man setting on a chair/throne, hand upraised over an archaic bow with rectangular figure below it and a bovine behind the man equal the name Ta-Seti (i.e., the bovine and bow standard).

SHADES OF MEMNON II

## *Two Kushites*

The Greco-Roman writers made it clear that there were two Kushite Empires one in Asia and the other group in the area we call the Sudan, Nubia, and parts of southern Egypt. The Greek writer Homer alluded to the two Kushite empires, when he wrote, "a race divided, whom the sloping rays; the rising and the setting sun surveys". The Greek traveler/historian Herodotus claimed that he derived this information from the Egyptians.

The Asian Proto-Saharans were also called Kushites or Ethiopians. The term Ethiopian comes from two Greek terms: Ethios 'burnt' and ops 'face', as a result Ethiopian means the 'burnt faces'. Herodotus and Homer, described these Ethiopians as "the most just of men; the favorites of the gods". The classical literature makes it clear that the region from Egypt to India was called by the name Ethiopia.

For example, the Elamites called themselves *KHATAM*, and their capital Susa: *KUSSI*. In addition, the Kassites, who occupied the central part of the Zagros Mountains were called *KASHSHU*. The Kushana, who help found the Meroitic civilization, formerly occupied Chinese Turkistan (Xinjiang) and the Gansu province of China. The Kushites in Asia, as in Africa were known for their skill as Bowmen. *Steu* was the name of the people of Ta-Seti.

The decipherer of the cuneiform writing of Mesopotamia, Rawlinson, said Puntites and Kushites were established in Asia. He found mention of *Kushiya* and *Puntiya* in the inscriptions of Darius. He also made it clear that the name Kush was also applied to southern Persia, India, Elam, Arabia, and Colchis (a part of southern Russia/Turkistan) in ancient times.

The Armenians made it clear that the ancients called Persia, Media, Elam, Aria, and the entire area between the Tigris and Indus rivers Kush. Bardesones, writing in his <u>Book of the Laws of Countries,</u> in the 2nd Century said that the "Bactrians who we called *Qushani* (or *Kushans*)". The Armenians, called the earlier Parthian: *Kushan* and acknowledged their connection with them. Homer, Herodotus, and the Roman scholar Strabo called Southern Persia *AETHIOPIA*. The Greeks and Romans called the country east of Kerma: Kusan.

From Iran the Kushites used the natural entry point into China along the path running from the Zagros to the Altai Mountains, and the Dzunganian gate. There is archaeological evidence indicating that farming communities village sites were established along this path of similar origin, which date back to 3500 BC. The archaeological data indicate that this agricultural economy spread from west to east.

The cultures of West Asia cannot be the oldest cultures because geologically speaking Mesopotamia is a very young formation. This area is built up by the deposits of the Tigris and the Euphrates which bring rich soil to the surrounding area when the rivers flood each year.

### Spread of Proto-Saharans into Arabia

The founders of the early civilizations of West Asia came from the Sahara. The first groups to separate from the Proto-Saharan group were the Ancient Egyptians, Cushitic-speakers and the Puntites, the so-called Semitic speakers. The Egyptians settled in Nubia, the Cushites and Semites migrated into the eastern desert regions bordering on the Red Sea. Other Cushitic elements migrated into Arabia and down into East Africa.

### Cushitic Speakers

The Cushitic speakers, now located mainly in East Africa formerly lived in Arabia and Mesopotamia. The Cushitic speakers were both herders and farmers. The Cushitic people are believed to have cultivated ensete since around 6000 BC. The Cushitic speakers and Puntite (Semitic) speaking folk were very close. The Puntite word for plow/ plough itself comes from the Cushitic speakers.

### Puntite Speakers

The Puntites main homeland was the Horn of Africa, which was called Punt in ancient times. The people of Punt were great seafarers. In the Sumerian text they were called *Meluhhaites* (Me-luk-haites). Puntite merchants sold carnelian, lapis lazuli, cattle, reeds and two types of wood. The majority of the Meluhhaites remained nomadic herders like the Martu people.

The Puntites lived in the Eastern Desert of Egypt for many years and on the Horn of Africa. The earliest representatives of this group are depicted on the Ivory Label of King Den (Udimu) of the first Dynasty of Egypt.

During the Neolithic subpluvial the Red Sea area had more rainfall. This area was blanketed with vegetation, they grew ensete, barley and dates and grazed sheep, goats and cattle. The Puntites inhabited North-east Africa and Arabia.

Puntites colonized Arabia during the Neolithic subpluvial. At this time Arabia was a vast savanna with marshes and lakes. What is now known as the Rub al-Khali or Empty Quarter, today, an arid mountainous area was then well watered. In Arabia Puntite and Cushitic tribes hunted and fished. Around 3500 and 2500 BC a group of people entered Mesopotamia from Africa that spoke African and Semitic languages. These people called themselves "black-heads" from about 2000 BC to the end of Sumerian history. The African-speaking group founded the Sumer Civilization.

The Sumerians and Elamites came to Mesopotamia by boats first used in the Eastern Sahara and on the Red Sea. The Sumerians were in control of Mesopotamia for many years. Then around 2334 BC, a group of Puntite Speakers called Akkadians under Naram-Sin or Sargon of Agade took over Mesopotamia.

This unity of the Akkadian and Ethiopian languages is supported by the Akkadians and Sumerians who claim they came from the Egypto-Nubia and Punt (Ethiopia) to west Asia. Most modern scholars such as Joan Oates, in Babylon suggest that Magan (Egypto-Nubia) and "Meluhha" (Punt) were southeastern Arabia and the Makian coast to as far as the Indus Valley. But according to Samuel Noah Krammer, the leading expert on the Sumerians and Akkadians, from the time of Sargon the Great (2334 BC) down to the first millennium BC, "Magan" and "Meluhha" was Egypto-Nubia and Punt (Ethiopia) respectively. According to these records ships from "Meluhha" and "Magan" brought trade goods to Mesopotamia.

According to W.J. Perry, in "The Growth of Civilization", the myths, legends and traditions of the Sumerians pointed to Nubia as their ancient home. Sir Henry Rawlinson, who deciphered the cuneiform writing traced the Sumerians and Akkadians back to Nubia and Punt. Sir Rawlinson, called the ancient Mesopotamian "Kushites". It was the French Orientalist Julius Oppert, who named them Sumerians, in an attempt to make them separate from the Kushites, a Black race of Africa. But Rawlinson, in the " Journal of the Royal Asiatic, was correct in calling them Kushites. The title "King of Kish", was highly prized by subsequent Kings of Sumer as a claim of suzerainty over the whole country.

Dierelafoy, in "L'Acropole de Susa" wrote, "I shall attempt to show to what distant antiquity belongs the establishment of the Negritos upon the left bank of the Tigris and the elements constituting the Susian monarchy.

"...Towards 2300 BC the plains of the Tigris and Anzan Susinka were ruled by a dynasty of Negro Kings". Herodotus, who visited the area in the 5th century BC mentions the dark skin of this people who he called Ethiopians. Sir Harry Johnston noted that the Elamites "appear to have been Negroid people with kinky hair and to have transmitted this racial type to Jews and Syrians".

The Sumerians learned all their knowledge from the Anu. The Sumerians expanded the dykes to hold back the floods of the Euphrates and Tigris rivers, and dug canals and reservoirs to store water and carry to the plains. This led to grand harvest yielding 200 and 300 grains per plant, in an area today where the Turks make a pitiful existence.

Sumerians built cities of unbaked bricks. Many of these cities such as Ur, Erudu and Uruk (Erech), Nippur, Agade (A-gaa-dee) (Akkad) have been excavated. The excavations of Erech and Agade support the Biblical accounts and skeletal remains of the ancient inhabitants of Chaldaea, show that they were Blacks. The Blacks were short with thin lips and noses.

The Sumerians said they came by sea to Sumer-Akkad. Enki, who founded Eridu situated on the head of the Persian Gulf is said to have come by sea. The Sumerians spoke two different languages one was Semitic, it was used by the Semitic founders of Akkad; and the other language was Sumerian, like the Egyptians said they had come to Mesopotamia from "*Magan*" or Egypto-Nubia, and "*Meluhha*" or *Punt* (northeast Africa). These areas are mentioned as early as Sargon the Great and Gudea. Both countries are frequently in the Sumerian and Akkadian records.

Sargon the Great (2330) wrote that the boats of *Magan, Meluhha* and *Dilmun* were anchored in his capital of Agade. Gudea wrote that he obtained diorite for his statues from *Magan* and wood for the building of temples from both *Magan* and *Meluhha*. The Meluhhaites were called "the men of the black land" or "the black *Meluhhaites*". The *Meluhhaites* are said to have traded in carnelian, lapis lazuli, metals, stones and mineral.

Dilmun, which is believed to be the ancient Indus Valley civilization, was considered to the Paradise by the Sumerians. According to Sumerian traditions Enki, had come from Dilmun. It is interesting to

SHADES OF MEMNON II

note that Sumerian is closely related to the Dravidian language, which was spoken in the Indus Valley in ancient times.

## *Elam*

The most important Kushite colony in Iran was ancient Elam. The Elamites called their country *KHATAM or KHALTAM* (Ka-taam). The capital of Khaltam which we call Susa, was called *KHUZ* (Ka-u-uz) by the Aryans, NIME (Ni-may) by the people of Sumer, and KUSHSHI (Cush-she) by the Elamites. In the Akkadian inscriptions the Elamites were called *GIZ-BAM* (the land of the bow). The ancient Chinese or Bak tribesmen who dominate China today called the Elamites *KASHTI*. Moreover, in the Bible the Book of Jeremiah (xlxx, 35), we read "bow of Elam". It is interesting to note that both Khaltam-ti and Kashti as the name for Elam, agrees with Ta-Seti, the ancient name for Nubia/ the Meroitic Sudan.

There were already Anu people living in Iran by the time the Proto-Saharans or Kushites began to settle West Asia. By around 3200 BC, or thereabouts, Kushite adventurers in search of wealth and prestige began to settle Iran. They were able to take these lands over because the former rulers of the land the Anu had suffered a decline in their influence in this area after the great flood which seems to have wiped out much of their civilization after 4000 BC.

The Kushites in Elam early settled the Susiana plains of southwestern Iraq and Uruk in Mesopotamia. They already arrived with their own writing and boats. It would appear that a trading network already existed in this region because the Proto-Elamites abandoned the Proto-Saharan script and used the cuneiform script, which like the Egyptian Hieroglyphics, was probably invented by the Anu people. Since the merchants in much of West Asia were already using cuneiform, it was most logical for the Kushites to continue to use this writing so they could dominate trade in this region.

The ancients were sure the Kushites had founded the Elamite civilization. According to Strabo, the Roman geographer the first Elamite colony of Susa, was founded by Tithonus, a King of Kush, and Pa of Memnon. Strabo in Book 15,chapter 3,728, wrote, "In fact, it is claimed that Susa was founded by Tithonus Memnon's Pa, and that his citadel bore the name Memnonium. The Susians are also called Cissians; and Aeschylus, calls Memnon's mother Cissia. Some scholars believe that Amenhotep III, may be Memnon.

Although this is the opinion of some researchers the fact that the ancient writers made it clear that Memnon came from Kush, suggest that he was not an Egyptian. It is more likely that Memnon's ancestors had lived in the Proto-Sahara. This fact is supported by the Elamite language, which is clearly related to Dravidian and Manding.

A tomb of Memnon is reported to have been formerly established in Troad, an area near Troy in northwest Anatolia, according to Martin Bernal, in volume II of BLACK ATHENA. This tomb was associated with Memnoides or Black Birds. This identification of Memnon with Black birds suggests that he was a member of the bird clan, which also founded the Shang dynasty. It should also be remembered that it was from Elam that the Manding and Dravidian explorers of Central Asia and China first made their way into East Asia.

The Elamites established an extensive trade network, which linked them to the Sumerians in the West, and the Proto-Dravidian and Mande speaking groups of Central Asia and the Indus Valley. They also had trade relations with Africa.

Archaeologists use ceramics to identify cultures. The ceramic style from Susa and Godin, parallel the ceramic inventory at Warka IV and Nippur XV in Mesopotamia. Moreover a distinctive style of chlorite (steatite) bowl manufactured at Yahya, with identically carved motifs have been discovered at excavated sites of Sumerian Early Dynasty II/III city.

The French historian Lenormant, observed that when the archaeologist Dieulafoy excavated Susa, he found that "the master of the citadel, is black; it is thus very possible that Elam was the prerogative of a black dynasty and if one refers to the characteristics of the figures already found, of an Ethiopian dynasty".

The Elamites later conquered Sumer. They called this line of Kings the "Kings of Kish'. This term has affinity to the term Kush, which was given to the Kerma dynasty, founded by the C-Group people of Kush. It is interesting to note that the Elamite language is closely related to the African languages including Egyptian and the Dravidian languages of India.

### *Europe*

Blacks also settled ancient Europe. As a result, we find that Troy was a great center of African civilization. The Aryan speaking Greeks were called Ionians and Dorians.

SHADES OF MEMNON II

The pioneers of Grecian civilizations were the Blacks who came to Europe from Africa. They were called Eteocretans (Real Minoans). Pelasgians, Achaeans, Gadmeans, Lelges, and Carians/Garamantes [4]. The Eteocretans early settled Europe. These people originated in the highlands of modern-day Libya, called the Fezzan. The Eteocretans allegedly founded Troy, Mycenae, Tiryns, Thebes and Orchomenos [5].

The Greeks often referred to the ancient Black Greeks as Achaeans and Pelasgians. The Pelasgians founded the cities of Athens, Thrace and Attica[6]. The Achaeans founded the cities of Argolis, Pylos and Messenia. The fact that Blacks founded these cities and Athens, explains why many people claim that Socrates was Black.

In addition to finding evidence of these Blacks in the Classical literature, we also find art pieces depicting these Blacks, such as the "Stag Hunt", "Lion and Spearmen Hunt", and the "Siege Scene" on the Silver Rhyton Cup.

### *The Far East*

Blacks early occupied the Far East. These blacks include the Africoid, Negrito and Australoid types. Febre d'Olivet said that: "The Black Race was dominant upon the earth and held the scepter of science and power; it possessed all Africa and the greater part of Asia.... The Black race existed in all the pomp of social state. It covered entire Africa with powerful nations sprung from it; it possessed Arabia and had planted its colonies all over the Meridional coasts of Asia and very far into the interior".[7] Harry Johnson observed that:

"The Asiatic Negro speed—we can hardly explain how, unless the land connections of those days were more extended through Eastern Australia to Tasmania and from the Solomon Islands to New Caledonia and even to New Zealand to Fiji and Hawaii. The Negroid element in Burma and Annam is therefore easily to be explained by supposing that in ancient times Southern Asia had a Negro population ranging from the Persian Gulf to Indo-China and the Malay Archipelago".[8]

In the upcoming pages we will review the rise of the **li min** 'black headed people' who founded the Xia and Shang civilizations of China. The Africans or blacks that founded civilization in China were often called **li min** 'black headed people' by the Zhou dynasts. This term has affinity to the Sumero-Akkadian term **sag-gig-ga** 'black headed people'. These **li min** are associated with the Chinese cultural hero **Yao**.

In the <u>Annals of the Bamboo Books</u>, we learn that Yao devised a calendar to help regulate agrarian work through proper use of ritual and music and created a rudimentary government.[9]

The <u>Annals of the Bamboo Books</u>, makes it clear that Yao "he united and harmonized the myriad states [of his dominion], and the [li min] black headed people were reformed by his cordial agreement"[10].

We also read that Shun, the successor of Yao, distinguished by his reputation as an obedient devoted son, noted to: "Ki [that] the Black headed people are suffering the distress of hunger"[11]. To help relieve the people Shun gave his throne over to Yu, the founder of the Shang Dynasty. Yu, in the <u>Annals of the Bamboo Books</u>, is reported to have noted that "...when a sovereign gives response to the people, he is kind, and the Black headed people cherish him in their heart"[12].

We know very little about the sounds of ancient Chinese because Ancient Chinese was different from Old Chinese and Middle Chinese and the modern Chinese dialects. This results from the fact that diverse ethnic groups e.g., Xia and Shang founded the Chinese dynasties: **Dravidian and Manding speakers founded li (i.e., Black Shang)**[13]. Classical mongoloids, and Zhou were founded Shang-Yin by the contemporary Chinese[14]. This explains the difference in pronunciation for Ancient Chinese spoken by the Xia and Shang peoples and Old and Middle Chinese or a variant there of, which was probably spoken by the Zhou people.

This view is supported by the meaning of certain Shang characters, which compare favorably to the ancient Proto-Saharan script used by the Harappans in the Indus Valley and the Manding script used in the ancient Sahara and Crete[15]. Winters outlined the spread of the Proto-Saharan script to Harappa, and throughout Saharan Africa and Asia by the Dravidians and Manding [16].

The clan emblem for the ancient Manding was the first lizard/dragon. A dragon is nothing more than a giant lizard. This dragon motif was also found in Iran and Babylonian Assyrian civilization and the Anau civilization in Russia, which had similar painted pottery to the pottery styles of Henan (Xia).

The Xia **li min** built their settlements near rivers, lakes and streams. They are mentioned in the Oracle bone writing. The sacred tree of the Xia was the pine. The Xia naming system was the same as that used by the Shang.

SHADES OF MEMNON II

The founder of the Xia Dynasty was Yu. His Pa was Gun. Myths about Gun are found throughout southwest Shanxi. Yu's son founded the Pa culture. The Pa culture was a megalithic culture. Great Yu was the regulator of the waters and builder of canals. He invented wetfield agriculture. The decline of the Xia Empire led to the rise of Shang-Li (Black Shang) as the leading state in the confederation. The clan totem of Shang was the bird. In the Yen ben Zhi, it is written that a Black of Xia impregnated the mother of Xieh, the founder of Shang:

*"Three persons including Jian Di went to take a bath. They saw that a black bird dropped an egg. Jian Di took and devoured it, became impregnated and gave birth to Xieh. Xieh grew up, assisted Yu in his work to control the flood with success".*

There were two Shang empires. The first Shang Dynasty we will call the Shang-Li (Black Shang) it was ruled by the li-Qiang "Black Qiang". For the last 273 years of the Shang Empire the capital was situated at Anyang. The Shang Empire based at Anyang was founded by the Yin nationality. We call this empire Shang-Yin. Thus we have the Shang-Li Empire and the Shang-Yin Empire. The Yin were classical Mongoloid people related to the Thai and other small Mongoloid Austronesian speaking peoples situated in Southeast Asia.

According to the Yin ben Zhi , the founding ancestor of Shang was Xieh a member of the **Dzu** clan. His mother was Jian Ti.

The use of the "black bird", as the Pa of Xieh, relates to the "black bird" as a popular totem of black ethnic groups in China. This passage indicates that the founders of Shang were of mixed origin. The fact that the bird myths such as the one above are mainly centered on the east coast of China also suggest a black origin for the Shang since this area was the heartland of ancient China.

The eastern coast was a major area of Black habitation in ancient times. The **egret** bird is one of the popular symbols of the southern Chinese ethnic groups.[17]

This view is also supported by many archaeologists including K.C. Chang whose evidence indicates that the Neolithic Mongoloid population of north China resembled the Oceanic-Mongoloid type, but not the modern Mongoloid group we find living in China and much of southeast Asia today.

The name Shang refers to a town, which was the early capital of the Shang-Li Empire. According to the Shang poem Xuan Niao: "Heaven bade the dark bird/ to come down and bear Shang". The black bird who founded Shang was Di Ku or Emperor Ku (/Ju). In the oracle bone inscriptions Jian's husband was styled emperor Ku/Jun. Ku is also considered the Pa of the ten 'black birds' in the Mulberry Tree tradition. The references to "black birds" in the Chinese literature relate to the African origin of the Shang rulers. Many of the Shang spoke a Dravidian language.

The founders of Shang are often called **Yi**. Yi means "Great Bowman". The symbol for **Yi** in Chinese is translated **dagung.** This character has two parts **DA** "great" and **Jung** "a bow". The name **Yi**, and its similarity in the name **Kuishuang** (Kushana) and **Kushshu** highlight the archaeological evidence pointing to a western origin for many elements of Chinese civilization. The bird totem of Shang suggests that the Shang were predominately Dravidian speakers. (Winters 1983,1985c)

The Dravidian speakers originally came from Nubia. They were related to the C-Group people. The Shang culture was founded by the Kushites thus the name Yi "Great Bowmen", thus corresponding to **Steu**, the name for the founders of **Ta-Seti** the first monarchy in history.

The **Yi** seem to have lived in both north and south China. Fu Ssu-nien, in Yi Hsis Tunghsi Shuo, makes it clear that the Shang culture bearers remained allied to the rest of the Yi people who lived in southern China. The founders of Xia are usually referred to as **Yueh**, as opposed to **Yi**. It would appear that most of **Yi** were Dravidian speakers while the **Yueh** were Manding speakers. (Winters 1983,1985c)

The first Shang king was **Xuan Wang**, 'Black King' (**Xuan** means black). He was also called the **Xuan Di**, "Black Emperor". The founder of the Shang Dynasty was called Xuan Niao "Black Bird"; another Shang king was called Xuan Mu "Black Oxen".

The Shang kingdom flourished in the Yellow River basin in the Henan province after 1766 B.C. They cultivated rice, millet and wheat. They used many metals including copper and tin.

Each Shang town had its own king. The nobles ruling the Shang cities recognized the **Shang Di** (Emperor of Shang) as the head of the confederation because his powers were considered to be ordained by Heaven or God.

The Emperor of Shang was recognized as both a religious and military leader. As a high priest the Shang Di made sacrifice and paid homage to the gods for the nation and the people.

SHADES OF MEMNON II

Written history begins in China with the Shang Dynasty (c.1500-1027).The source of Shang history are references to this dynasty in ancient Chinese books, archaeology and the oracle bone inscriptions. After heating the bones of animals, the Shang priest would interpret the cracks and answer questions on various subjects relating to everyday Shang life. Other Shang records were kept on tablets of wood and bamboo.

The Shang are best known for their work in bronze. Shang artists made fine pottery and bronze vases of different shapes, often standing on three legs. The bronze works, along with works of art made from ivory and jade illustrate the high level of Shang technology.

The Shang-Li capital was established at Zhengzhou. There were 30 kings of Shang. Sixteen of the rulers were Shang-Li, the other fourteen that ruled at Anyang on the Yellow River. The Anyang Shang were classical Mongoloid not Yueh people.

Artifacts discovered at Panglongzheng, Hubei, far to the south in the Yantze River Valley, show bronze vessels 'culturally homogenous' to Zengzhou in every respect. At this time China's environment was different. China was much wetter and warmer several millennia before the Christian era. Many animals found only in Southeast Asia and southern China today lived in the north. In the Anyang area during the Shang period there were formerly two harvests of millet and rice. There were also elephants and rhinoceros in this area according to the oracle bone records.

During the Shang period the **li min** wrote much information on bones and turtle shells. This form of writing is called oracle bone writing. This writing is analogous to the Manding, Harappan, Proto-Elamite and Proto-Sumerian syllabic scripts.

The plants cultivated by the Shang had first been domesticated by the **li min** in south China and later taken northward as they colonized northern China.

These sun signs may refer to the ten clans that formed the basis of the Shang people.  Allan has discussed the possibility that the myth of the Mulberry Tree from which ten suns rose probably relate to the rise of ten founding Shang clans by ten suns (sons) which are identified as "black birds" (Allan 1981, p.294).

In the Mulberry Tree tradition one day ten suns rose from a mulberry and the Archer Yi, shot down nine of them. These suns in reality were birds. This bird myth probably refers to the "black birds" that founded the Shang Dynasty. The fact that only one of the ten birds survived the arrows of the Archer Yi, may relate to the unification of the ten clans into the Shang dynasty.

Both the ancient Chinese and Africans had similar naming practices. As in Africa the Shang child had both a day name and regular name. The Shang child was named according to the days of the **zun**, on which he was born. There were ten days in each **zun**. These days are called the ten celestial signs.

Shang society was based on totemic clans called **zu**. The clan signs are visible in clan emblems in bronze and oracle bone inscriptions: they were based on animal signs. The symbol of the Shang was the **bird**.

In 1027 B.C. the Shang Empire was conquered by the Zhou. The Zhou, who founded the first dynasty in China related to the contemporary Chinese people were originally nomads. A large bronze **gui** (bowl) , sat on square base dating to 1000 B.C., describes the Zhou defeat of the Shang:

"King/Wu son of King Won/conquered Shang, on the morning of the day **jia zi**. Having seized the/Shang/**ding** cauldrons and vanquished the dark Shang/King   /King Wu/ overthrow Shang./On the seventh day/ **xim wei**, King/Wu/ while at Lansai reward his minister Li with bronze,/ Li/ used it to make this precious vessel for/making sacrifices to his ancestor/ Tang ong".

The **li min** of Shang were uncooperative when the Zhou rulers came to power. The Tai clan, which entered Shanxi and adopted the Shang culture, led the Zhou. The Annals of the Bamboo Books report that one of the Zhou Emperors: "Tai Kang was on the throne as a sham sovereign. By idleness and dissipation he obliterated his virtue, until the black headed people all began to waver in allegiance".[18]

The diverse origins of the Zhou and the **li min** is evident from the statements of Duke Muh of Shanxi, in the Annals of the Bamboo Books.Here Duke Muh, noted that a good minister "... would be able to preserve **my descendents**, and my black head people".

Although the **li min** were little better than slaves they contributed much to Zhou civilization.  In the Chinese book the Ode Sang Yu, the Earl of Juy, mourned: "Every state is being ruined there are no black heads among the people".

In summary the **li min** "black headed people" of China originally came from Iran and the Fertile African Crescent. They entered China both by land, from Iran and by Sea. Once in China these **li min** in the

## SHADES OF MEMNON II

North and South were engaged in almost constant trade until the rise of the Zhou dynasty. The evidence of this early culture is evident in the artifacts recovered from the Lungshan, Yangshao, and Erlitou cultures.

It would appear that these **li min** spoke related Dravidian and Manding languages, which are a substratum language of Chinese. They remained disorganized in independent city-states until the members of the (Na) Kunte clan led by Hu Nak Kunte entered China from Elam in the later part of the 3rd millennium B.C. It was these **li min** who founded Xia, the first monarchy in China. It was from the Xia and later the Shang Dynasty that China derived its political system and government.

## *ANCIENT MIGRATION STORIES OF MEXICO*

The Maya were not the first to occupy the Yucatan and Gulf regions of Mexico. It is evident from Maya traditions and the artifacts recovered from many ancient sites that a different race lived in Mayaland before the Mayan speakers settled this region.

Friar Diego de Landa, in <u>Yucatan before and After the Conquest</u>, wrote that "some old men of Yucatan say that they have heard from their ancestors that this country was peopled by a certain race who came from the East, whom God delivered by opening for them twelve roads through the sea".

Other traditions recorded by Sahagun also record the settlement of Mexico by a different race. Sahagun says that these "Eastern settlers of Mexico landed at Panotha, on the Mexican Gulf. Here they remained for a time until they moved south in search of mountains". This tradition is most interesting because it probably refers to the twelve migrations of the Olmec people. The stone supports this view. Reliefs from Izapa, Chiapas Mexico published by the New World Foundation. In Stela 5, from Izapa we see a group of men on a boat riding the waves.

The most important ancient African site in Mexico was the Olmec civilization, which lasted from 1500 to 100 BC. Some scholars believe that the Olmec civilization lasted up until AD 600. These Africans built beautiful plazas in front of their temples where they placed huge carved heads 8 feet high, painted black and weighing tons.

The Olmec Empire was spread from Yucatan in the East, to Guerreo and the Pacific coast on the West, through Guatemala, Salvador and Costa Rica on the Southwest. Here the Olmecs continued to use the Proto-Saharan script, which was later adopted by the Maya Civilization.

Their efficient agricultural practices supplied them with abundant food to feed the large Olmec population.

Around the time the Manding speaking Olmec arrived in Mexico, the Gulf area was sparsely populated. The Olmec seem to represent trader-colonists because both men and women lived on the habitation sites. If the Olmecs had been only a group of merchants we would not find so many sculptures of African women in addition to men on Olmec sites. The Olmec called themselves Xi (Shi).

The decipherment of the Olmec writing indicates that the Olmec spoke one of the Mande languages closely related to the Manding group. As the ancient Mande of Tichitt and along the Niger River, the Olmecs were mound builders. Ancient Mexican traditions say that some of their ancestors came from a country across the sea, led by Amoxaque or Bookmen. The Mexican term Amoxaque, agrees with the Malinke-Bambara term A ma nkye, "he is a teacher". The Olmec had a syllabic writing system. The most famous Olmec inscriptions are the La Venta celts. In addition to writing inscriptions on celts and stelas the Olmec invented paper around 1000 BC.

The Olmecs were accomplished artists, scientists and engineers. Their civilization was highly developed. It influenced all the later civilizations in Mexico. The Olmecs constructed complex earthen pyramids and large sculptured monuments weighing tons. Under the preclassic Maya pyramids we find dirt and rubble. This suggests that the earthen mounds over the Olmec tombs were covered with a stone pyramid in preclassic Maya times. The Africoid somatic traits of the Olmec colossal heads astonish most archaeologists. The so-called epicanthic fold is associated with the African type. Large stone characterizes the art of the Olmec monuments, especially the heads of the Africoid rulers found at LaVenta and San Lorenzo. In addition to this monumental art, Olmec personal art includes human figurines, ceramics, small stone sculptures, masks, and axes.

## *OLMEC AFFINITY TO ANCIENT CHINESE CIVILIZATIONS*

Many researchers had detected affinity between the ancient civilizations of China and the Olmec civilization. These scholars have wondered why the civilizations share many characteristics. The answer is that both the Olmecs and founders of Xia and Shang came from the Proto-Sahara. Moreover as shown in Chapter 25, some of the founders of the Xia and Shang Dynasties spoke Manding the same language spoken by the Olmecs. It is interesting to note that the Olmec Bird cult is analogous to the Bird

Clan of the Yueh people. Moreover the fact Xi, was the name for the first civilization of China, may go back to the fact that the Manding or Xi people founded both the Xia civilization of China and the Xi (Olmec) civilization of Mexico.

The unity of these civilizations makes it clear why the World of Memnon was not isolated in Africa. As we know, Memnon was at Troy to help a relative. This should not be a surprise, in ancient times the relatives of Memnon—the Kushite—were established throughout the world. A world given vivid detail in <u>Shades of Memnon</u>.

1 Clyde Ahmad Winters,"Tamil,Sumerian and Manding and the Genetic Model",International Journal of Dravidian Linguistics 18,(1989) no1.

2 Clyde Ahmad Winters, "The Proto-Culture of the Dravidians, Manding and Sumerians", Tamil Civilization 3, no.1 (March 1985a) ,pages 1-9.

3 Ibid., pages 7-9.

4 G.W.Parker, "The African Origin of Grecian Civilization",Journal of Negro History. 2(3) (1917),pp.334-344;and G.W. Parker, The Children of the Sun. Baltimore,Md.: Black Classic Press (1981).

5 Clyde A. Winters, "Les fondateurs de la Grece venaient d'Afrique en passant par la Crete", Afrique Histoire, no8,(1983) pp. 13-18.

6 Plutarch, in Theseus 12; Ovid in Metamorphosis 7, 402 ff and Herodotus 7, 91.

7. F. d'Olivet, Hermeneutic Interpretation. (1915)p.640.

8. Harry Johnson. Negro in the New World, (1910) p.15.

9. C.O. Mucker, China's Imperial Past. Stanford:Stanford University Press, 1975.

10 Terrien de Lacouperie,"The black heads of Babylonia and ancient China ", The Babylonian and Oriental Record, 5 (11),(1891) pg. 237.

11 Ibid., 237.

12 Ibid., 237

13 Clyde Ahmad Winters, "Blacks in Ancient China,Part 1:The Founders of Xia and Shang", Journal of Black Studies 1,no2 (1983c); Clyde Ahmad Winters, "The Far Eastern Origin of the Tamils", Journal of Tamil Studies , no27 (June 1985c), pages 65-92.

14 Clyde Ahmad Winters, "The Proto-Culture of the Dravidians, Manding and Sumerians", Tamil Civilization 3, no1,   (March 1985a) ,pages 1-9.

15 Clyde Ahmad Winters, "The Indus Valley Writing and related Scripts of the 3rd Millennium BC", India Past and Present 2, no.1 ( 1985b), pages 13-19.

16 Winters, "The Far Eastern Origin of the Tamils", passim.

17. F. Mirth, History of China, (London 1969) pp.197-198.

18. Lacouperie, 1891, p.237.

SHADES OF MEMNON II

# PRELUDE: TOGETHER FOREVER

The crowd of grieving relatives were gathered in the darkened hospital room. Forming a semicircle around the bed where the still form of young Craig Martin lay, most silently wept. All of them had expected this day to come and there was a general feeling of relief that the suffering, both Craig's and the family's, would now come to an end. So they had driven and flown in from all over the country. They had come to say good-bye.

It had been several weeks since Craig had been horribly wounded by a stray bullet on his way home from school. He had lost an eye, and the doctor told them that his chance of coming out of the coma was good for only a few days. It had now been over a month and the grim decision had finally been made.

Suddenly the door opened, letting in a stream of light from the well-lit hallway. In walked a striking young woman wearing a long black leather coat. As she gazed around the darkened room, those inside noted her long luxurious braids and large, light brown eyes. The silence was broken by whispers as a question flitted from person to person: "Is that her? Is that her?"

The young woman immediately walked over to Craig's mother and they held each other in a tearful embrace.

"Hello Deena," Mrs. Martin said. "I'm glad you came."

She hugged Mr. Martin also, dabbed a tissue under her eyes, then walked over to the bed. As she gazed down upon the still form of the man she loved, memories came rushing in like a giant wave. She remembered how they had met: both reaching for the last textbook in the school bookstore, how they had argued before reaching the compromise of studying it together in the library until the new books were shipped in.

Deena recalled with a smile how she had considered Craig to be low class. Kind of cute, but certainly not her type. She had come from a well-off family, drove a Porsche to school, while Craig took the bus. She remembered how she had tried to resist, but it was his heart, Craig's open and giving heart, that had melted hers.

It was the little things, like sharing his lunch with her when she knew he had no money to buy more. It was walking her to her car in the underground garages where she parked, keeping her safe and making her laugh along the way.

## SHADES OF MEMNON II

He never made a pass at her, until one day she made a pass at him. She remembered sticking the key into the door, then turning suddenly to grab the front of his jacket and pulling him close. They kissed so deeply that a mugger could have easily snuck upon them as they leaned against her car. And then it was on. They were inseparable. Their lovemaking was so intense, so strong and so transcendent, they knew it was beyond the physical. It was during those most intimate moments that she knew they were meant to be together forever.

Mr. and Mrs. Martin observed how Deena looked at their son and began ushering everyone else out of the room. They were the last to leave and closed the door behind them. Deena prided herself on being a strong woman, but as she thought about what could have been, her strength melted away. Dropping to her knees, she found herself sobbing on the edge of the bed. Craig had not asked her to marry but she knew it was coming. She knew she was going to say yes and she knew they were going to be happy. Now all of that had been taken away, she thought, "because of some fool with a damn gun."

Looking up, Deena saw her reflection in the window. Her makeup was running down her face with the tears, but she didn't care. Gazing up at Craig's bandaged face, she took his limp hand in her own. Feeling his warmth for the last time. She glanced at the beeping machines attached to him and had to agree with his parents: Craig wouldn't want to go on like this.

As she took his hand, Deena concentrated on their happiest times, expecting then to get up, never to touch him again. But suddenly Craig's hand snapped closed upon hers and a white light exploded in her mind. She lost all sense of space and time, as images rushed into her mind: First she saw Craig speaking to a strange tall man, then a whirlwind of confusing images flashed by, like a movie on fast forward, accompanied by a dizzying array of sounds and emotions.

Without warning the white light in her mind exploded again and she opened her eyes. Feeling a sharp pain in her hand, she looked up to find Craig's exposed eye wide open and gazing into hers. Startled speechless, Deena saw his lips moving but could hear no sound. Bending closer to his mouth, she listened as a word gasped weakly from his lips. Then his eye closed again and his hand slid away from hers.

"Mrs. Martin!!!! Deena screamed. "Mr. Martin, come here!!!"

The door to the room burst open as Craig's parents rushed in.

There Deena stood before them with the strangest look they had ever seen on anyone's face.

"What is it child?" Mrs. Martin asked, as her husband surveyed the room.

"Don't do it, Mrs. Martin." Deena said breathlessly. "Please don't cut him off the machine!"

Mr. Martin shook his head. "I'm sorry Deena, but we can't let him go on like this..."

"But you can't!"

"You know he wouldn't want this," Mrs. Martin said, approaching to embrace her.

Deena jumped back.

"No!" she cried. "He's not gone! He's not gone! I swear to you he's not..."

The Martins looked at each other.

"What?" cried the tearful mother.

"Somehow he knows what's happening," Deena cried. "He's going through something. Something strange. But he's not gone..."

"Now hold on young woman," Mr. Martin replied with a mix of sadness and anger. "We finally came to accept this...why take us back through it again..?"

"What are you saying child?" added Mrs. Martin.

"Wait!" cried Deena. "He was just awake and said to wait!!"

The Martins looked at each other again, shaking their heads in disbelief. Mr. Martin walked over to Deena. Gently, but firmly, he tried to guide her into a chair.

"Maybe you should just sit down. We'll have the doctor get you something..."

"Nooo!" Deena cried, pulling away, "Look!"

Deena held her hand palm out. Blood dripped from four small wounds in the shape of fingernails. She then held up Craig's limp hand. Blood dripped from the fingertips.

Mr. and Mrs. Martin gasped.

"He was just awake," Deena cried tearfully. "He grabbed my hand. Mrs. Martin please don't cut him off!"

The Martins came close and examined both hands.

"She couldn't have done this to herself," Mr. Martin said finally.

"I...I know," replied Mrs. Martin as she pulled Deena close.

## SHADES OF MEMNON II

"Oh my dear child" she said. "I don't know how, but you've saved our boy's life tonight."

Then she turned toward the door.

"Lenard! Cathy! All of ya'll come in here!

All of the relatives filed back into the room.

"It's time for ya'll to leave," Mrs. Martin announced. "Our boy ain't dying tonight!"

And somewhere deep inside the mind of Craig Martin, the story of Memnon continued...

SHADES OF MEMNON II

*"And Swarthy Memnon In His Arms He Knew,*
*His Pompous Ensigns, And His Indian Crew."*
*Virgil, "The Aeneid" - 31 BC*

# CHAPTER 1: "ALIVE FROM THE LABYRINTH"

The voyage to Keftui lasted a full moon. During this time I slept in the warrior's quarters, strictly avoiding any contact with Nala. I had several conversations with Kho-An-Sa though, who informed me of my task and how it should be accomplished. On the last day of the voyage, as we conversed on the deck of the ship, the lookout announced that the land of Keftui had appeared upon the horizon.

"The time has come, Memnon," said Kho-An-Sa as we watched the land grow larger on the horizon. "This may be the most difficult challenge that you have faced. Are you prepared?"

"I am prepared," I said.

When the ship glided into the docks of Keftui I was very pleasantly surprised. A land of beautiful green hills and cultivated fields stretched out as far as the eye could see. Fabulous temples of carved white stone stood atop many of the hills, each surrounded by lines of well-built houses of stone and mud brick.

Beautiful trees and colorful bushes lined streets everywhere, indicating that the builders of this city had a fondness for natural things. It seemed strange to me that the horrible stories I had heard of mad King Minos could come from a land such as this.

Men on shore threw a ramp to the deck, then Kho-An-Sa, I and two warriors climbed down onto the docks. There we were greeted by a group of warriors and led to waiting chariots. After securing our weapons and bags, we trotted away from the sea, turning onto a cobble paved road inlaid with beautiful blue stones. Far ahead in the distance, upon a huge flat hill, was a temple larger than all of the others. As we made our way towards it, I noticed the people gathering to watch us pass by.

The population was a mix of Tamahus, Kushites and some who seemed to be blood mixtures. I noted that most of the Kushites were bearers and workers, while most of the Tamahu walked ahead or behind them carrying nothing. I shook my head in disgust. Just as they had been in Petra, it seemed that the Kushite population had been enslaved.

We rode up to the gates of the temple, dismounted, and climbed up the steep white stairs. Two huge doors swung open, revealing a long hall filled high columns and vividly colored wall paintings. When we stepped inside several guards approached, demanding our weapons. I stepped back defensively, glancing at Kho-An-Sa.

"It is all right, Memnon," he said. "Give them up."

With great trepidation, the two other warriors and I unstrapped our weapons and handed them over. The man who took mine had a look of astonishment upon his face as the jeweled hilts sparkled before his eyes. Kho-An-Sa stepped close to him and spoke the northern language in a low, menacing voice, while closing his hand into a fist.

The man's complexion turned pale as he seized his chest in pain. He tried to speak, but found he had no voice, until Kho-An-Sa opened his closed fist. Gasping for air, he spoke apologetically as we walked away.

"Fear not for your blades," said the magician, "I gave him a taste of what will happen if your weapons are not taken care of."

As we walked along, another man appeared who had an air of authority. He spoke to the others briefly, then led us toward another hall. Kho-An-Sa pulled me close and spoke softly.

"We go now to the throne room. Be very careful and do as I do. Stay close and I will translate for you."

As we started down the hall, Kho-An-Sa looked over his shoulder and again shot a cold stare at the man holding my weapons. Perspiration rolled down the guard's face as he turned away. I had no doubt that he believed Kho-An-Sa's warning.

We were led through the hall to another set of doors, which swung open into another hall even more beautiful than the one before. It too had vividly painted walls depicting many activities. Dancing and singing dominated the scenes, along with images of deities and ancestors.

But one thing I noted troubled me. Someone had painted over the men in the scenes in an effort to portray these clearly Kushite people as light skinned. No women were depicted at all, but there were a number of suspicious blank spots. I believe what I was seeing was the price of Tamahu conquest.

They marched us up to a dais that towered above the floor, with young Tamahu and Kushite boys sitting upon it's shiny stairs. Upon the very top sat a huge golden throne with a tremendously fat man sitting upon it. He was holding a small boy in his lap, caressing and kissing his face and speaking softly to him. The man who led us bowed before the throne and began speaking. Kho-An-Sa translated for me.

"Hail, O Great Sun Minos," said the warrior reverently.

"Sire, I have fetched the one called Kho-An-Sa and his warriors."

The king didn't look up.

"Yes, yes," he said curtly, continuing to stare into the child's face.

"Sire..." repeated the warrior. "I have fetched the one..."

"Shut up, shut up, fool," the king screamed in a high shrill voice. "Don't you think I can see? Don't you think I see?"

The man threw himself on the floor before the throne.

"Great Sun," he cried in dismay, "I meant no disrespect..."

The fat king rose and put the boy down. Shaking with rage, he pointed a pink, bloated finger at the man before him.

"That's your problem, Brid. You don't have enough respect. You've exceeded your place once too often. You are hereby ordered to stay upon your belly for a full moon. Don't let me hear about you getting up for any reason."

He then sat his huge bulk back upon his throne and started giggling.

"Hee, Hee, Hee, Hee, Hee, Hee, Hee!"

It was an troubling, evil sound that I will never forget and went on for several moments. He then stopped abruptly, looking out at the guards and court members gathered before him.

"If anyone sees Brid upon his feet or knees, you kill him. If anyone sees anyone watching Brid get up and they don't kill him, then kill that person. If anyone doesn't kill Brid for getting up, I'll kill you."

Kho-An-Sa and I looked at each other as he translated the absurdities of King Minos. Clearly the stories about the madness of this king were justified.

"Hee, hee, I'll kill you, I'll kill you" the king repeated in a singsong voice. He patted another boy on the head as he sat down, then finally turned to address us.

"Well, what do you want?"

Kho-An-Sa stepped forward and bowed.

"Great Minos, we have come on pressing business. I have heard of the trouble you are having with the rebels from Mycenea..."

"Trouble?" the fat king replied, "who says we're having trouble?"

"Err, you did king Minos. In a letter to our associate, Aias."

"Oh. Oh yes. So I did."

At this point Kho-An-Sa could no longer translate as he and the king engaged in intense conversation. As they talked Kho-An-Sa pointed and gestured to me several times. The fat king nodded at me occasionally, then finally beckoned me to approach the throne. As he talked,

SHADES OF MEMNON II

Kho-An-Sa resumed translating.

"So," the fat king began, "you are the warrior sent to help subdue the rebels."

I bowed respectfully.

"Yes, great Minos. I will do what I can."

"Well listen young man, we don't usually put Kushites in positions of authority in this land. It doesn't look good. But your master says you are a gifted warrior, so we may make an exception. First though, let us see if you really are a great fighting man."

I looked into the king eyes. There was an evil gleam about them.

"What do you propose, great Minos?" I asked suspiciously.

The king smiled.

"Step forward, son of the great Memnon of Troy."

I looked at Kho-An-Sa. He nodded affirmatively, then I took a step toward the throne. Suddenly, the king let out a cruel peal of laughter and touched something on the side of his golden chair.

Immediately the floor gave way beneath me and I slid down a steep, pitch black tunnel. After long moments I saw light ahead and tumbled briefly through the air, landing in a painful heap upon a hard stone floor.

As I rose to my feet a terrible odor assailed my nose, like a 100 year old stable never cleaned. Leaning against a cold stone wall, I tried to regain my composure. A quick look around revealed flameless lights of the sort in Daedalus' caves. More lights appeared as I began my search for a to find a way out.

It was soon clear to me that I was trapped in a labyrinth of some sort, with confusing twists, false starts and dead ends designed to baffle its hapless victims. The walls were about forty cubits tall, smooth and quite unscalable, while falling mortar and slight discoloration provided clues to the great age of the construction.

Suddenly I was startled by the bellowing of a large and powerful animal. Then I heard the sound of hooves upon the stone floor. The steps of the beast grew closer when it bellowed again and I recognized the powerful cry of a bull in heat. But this left me confused. For the hooves I heard resounded with the rhythm of just two feet.

I did not know how close the creature was, but I seemed to be heading towards it. Since I was unarmed, and in it's territory, I turned back the way I had come. Besides, I considered, the way out could lie in any direction. I just hoped to reach it before the animal I heard reached me.

The maze seemed endless as I dashed to and fro, desperately trying to put distance between myself and the dangerous beast. As I made my way along the dark corridors, my feet struck something. Looking down, I saw a pile of white objects that rattled as I shifted my foot. Bending down closer, I found it was a pile bones. I stared for a moment, then tore my eyes from this grisly sight and went on. But soon I stumbled upon more bones and even some full skeletons. The remains were fresher and less decayed as I pressed on, until I was surrounded by the bodies of recently killed men. There were twelve of them, all large warriors, with their clothing torn off and weapons scattered nearby.

With the thought in mind to defend myself when the monstrous bull came for me, I snatched up a sword and tested it's feel. But then I looked closely at the dead warriors. They too had had the same thoughts and it had done them no good. And I noticed something else also. A strange look about the bodies. I did not understand exactly why, but something about the way the warriors died did not seem right to me.

All of them lay on their stomachs, the flesh and bones of their behinds and midsections broken and shredded. Sticky pools of drying blood were everywhere. As I observed this gruesome sight, the terrible bellow rang out again.

As I looked around the scene a desperate plan came to me. I tossed down the sword and picked up a spear near one of the dead warriors. Checking the blade, I found it to be sturdy and sharp. Then I turned to the wall, found a loose section of mortar between the stones and plunged the blade into it. Burying it deep, I leaned upon it to test its strength. It seemed to hold well, so I turned around to gather more spears.

A strip of cloth from one of the dead warriors provided an adequate harness and I strapped a dozen more spears to my back. The creature's bellow sounded no more than a corridor away as I jabbed another spear into the wall. Seizing a light, I climbed cautiously onto my makeshift ladder. Carefully and slowly, I continued the process, gradually rising above the floor of the labyrinth. I was little more than halfway when the creature finally appeared.

My eyes widened when it came into view and I had to stop myself from gasping in astonishment. The creature was huge, larger than any bull I had ever seen, and it indeed stood upon two legs. Twice as tall as a man, it had the head of a large bull, with two long horns and a thick

SHADES OF MEMNON II

manlike torso covered with hair. Its legs were thickly muscled and hooved and its hairy arms were wider around than my whole body at the waist.

There was a gigantic double ax over thrust over its shoulder and it breathed in short powerful bursts. But the most horrible thing was what I saw as it came closer.

I could see that it's giant male organ was fully erect, as it shifted its huge bulk, apparently confused by the disappearance of its prey. With each step, the horrible, bulbous member pulsated with excitement and I then realized how the others in this place had died.

Slowly I pulled another spear, inserted it carefully into the wall and took another step up. Resting carefully, I held my breath as the creature walked in a circle, continually sniffing the air. I pulled another spear, pushed it into the wall and lifted a leg up and the move was successful, until I brought my foot down. Then the spear quivered and I watched in dismay as a chunk of mortar plunged down.

The chunk shattered against the floor and the creature whirled around. It's eyes locked onto the wall beneath me. Slowly it directed its gaze up and when it's saw me, let loose a terrible roar. As it's bellow split the air, I knew that there was no way to survive a fight with this creature.

There were only a few cubits to the top, but I knew the beast would not let me climb them. Even now it approached the wall, lifting the ax to cut me down. I untied the knot holding the spears and they tumbled away. Then I took a step up, snatched the spear I had just inserted out of the wall, and tossed it at the creature.

It's eyes glowed blood red as it plucked the weapon from the air, snapping it like a small twig. Balancing myself on the spear beneath me and holding onto the torch with my teeth, I leapt for the top of the wall. As my feet left the spear I felt a rush of air. I knew it was the huge ax, barely missing my legs.

My hands grasped the edge of the wall and I scrambled to the top. As I crawled over, the creature bellowed again, mad with rage and frustration. It kicked a dead body, then picked it up and flung it at me. When it missed, the creature seized another body and tossed it also. Then another, and another, until I was under a barrage of decayed flesh and bones.

Making myself a small target, I crawled along the wall until I was out of the creature's throwing range. Then I stood up, holding the light

SHADES OF MEMNON II

ahead to make my way. I could see that I had indeed been right. It was a vast labyrinth, of amazing complexity and ingenuity. From the looks of it, no one could possibly get out before the monstrous creature managed to destroy them. But I had made it to the top of the walls, something I am sure that the creators did not anticipate. Checking my surroundings further, I noticed that the ceiling of this place was of solid rock. Someone had accomplished an amazing feat of engineering, creating this place from a vast underground cave.

In the far distance I saw what looked like a large door and decided to make my way toward it, the roars of the creature continuing as I hurried on. Often I had to leap from wall to wall, knowing that if I slipped, the monstrous creature awaited me. Luckily I did not slip, and, after a long while, the end of the vast maze came into view.

There a wall loomed, dominated by a gigantic door made of metal, no doubt to keep the creature in. This made me contemplate for a moment: If the door was designed to keep the monster in, then surely I could not make use of it. So I kneeled down and scanned that area for some other way out.

Several cubits from the door I saw a small opening. I didn't know exactly how large it was, or if it led to a way out. But the monstrous creature's roars were getting nearer again and I realized I had no choice. I walked to the end of the wall, gazing at the long cubits down to the bottom. A leap from this height could cripple a normal man on the stone floor, but, trusting that my hardened bones would see me through, I braced myself and jumped.

I landed on my feet, nearly dropping the light from the impact. My soles were stinging sharply, but I was otherwise unhurt. Just in case, I ran to the door and tested it, to find it locked from the outside as I had thought. I ran to the smaller opening to find rotting vegetables and grasses piled underneath it. Clearly the portal used for feeding the creature. I pushed my head and shoulders in and found that I could fit, but I had no way of knowing if it continued wide enough all the way to the top.

Just then an earsplitting bellow broke my contemplation and I turned to see the creature emerging from the labyrinth. It spotted me immediately and pounded its hooves upon the stone floor.

I really had no choice now. As the beast came running, I threw down the light and crawled quickly into the opening. It was narrow and cramped, but I could push forward with my hands and feet.

Scooting up the angled passageway in total darkness, I heard the bellow of the creature, and then felt a terrible jolt. Then another bellow and another jolt, as it pounded against the wall in anger and frustration.

The creature continued battering and bellowing for a long time. But the jolts became less and less powerful as I moved further on. The tunnel was pitch dark, and at times I crawled along in a nearly vertical position. What saved me from plunging down was the poor construction of the passage. Luckily it's roughly hewn, lumpy surface served as hand and footholds, for without them I would have surely been doomed.

I had no way of knowing how long I was in the passage, but my limbs were aching terribly when at last I saw light. It gave me renewed strength and I climbed vigorously toward it. After long moments more, I seized hold of the opening and poked my head through. There before me were two women holding a large box of vegetables. Surprised, they dropped the box, causing the contents inside to tumble. One woman seized her chest and fainted, while the other turned and ran from the room. I climbed from the passage and collapsed to the floor.

Looking up, I found myself in a kitchen. The fragrance of the food was quite pleasing. But before I could call out for anything, I found myself surrounded by a group of fearful women, brandishing brooms, mops and cooking utensils. I looked up at them, smiling weakly. After surviving the maze and the creature that dwelled in it, I thought it unseemly to fall before a group of cooking women on an empty stomach. They jumped back as I reached into the pile of vegetables, seizing a hefty carrot. I took a huge bite of it and chewed hungrily.

"Take me back to Minos," I said between mouthfuls. "But first, give me a plate of that food."

Moments later two warriors arrived. Looking me over as I ate, they first questioned the women. Then a man arrived that I recognized from the king's court. Shaking his head in disbelief, he instructed the women to give me more food, which I devoured gratefully. After conferring with the other warriors, he led me from the cooking area and down a long hall.

All the warriors we walked near stopped in their tracks, whispering to each other and pointing. Finally, we stopped before a door upon which the warrior knocked once. It opened, and there before me stood Kho-An-Sa.

"Memnon!" he cried.

# SHADES OF MEMNON II

I stepped into the room and the magician directed me to a chair. He looked at me for a moment with the same astonishment that everyone else had since I emerged. Then he got up and threw his hands into the air.

"I should have known," he said laughing. "Memnon, do you know that you are the first to ever come back alive from the labyrinth?"

"Kho-An-Sa," I said. "Right now I neither know nor care. I have need of rest."

"Of course, of course," the magician said.

He led me to his own sleeping chambers and pointed to the bed. As I fell into it, Kho-An-Sa started questioning me.

"Sleep, young panther," he said, "But first I must know: How did you do it?"

I opened my mouth to answer, but my eyes slammed shut and I found myself asleep instead.

The next day we stood before the throne of Minos again. I was dressed in the finest Keftuan robes Kho-An-Sa could procure and the magician himself stood beside me with his chest protruding. As Minos sat before us, I could barely control my rage. I was prepared right then to carry out my mission, not for Kho-An-Sa, but for what the fat king had put me through in his labyrinth. And for all the poor victims of the creature that I saw there. As the king spoke, Kho-An-Sa translated again.

"I must say, young man," Minos began, "I didn't think much of you, but you certainly have impressed me."

I nodded. Kho-An-Sa had instructed me to remain silent before the king, who leaned forward in his throne as he continued.

"You are the only one to ever come out alive," he went on. "But you didn't hurt my pet while you were down there did you? Tell me you didn't."

I could hardly control myself as I looked into the face of the piggish king. Luckily, Kho-An-Sa spoke for me.

"No, great Minos. Your "pet" is alive and well."

"That's good, that's good," the king replied. "He's been with the family for such a long time. We love him so."

The king became silent for a moment, as if debating something inside his head. He looked me up and down as he addressed Kho-An-Sa.

"Look here magician," Minos began, "I'm looking for a new general for my army. Since you are leaving him here with me, I want your warrior to take the position."

Kho-An-Sa translated this and I looked at Minos as if he had lost his mind. Before I could open my mouth, Kho-An-Sa spoke for me again.

"He thinks that it would be an honor to serve as your general Minos," Kho-An-Sa answered. "He will do it gladly."

"Well, I like that enthusiasm," the king replied. "You know good help is so hard to find in these times. Brid was the general but he's crawling on his belly like a snake now."

The king pointed to the warrior he had abused upon our arrival. He was there before the throne among the others, still laying upon his stomach in utter humiliation. I began to shake my head, but Kho-An-Sa elbowed me.

"Bow, Memnon, bow."

I bowed down, feigning a thankful manner, but I was feeling anything but grateful. I had no experience at running an army, and had no idea what the job entailed. But Kho-An-Sa urged me to go along with it, so I did.

Minos clapped his hands. Then a warrior brought forth my weapons and I seized them quickly from him. It felt good to hold them and I checked to make sure every jewel was still there. The king clapped again and several women stepped forth from the crowd.

"I have heard that you have need of a skilled woman. Well these are some of the local temple women, and I think, a few of my wives. I have no need for them, so take any one you want. Or take them all, I don't care."

I bowed once more and Kho-An-Sa spoke for me again.

"Thank you, great Minos," he said. "He will be very happy I am sure."

"Good," the king replied. "Tomorrow we will have a feast to celebrate."

"Celebrate what, great Minos?" asked Kho-An-Sa.

Minos put his hand to his chin and thought for a moment.

"Why, the new general and his escape from the labyrinth, that's what. It does not matter really, because I always have feasts. Come back tomorrow, good day."

Some of the courtiers tried to approach the throne, no doubt with business of their own. But Minos would hear none of it as he waved them away rudely.

## SHADES OF MEMNON II

"Good day! Come back tomorrow. Good day! Good day!"

As Kho-An-Sa and I left the throne room, Brid slithered by us on the floor. Pausing near us, he looked up, giving me a bitter scowl before crawling away.

"What have you gotten me into Kho-An-Sa?" I asked

The magician rubbed his hands together and smiled slyly.

"Ahh, young panther," he said. "This is better than I had hoped for. You will be able to carry out your assignment much more efficiently now. You will see."

The next morning the banquet hall was alive with the sights, sounds and fragrances of revelry and feasting. Walking through the entrance, Kho-An-Sa and I were nearly bowled over by servants carrying large platters of smoking food and tall jugs of drink. We were directed to two chairs at the huge feasting table near King Minos, who greeted us with greasy smile as he stuffed the royal face with the leg of some hooved animal. Once again, Kho-An-Sa translated the northern tongue.

"Kho-An-Sa! Young Memnon!" he cried. "Do join in the feast! What will you have? Lamb? Dove? Wait, I know what you want."

He shouted at a nearby servant girl.

"Wench! Bring us the suckling pig! Be quick about it."

The magician and I looked at each other as Minos went on offering the table's fare. He went on and on about the culinary delights of Keftui. Finally, Kho-An-Sa slipped a few words in, telling him about my eating requirements.

"Oh," said the king, "he's one of those. Well, we have plenty for him also. He'll not miss this feast."

The servants brought me a plate of delicious fruits, vegetables and various breads. They also gave me a large flask of grape wine, which the Keftuans were famous for. As we dined, dozens of musicians played various instruments and dancing girls whirled around the room.

One in particular interested me, a tall, lithe Kushite woman, whom I recognized from the group of females offered to me by the king. I tried several times to catch her eye, but she seemed to be in a dancer's trance. Floating like a bird one moment, writhing like a serpent the next, she was oblivious to her surroundings, taken by the movements of the dance.

The king clapped his hands and the dancers left the floor. Then a group of men appeared carrying large wooden posts and boards. As they

50

arranged the pieces, a tall wooden fence of the sort used to cage sheep and cattle took form. When all the parts were in place they checked the sturdiness of the structure, then left the hall.

I looked around at the feasting throngs to find the room totally silent. Everyone had stopped eating, leaning forward in their seats in tense anticipation.

Suddenly four of the fence builders came back, this time leading a full grown bull, it's head completely covered by a large sack. It was very docile due to the bag and was led right up to the fence and through the gate. Three of the men exited and closed the gate, leaving one man inside with the animal. Untying the bag rapidly, the man snatched it from the bull's head and ran for the walls of the fence.

The bull huffed loudly, shook it's head and looked around. Then, as if angry at being put on display, it let out a tremendous bellow like the creature in the labyrinth. As the man with the sack scrambled over the gate, the bull saw him and charged. His legs cleared just as the bull's horns crashed into the wood and the banquet hall exploded with gleeful applause.

I looked around at the crowd with much displeasure. I could not believe they could find so much joy at the near death of the bull keeper. This was just the sort of barbaric behavior that I had mentioned those long months ago in the House of Life. I wondered if Master Shu Ha would argue with me now about the mindset of most Northerners.

Bloodlust and a callous disregard for life was the manner of all the Tamahus in the room. Only the Kushites, who were all servants, displayed sadness about the spectacle of the bull. I was later to learn exactly why.

King Minos clapped his hands once more and the room became silent again. All waited in anticipation again, their eyes upon the entrance to the hall. Suddenly a cadre of Kushites entered, beating large drums and dancing rhythmically. There were about twenty of them, forming two lines facing each other on either side of the gate. The drumming continued for a few moments more, then they abruptly stopped. Suddenly the dancing girl appeared that I had noticed before, slowly walking toward the fence.

Several Kushite servants bowed their heads and made hand signs in the air as the dancer walked between the drummers and right up to the gate. Opening it quickly, one of the bull keepers shoved her inside, then

SHADES OF MEMNON II

quickly slammed it shut.

This was too much for me. I stood up immediately, grasping the hilt of one of my weapons. But Kho-An-Sa seized my arm and pulled me down close to him.

"Do not interfere Memnon," he whispered. "You cannot change the ways of a people."

I would have pulled away regardless and rushed to the assistance of the young woman, but as I looked on I knew I would be too late. Already the huge bull had its horns lowered, charging relentlessly towards the defenseless woman.

SHADES OF MEMNON II

## CHAPTER 2: "I AM YOUR FRIEND, GREAT ANU"

The powerful bull charged down upon the helpless woman, who simply stood there, showing no apparent fear. The sheer cruelty of the exhibition appalled me and I wondered why she made no move to save herself. My answer came in the next instant, as the woman sprang suddenly to life in an amazing feat of bravery and dexterity.

Leaping high into the air at the very last moment, she seized the beast by the horns. Then, using the force of the bull's own charge to propel her, she pushed off it's horns and whirled gracefully over it's broad back, landing lightly at the animal's rear.

The crowd in the hall went wild with applause as the beast turned for another charge. Again the woman repeated this astounding feat of acrobatics, leaping above the deadly horns without a sign of fear or nervousness. To those of us watching, her death-defying moves were as graceful and beautiful as her dance. But to the bull she was a hated target, tauntingly defying its every effort at destruction.

Time and again the animal charged in fury, each run becoming weaker, while the woman seemed never to tire. Finally the animal leaned against the fence, huffing loudly, legs shaking with exhaustion. Then, bellowing once last time in utter frustration, it collapsed to the floor, defeated.

The revelers applauded again as the gate was opened and the young woman emerged. Walking calmly from the hall, she paid no attention to their adulation, as the bull-keepers dragged her horned opponent behind her. Minos clapped his hands again, and the fence was dismantled and carried away. The fat king was greatly pleased as he turned to Kho-An-Sa and I.

"Are you enjoying the entertainment so far?" he said.

"Why, yes, great king," replied the magician. "It was...thrilling."

Staring down at my plate of food, I tried hard not to let the king see my disgust at his cruel "entertainment." Luckily he seemed more concerned with boasting than he was about my disposition.

"This bull-jumping is something the natives have been doing for many years," he declared.

"So I have heard," replied Kho-An-Sa.

Biting off another chunk of meat, Minos chewed sloppily, swallowed loudly and continued.

## SHADES OF MEMNON II

"They were doing it as a part of some foolish practice. A religion I do believe, which we put a stop to. Now they only jump bulls to entertainment us. Is that not special?"

"Charming," replied Kho-An-Sa.

"Wait until you see the next event. We know how to have a good time in this land, you'll see."

We dined for a while longer, all the while listening to Minos' ceaseless prattling about this or that custom or tradition they had usurped from the native Keftuans. Finally he stopped talking and clapped his hands once more.

The hall became silent again, as twelve striking Kushite men strolled into the room. All of them were nearly my height, extremely muscular, with jet-black skin oiled to a shine.

As each came forward to bow before the king, I noticed that their hands, feet, elbows and knees were bound with white cloth. All wore headbands of different colors and had the sort of tough demeanor developed only after many years of combat.

Flexing and stretching as they spread out, the men formed a semicircle and stood awaiting their orders. Smiling gleefully, Minos snapped his plump fingers and two of the warriors approached each other.

One warrior wore a headband of brilliant green, the other of intensely bright red. Both looked quite formidable as they bowed to one another, crouched into fighting stances and began circling like two big cats.

Suddenly one exploded with a quick and brutal kick, which the other fighter dodged even more swiftly. Then the two men rushed together, feet and arms flying in a barrage of blows and counter blows. As they rained punches upon each other with blinding speed, I understood the need for the protective cloth: The blows produced sounds unlike flesh hitting flesh, resounding like wood smashing wood at one point, and metal striking against metal at others.

The sounds they emitted puzzled me, while their speed and technique was intriguing. I had not seen such skilled hand-to-hand fighting since the warrior's festivals of Kamit. There the Medjay warriors would spar to show their skills and to attract interested youth to the ranks. I was always very interested.

But this was a much different fighting art than that of the foot fighting in my land. It was much more brutal, used more sheer force and less rhythm. Yet there was a strange grace about it that appealed to me. Minos noticed my interest and commented as we looked on.

"It's called Pan-Kau-Ra-Shen," he said. "And there is much more to it than the movements that you see. Keep watching."

Nodding, I did just that, as a change in the combat style took place. Neither man could land a solid blow due to the excellence of their blocks and counter strikes, so they seized each other and began to grapple. In this they also seemed evenly matched as they thrashed and twisted, arms locked together like links of chain.

Suddenly the man in the green headband began to breath loudly, in a strange rhythmic pattern. Then the other fighter began to do the same. As the sound of the breathing reverberated, Minos and the other revelers leaned forward in anticipation.

Tense, quiet moments went by, as the bodies of both fighters began shaking like leaves in the wind. An ear splitting sound resounded off the walls as a long crack ripped through the stone floor beneath the fighters feet. Then, as if the grip of a giant hand, the fighter in the red headband was violently wretched from the other and thrown back through the air.

Head over heels he tumbled, until two of his fellow warriors leaped up and caught him. As they seized upon him his body hesitated in midair, still caught in the grip of the powerful force that propelled him, before falling into the arms of his fellows.

The crowd exploded with applause again as the warrior in the green headband bowed before the king and the other was carried away sense-less. I did not understand what had happened and looked at the king for some explanation.

"That was the inner power of Pan-Kau-Ra-Shen: the inner force called "pneuma," said Minos. "It is only used by the masters of the art because it is very dangerous. This too was a common practice with the natives, but now only elite guards, such as these men, are allowed to learn it. And we make sure they are loyal to us."

"I can understand why," quipped Kho-An-Sa. "It is a very powerful art."

"Indeed it is," replied Minos. "Let us see more."

Minos clapped his hands again and more of the fighters engaged. I was awed by further displays of the skill of these warriors and the wonders performed using the inner power of Pan-Kau-Rau-Shen. I understood that this "pnuema" was just another word for the life force,

Rau, and wondered what effect their training would have upon me. I could have watched the warriors all day, but their exhibition soon ended and Minos sent them away.

"Now we will have the final entertainment," the king said. "I think you'll like this most of all.

The king pulled a manservant close, whispered into his ear, then watched him leave to see to his wishes. Moments later the servant came back, leading a large group of musicians. Some were drummers who had performed for the dancers before, along with flutist players and strummers holding various stringed instruments. Stopping before our table, they stood poised to play on the kings command.

Then four other men entered pulling a cart, upon which sat a small wooden box wrapped in chains. It's aged wheels rattling, they pushed it near our table and unlocked the chains. Then they tapped the side of it, causing a wall of the box to fall away.

There inside stood the shadowy figure of a very small person, which I at first took to be a child. But when they reached in and dragged him into the light, I knew exactly what he was. It was an Anu.

As they lifted the little man down to the floor, I saw that he was naked except a small cloth covering his privates. His tiny wrists and legs were shackled with golden chains and a silver collar gleamed from his neck. He blinked once, his eyes becoming accustomed to the light, and I saw that he looked like the little men Neftiji and I had seen on the Island of the Ka.

With a long, goat-like beard jutting majestically from his face, his reddish-brown skin glowed in the torchlight. Though he was beautiful like the other Anu I remembered, he looked weak and was clearly underfed. Brutal laceration upon his arms and legs were proof of many beatings.

One of his keepers attached a long leash to his collar, then unlocked the chains from his limbs. The box was wheeled aside and the keeper backed away, unwinding the lease as he went to give the Anu some slack.

"Now," said Minos. "You will see a rare sight indeed.

I knew well how rare it was to see the people of this ancient race and I remembered how joyful and free they were on the Island of the Ka. My heart was tearing apart to see this one treated so harshly.

"Why must you keep him bound?" I asked.

"You don't know much about the Anu, do you?" Minos replied. "If we let him walk freely, not all the guards in this place could keep him from escaping. Now just watch."

Minos nodded his head and the musicians started to play. Then the little man began to dance. Though he was on a leash, he moved with a rhythm and grace that I had never seen. Each section of his body seemed to have a mind of it's own, moving independently, yet in perfect time with the whole. Suddenly I recognized his movements. It was the Dance of Peace done before the shrines of ancestors in Kamit. But I had never seen it performed like this.

As my eyes followed him, each movement sent waves of pleasure through me as if I had taken a powerful herb. All the pain and anger I'd felt during the past months simply washed away, replaced by warm serenity and peace.

The little man's feet seemed at times to hover above the floor and a small glow emanated from the top of his head as he performed these wonderful movements. Looking around the room, I saw many of the Tamahu revelers looking sad and thoughtful, while most of the Kushite servants openly wept.

When it seemed that the entire room would burst with tearful emotion, the musicians changed the tune and the little man began to dance differently. This time it was a happy, joyful dance, causing the revelers to clap along as he bounced and weaved. I found myself clapping also, as the Anu approached our table.

Stopping near each person momentarily, the Anu gave us a special, close up show. He danced near Minos, who clapped with childlike glee and near Kho-An-Sa, who, barely suppressing a smile, clapped along also. When he came near me I found that he was doing far more than the eye could see. Some force from his body, pushed outwards by his movements, pulsated against me with a life of it's own.

Wrapping itself around me like a solid sort of mist, the force pulled joy from inside me I did not know I still possessed. All the good feelings I had ever experienced resurfaced as the power of the little man's dance enveloped me.

Clapping my hands joyously, I raised my hands higher to do it more vigorously, when suddenly the Anu's dance ceased. Eyeing my right hand closely, he bowed his head and nodded. I did not understand the meaning of this and looked around at the others at the table. No one, including Kho-An-Sa and Minos, seemed to understand either.

The Anu's keeper jerked the leash, but still he did not move. I leaned closer to see if he was injured in some way and he seized my hand, gazing intently at my ring. Then he looked up and our eyes met.

## SHADES OF MEMNON II

It was then that I realized: Here was the one I had come to the court of Minos to find. This Anu was the one who could help me if I first assisted him.

Our eyes locked for a long moment, then his keeper and another man seized the Anu and dragged him away. The music had stopped, and when I looked up, everyone was staring at me. Kho-An-Sa looked at me inquisitively and Minos had one eyebrow raised.

"What was that about?" the king asked.

Glancing at everyone around me, I shrugged my shoulders.

"I...I do not know," I lied.

"No matter," said Minos. "The Anu shall be punished by his owner for this. And Brid had better give it to him good for ruining my entertainment."

"The Anu belongs to Brid?" I asked.

"Yes," replied Minos. "He seized him many moons ago on some adventure or another. I thought he had tamed him by now. It is a shame we cannot see the rest of his performance."

They put the Anu back in chains and led him to his wooden cage. As they lifted him to the box, our eyes met once more, then they slammed it shut once again. I shook my head as they wheeled the box away. I did not understand how they could treat a being who brought them such joy in such a terrible manner. I only knew that I must free him no matter what the cost.

The feast continued for some time, as an array of jugglers, wrestlers and other entertainers paraded before us. But I paid little attention to the rest of festivities, my thoughts continually returning to the Anu. I had to get him away from Brid, and I thought I knew a way to do it.

Later, after the festivities had come to an end, Kho-An-Sa and I strolled back to our quarters, our bellies full and our bodies ready for rest. He seemed to be in deep thought as we walked along, nodding to himself and pursing his lips as he engaged in some internal conversation.

"Memnon," he said finally, "I will leave on the morrow. My business with Cronn beckons..."

I nodded.

"It may take six, seven moons or more. While I am gone, you are to carry out your mission. The object you seek is a dagger, called the Blade of Shai. I have heard rumors that it may be kept in the Labyrinth. Find out if this is so, but wherever it is you are to get it. Then find a method of disposing of that fool Minos."

"Yes, Kho-An-Sa," I replied.

The magician stopped walking and looked at me intently for a long moment.

"And Memnon, never forget that your sister is in my power. I know you do not "like" the task I put before you, but you will see that it is done."

I looked into the piercing eyes of the magician.

"I understand my position. I will do as you ask."

Kho-An-Sa smiled.

"Good. Now let us retire. I have a special present awaiting you in your quarters. I recommend you keep it if you wish to stay strong."

"What is it," I asked.

"You will see, you will see," he replied, smiling.

I rushed to my quarters quickly, eager to see this "present" from Kho-An-Sa. When I threw open the door and stepped inside, there upon my bed lay one of the women presented to me by Minos. She was a beautiful Tamahu, wearing a fine blue robe that caressed her ample curves tantalizingly. Tossing her red hair, she flashed her green eyes sensuously, and I thought for a moment about going along with Kho-An-Sa's wishes. Then I remembered what he had done to me with Nala.

As she opened her arms invitingly, I stripped off my robe and approached the bed. Climbing onto the soft sleeping blankets, I embraced her gently and turned her body so that her back was to me. A low moan of pleasure escaped her lips as she pulled up her robe, poking her rear out for whatever I had in mind. Greatly pleased that she was so cooperative, I placed my foot firmly on her backside and booted her from my bed.

Shrieking sharply, she tumbled away, landing on the floor with a noisy thump. Rising after a moment with a confused look, she found me shaking my head and pointing to exit. Finally getting the message, she walked hesitantly through the door and closed it behind her. Pulling the covers over my head, I smiled and went to sleep.

Kho-An-Sa's ship left at dawn the next morning. As I watched its sails puff with wind and pull the vessel out to sea, I thought of my sister and of the odd fate that my life continued to bring me. I knew that I must to find some way of freeing Neftiji, but first I had to see to the present situation. That meant freeing the Anu. And since that might require fighting, it was imperative that I find myself a skilled woman.

I spent most of the day trying to communicate my needs to those

## SHADES OF MEMNON II

around me.  Without Kho-An-Sa to translate I was at a great disadvantage with the Northerners, but I found the tongue of the Kushite natives close enough to Kamitic to get along.

On the advise of a few of the natives, I had decided to investigate the skills of the bull jumping woman, and by late that evening, I had learned of her whereabouts.  After a brief meeting with Minos and a Kushite interpreter to express my intent, I set out immediately to see her.

The woman was one of Minos appointed wives and lived on the other side of the palace, in the section set aside for royal women and concubines.  Men were not usually allowed inside the inner chambers, but I had a special note from the king to enter.

After following the directions given to me, I found myself before a huge golden door, covered with inscriptions and paintings of women.  Seizing the large round knocker hanging from the entrance, I pounded three times as I was told.  After a moment the door opened a crack and I could see an eye and part of the face of an old Kushite woman.

"State your business here, please," the woman said.

I pushed the note through the crack and she slammed the door shut.  After a moment she opened it wide, inviting me to step inside.  We walked through a short dark hallway which led to a tremendous room dominated by a large swimming pool.  Sweet perfumes assailed my nostrils and women were everywhere: swimming in the water, lounging on couches and sitting in groups grooming and gossiping.  There were Tamahus and Kushites, all nude or nearly so, and most of them really quite beautiful.  When they saw us enter they swarmed towards us, smiling, giggling and batting their eyes invitingly.

"Look!" one woman exclaimed. "It's a man."

"A Kushite man!" said another.

"A beautiful Kushite man," another added.

"Is he the one?"

"I think he is!"

"Oooooooooooooh!" they all cried in unison.

The women started touching me, shoving each other aside and pulling each other's hair, until the elder who let me in seized my arm and dragged me away.  Beating the young women back with a small stick, she pushed me into a nearby room and shut the door.  As the locks tumbled I heard the elder scolding, then groans of disappointment from the women.

As I stood near the door, I could not suppress the smile growing upon my face.  I found the adoration of the women was very intriguing and considered letting one or two in with me. But, thinking better of it, I sat down upon a nearby couch to wait.

A few minutes passed. Then the locks tumbled again and the door opened. There before me stood the woman who had defeated the bull. Dressed beautifully, she wore an elaborate gown of purple, highlighted with spirals and streaks of bright gold. On her head was a silver band inset with various jewels, matching a necklace drawn tightly around her throat. She was quite radiant, with a regal and strong demeanor.

"Greetings," she said. "I am Maa-Ra."

"Greetings, sister. I am Memna-un."

"I know who you are," she said with a sly smile. "You escaped the labyrinth. Everyone is talking about you..."

"Oh, are they?" I replied.

"Indeed. The women outside would tear down this door to get to you if they did not fear punishment."

I smiled back at her.

"Then it is best that they don't get in," I replied jovially.

"Yes," she agreed with a smile, "it is best that they don't. Now then, what is it you wish of me?"

Clearing my throat nervously, I looked down at the floor. I had never asked a woman for intimacy before. I did not know how to say it.

Maa-Ra stepped forward and touched my face, raising my chin until our eyes met.

"I think I know what you want. The king says that you have the need for a skilled woman?"

I gulped long and hard.

"Why...yes. I do...but I would never take a woman against her will. I would not do that."

Maa-Ra stepped back with a surprised look.

"You are much different from others who have been sent to me. But before I decide, I would learn more about you. Come."

She took my hand and led me to a low table on the other side of the room. There we sat cross legged across from each other as she reached into her robe. Pulling her hand out fist closed, she closed her eyes and moved her mouth in a silent prayer. When she opened her hand several cowrie shells tumbled from her grasp.

When they settled upon the table, Maa-Ra surveyed them for a few moments. Then she turned her face up toward me, her eyes far away as she rested her head with the oracle.

## SHADES OF MEMNON II

"You are on a journey," she said.

"Yes," I replied.

She gathered the shells and threw them again.

"You seek...salvation...but not for yourself."

"Yes," I repeated.

She threw the shells once more.

"You are a good man...but you are... bound by evil."

I looked at her and nodded. Then she gathered up the shells and put them back into her robe. With the faraway look still in her eyes, she stood up before me.

"Someone has a message for you. Come I will help you to hear it."

Maa-Ra took my hand and led me over to the couch. With a snap of a strap, her robe fell, revealing a wonderfully curved form that filled me with desire. I disrobed also and we tumbled upon the couch. When our bodies joined, I felt a charge of life force course through me like lightning.

Maa-Ra's body was shaking with pleasure, and with each quiver, I saw lights of various colors flash around her. Overjoyed, I at last felt the void inside me fill rapidly with Rau. Maa-Ra was indeed a very skilled woman.

We continued our embraces for long minutes more, when suddenly Maa-Ra began shaking violently, her head snapping from side to side as if she were in great pain. I was startled and tried to pull away, but she held me fast with a strength beyond her womanly frame. Then a voice rang out that was not hers.

"Memna-un!"

I recognized the voice but I could scarcely believe it. The sound emerged from the mouth of Maa-Ra, but it was the voice of Meri-Ta, my Mut.

"Memna-un! Listen!"

"Yes Mut," I replied.

"Listen to me! I observe your spirit from the inner planes! Something has been done to you!"

"I know Mut, I know. I will never be with Nala again..."

"Noooo! Not her! Something has been done to you. If you give in to it you will never free your sister. Never fulfill your destiny."

Maa-Ra's body was pouring with perspiration. Though she too was empowered by the force of our union, manifesting the spirit of my Mut was taking a terrible toll. Her grip upon me loosened and her shaking began to subside, so I spoke quickly, desperate to hear the message before the connection was broken.

"What is it Mut? Quickly, what is it."

Her reply seemed far away, fading more with every word.

"Shed no blood, Memna-un..."

"But Mut...!"

"Shed...no...blood..."

Then she was gone.

When Maa-Ra came back to herself, I was already dressed and sitting on the edge of the couch. Her soft hand touched my shoulder, but I continued to stare ahead at nothing.

"What is wrong Memna-un?"

"You heard her, Maa-Ra. How am I to accomplish my goals without the shedding of blood? My sister and I have been abused by evil ones whose blood surely deserves shedding."

"I do not know Memna-un. But surely your Mut meant well."

"I am sure also, but... I cannot understand."

Then I thought for a moment.

"The Anu! I was sent here for him. Perhaps he would know."

"The little man?" Maa-Ra asked.

I nodded affirmatively and Maa-Ra looked concerned.

"He is owned by Brid, Minos' general. How do you propose to get him?"

"He is the former general. Minos appointed me to his position. I think I have something to trade for the Anu, but I need your help Maa-Ra."

"I will do what I can," she replied.

The next day I walked with a spring in my step as Maa-Ra and I sought the whereabouts of former general Brid. Not since my time with Nala had I felt so alive. The Rau-force coursed through my body with each breath, especially when my hands came near my weapons. I also noticed that my eyesight, hearing, all my senses were heightened as we strolled though the military wing of the palace. A warrior directed us to nearby quarters and we knocked on the open door. A bitter and angry voice bid us to enter and we stepped inside.

The room was a large, sumptuously furnished living space with a huge purple rug in the middle of the floor. Upon this rug lay Brid, flat

SHADES OF MEMNON II

upon his belly, a flask of wine in his hand. He was pouring it sideways into his mouth, spilling much of it as he guzzled without care. On the floor nearby were other flasks and larger jugs, as well as the remains of meals he had eaten. I looked around to make sure we were alone and closed the door. When we approached him, Maa-Ra translated as I began to speak.

"Greetings, Brid," I said.

"What do you want!" he shot back rudely.

"Brid," I began, "I would like to talk to you. As a man. Please stand up."

He looked up at me suspiciously. Then shot a hateful glance at Maa-Ra.

"Minos sent you here didn't he?"

"No he did not. I come of my own accord..."

"But what else could you want from me?" Brid went on. "You have my generalship. You are famed for escaping the labyrinth..."

Then he pointed at Maa-Ra.

"Minos even gave you the run of his women, including this disgusting half-breed. What more could you want? To laugh at my plight? Is that it?"

"No Brid. That's not it."

I got down on my belly and crawled towards him. He was surprised, but still very suspicious.

"What is this? Are you mocking me?"

"No Brid," I replied. "I don't agree with what Minos has done to you. But if this is the only way I can speak to you as an equal, I will do it."

Several emotions flashed across Brid's face. Finally he shouted words at Maa-Ra, who walked over and locked the door. Then he got to his feet.

"This better not be a trick."

"It is not," I said, standing up before him.

Brid stretched his arms and legs heartily. He was a big man and the heaviness of his body had taken its toll since he was forced to crawl about. Scuffmarks and welts covered his knees and elbows from days of his cruel punishment.

"Well what is it? What do you want?"

"I want the Anu!"

"What? No!" Brid exclaimed. "Never! Do you know what it cost me to catch him? He brings me great profit. Why should I give him to you?"

I looked at Maa-Ra as she translated his tirade. I had to handle this delicately or blood would surely be spilled. I was not leaving without possession of the Anu.

"Not even for your generalship?" I asked.

Brid's raised his eyebrows.

"Hmmm, my generalship you say?"

"Look here Brid," I replied. "I am only going to be here a short time. In a few moons my master will return and I will take my leave. I have no wish to be a general for Minos or anyone."

Brid looked puzzled.

"You don't? Then why would Minos...?"

"That I do not know. But I am willing to act as general in name only and let you do your job as you have been. Also, I will ask Minos to cease this punishment so that you may teach me what I need to know. And by the time I leave here, we will conspire a way for you to get justice for what Minos has done to you."

Brid put a hand to his chin as he considered my offer.

"All this, in exchange for the Anu?"

"In exchange for the Anu."

"Well, then, I will just have to catch another. I agree to your terms."

Then he pointed at Maa-Ra.

"But must this half-breed be involved?" he asked scornfully.

I could not understand what Brid had against Maa-Ra, but I wouldn't allow him to mistreat her.

"She is my helper Brid," I answered. "She remains with me."

Brid shook his head. Then we clasped hands to seal the deal and he left the room. He returned momentarily, handing me a note and several keys.

"He is kept out near the stables. Give this message to the guards and they will give you leave. These are the keys to his cage and chains. Never take the silver band from his neck. It possesses the magic which binds him. He will escape immediately if you remove it."

I thanked Brid heartily and clasped hands with him again. As Maa-Ra and I headed for the door, a last bit of advice left with us.

## SHADES OF MEMNON II

"Remember to beat him regularly, or you'll spoil him," Brid shouted. "And dance him twice a day to keep him in shape."

We left Brid and made our way to the stables. Following the odors natural to the area, we soon found ourselves surrounded by warriors, chariots and horses. A helpful horse keeper led us to a small wooden building under the watch of two guards. I handed them the note and they stepped aside immediately.

After informing Maa-Ra that I wished to go in alone, I stepped inside the dank and foul smelling stable. A dim light shined from a small lamp hanging from the ceiling, illuminating the gloom. Shutting the door, I spied the familiar cart pushed back into a corner.

The Anu's cruel cage was perched atop it and on the ground before it sat a bowl of molded vegetables. Kicking the bowl aside angrily, I unlocked the chains and pulled them loose. Then the wall fell away, revealing the shadowy figure of the Anu, his arms held defensively before him.

"It is all right," I said gently, "I am your friend, great Anu."

Slowly and gently, I put my hand forth. The little man's eyes lit up in surprise as he spied the ring once again. Then, placing his shaking hand in mine, he stepped forward. As I lifted and placed him upon the ground, he winced in pain due to the fresh marks of a recent beating. My heart suddenly flooded with grief as I realized this new pain was probably incurred due to our last meeting.

Managing a reassuring smile despite these feeling, I lifted the keys before his eyes.

"It is a new day my friend," I said with a nod. "No one will hurt you again."

Unlocking the chains from his legs, I threw them aside. Next I freed his arms, tossing those chains over my shoulder. Lastly, I unlocked the silver collar from his neck and glanced at the curious markings engraved on it. With great contempt I tossed it to the ground and stepped on it.

The Anu lifted his tiny arms and looked at them. Then he stretched his legs and rubbed his ankles. Then he reached up, touching the swollen scars upon his neck. Gold colored tears shined from his eyes as he looked up into mine.

"I am Hra-Twa," he said in perfect Kamitian. "I thank you for freeing me this day."

I smiled at Hra-Twa, bowing before him as he had done before me days ago. My mind reeled with many questions, but before I could ask one, I thought I heard a sound behind me. Suspecting treachery from Brid, I pivoted swiftly, my hand grasping one of my weapons. To my relief the door was still closed and no one was there, so I turned back to speak to the Anu. But I found that my new friend was gone.

SHADES OF MEMNON II

# CHAPTER 3: "I AM PERSUS"

I called out Hra-Twa's name, but there no answer. Then I searched the stable thoroughly, looking under the cart, in the box and beneath the piles of hay, but to no avail. In the time it had taken to turn my head, the little man had disappeared without a trace. Confused and saddened, I walked out and asked Maa-Ra and the guards if they had seen anything. As I suspected, they had seen me go in, but observed no one else come out.

Stepping back inside, I pondered the situation. Why had the Anu left so abruptly? Could I have been wrong? Was there someone else here I had been sent to find? Thinking it best to pretend I had the Anu in my possession, I tossed his bonds into the box, chained it up again and wheeled the cart from the stable. As Maa-Ra and I pushed it back to my quarters, I pretended that Hra-Twa was inside.

I spent the rest of the day with Maa-Ra evading questions about the Anu. By nightfall she realized it was a subject I would not discuss, so she began to tell me about her land and peoples: How they lived in peace until two generations ago, when they were invaded by the forces of the first Minos, the mad grandPa of the current mad king.

She told me how, after years of valiant struggle, they were defeated by deceit and trickery: Having reached a peace agreement, they were to exchange children as mutual hostages, but instead were duped into giving over hundreds of their loved ones in exchange for an empty boat. Rather than see their children tortured and killed, they chose surrender.

This answered many questions for me, including how a people with the secret of the great fighting art I had seen could be defeated. To that very day, Maa-Ra told me, they kept thousands of hostages in a secret location as a safeguard. I asked her if they had attempted rebellion.

"Oh, yes, there was one great uprising," Maa-Ra replied. "But it ended in the death of many children. This we could not bear, because we love our little ones more than life."

"And so no more attempts were made?"

Maa-Ra shook her head sadly.

"As time went by many became resigned to this fate. Also, there is the place of those of us who have been born blood mixtures. We have many positions of power under the Tamahus and our loyalties lie mostly with them."

"And where do your loyalties lie?" I asked.

"My Pa was one of the few high-ranking Kushites of his time. My Mut was a cousin of Minos' Pa. I was allowed to study and become a priestess because of this. But each day I see the hypocrisy and cruelty that has come to this land with my Mut's people..."

"And so?" I asked, taking her by the hand.

"And so I am a woman in the middle. I would like to stand with those who are being oppressed," she replied. "But how can I turn my back upon the people of my Mut?"

I nodded and pulled Maa-Ra down onto a nearby couch. She responded by wrapping her hands around my neck and pulling me closer.

"It is a subject I must give more thought to," she said. "But I do know that my desire is for a Kushite man like my Pa..."

Then she unfastened her robe.

"My desire is for a man like you..."


After a long and pleasurable night, the next morning we accompanied Brid for an audience with the king. When we arrived in the throne room, Minos was sitting in his golden chair, piggishly eating from a large tray of food placed before him. Once again the room was filled with petitioners, all carefully waiting until the king finished to present their grievances and requests. Finally he finished with his repast, shoved the tray into the arms of a servant and began to give audience to those before him.

As Brid and I waited our turn, Maa-Ra translated the proceedings for me. Minos gave one absurd decree after another: Suggesting that land disputes be determined by knife fights, an inheritance be resolved by awarding the more handsome son and ruling that a trade dispute be resolved by each party destroying the remaining property of the other. There was no justice in the court of Minos, and I wondered how he had survived thus far without a knife in his back. As for our case, I knew I had to cater to his absurd cruelty to win it.

Finally our turn came and we approached the throne. Minos smiled as he greeted Maa-Ra and I, but frowned as Brid crawled up beside us.

"What do you want Brid?" he hissed. "You'll find no mercy from me. Your punishment is not over yet..."

Then I stepped forward.

"He is here at my behest, great Minos."

"Your behest?" he shot back. "You're the new general, what need have you of him?"

"Great Minos, if you please," I began humbly. "My request is that you release this man from his punishment so that he may serve me."

"Serve you at what?"

"Great king," I replied. "I am new to your land and new to the position you have granted me. I need Brid to show me the best way to defend your interests. He cannot do this on his belly."

Minos rubbed his fat chin as he thought.

"I don't know...I decreed his punishment..."

"Great Sun," I said reverently, "if you release him to me as my manservant, I will treat him like the lowly worm you have shown him to be. His punishment will continue."

Minos' eyes shifted from side to side, his lips twisted into a great smile. Then he burst out in laughter.

"Ha, ha, ha, ha, ha, ha, ha! A lowly worm! Yes, that's what he is."

Then he pointed at Brid.

"Brid, will do your general's bidding as the lowly worm you are if I allow you on your feet?"

Brid looked up, his eyes burning momentarily with searing hatred. Then he lowered his head.

"Yes. Yes, great Minos. I will serve him..."

"Serve him as what? replied the king sarcastically.

I heard Brid swallow hard.

"As...as the lowly worm I am..."

"To your feet then! As long as you know what you are you can stand like a man. But don't forget: you are a worm. Now get from my sight!"

We left the throne room of Minos quickly amidst snickering and laughter from the crowd of petitioners. Brid's head hung low and he rubbed his limbs slowly, wincing in pain from the swollen welts. He refused to look me in the eye and I could not blame him. Never before had I seen a grown man so humiliated.

When we arrived at his quarters, Brid immediately seized a flask of wine and started pouring it down his throat. Maa-Ra and I watched him drain it and reach for another. But as his hand wrapped around it, I seized his wrist.

"Stop, Brid," I said. "I need you with your mind intact."

## SHADES OF MEMNON II

His eyes narrowed to two hateful slits as he tugged against me.

"Leave me!" he screamed. "Leave me alone in my shame."

I tightened my grip upon his wrist until he let the flask go. Then his eyes softened almost to tears.

"Brid," I asked carefully, "why does the king seem to hate you so?"

He turned around, walked to the far side of the room and began pacing back and forth.

"I may as well tell you," he said, shaking his head. "It matters not if it gets back to him. I am as one dead regardless."

He beckoned us and we all seated ourselves on floor pillows. Then Brid poured us all a cup of wine.

"It is because I criticized him...actually I merely commented. It was in private. No one else was nearby. Not like when he humiliates me..."

"Commented on what?" I asked, taking a small sip of wine.

"On...on..." Brid began. "You have seen him with the young boys, have you not?"

I nodded, slowly beginning to understand.

"Young boys," Brid continued. "He is obsessed with them. It is common to have a male youth from time to time among my people, but Minos shuns the duties of kingship. He never visits women."

I looked at Maa-Ra.

"This is true, Memnon," she said. "He has 100 wives and 300 concubines. None have spent a night with him..."

Brid nodded and drained his cup briskly.

"I...I merely commented that a son should be produced to carry his line and he became furious. He did not have me killed because of my political affiliations, but since then he has taken every opportunity to humiliate me."

"I understand," I replied.

"Do you? Do you really understand? He has used you, Memnon, to take away everything from me. When you escaped from the labyrinth, your fame became my undoing. Even my allies dare not argue against you taking my position, even though you are a Kushite."

I felt sorry for Brid and placed my hand upon his shoulder.

"You have my word man, that I will return your position to you and find a way to get you justice before I leave here. And while you teach me what you know, I will treat you like a man, not a worm."

For more than a moon it was necessary for Maa-Ra to sit in on the teaching sessions with Brid and I. After that I knew the northern language well enough to release her. And it was well that I did, because Brid began teaching me things he did not want her to know. Secret things about the defenses set up to ensure Keftui could not be invaded. And the contingencies against home grown rebellion, including the whereabouts of the island of hostages. Both of these subjects I observed very carefully, because, unbeknownst to Brid, I wished to see the Keftuan Kushites freed.

As time went by I developed much respect for Brid and his courses in military thinking. With boards, maps and mock armies, he taught me strategies, tactics, plans and counterplots. He taught me to study the enemy, the battlefield, and to look for any advantage at all to push my forces to victory. As a veteran of many skirmishes and conflicts, Brid was excellent in the art of violence men call war. And after two moons of his instructions, I felt I could make war too.

My chance seemed to come, when, on the first day of my third moon in the land of Keftui, a courier arrived with a note bearing the royal seal. Brid scanned it quickly and handed it over to me. Though my reading of the their language left much to be desired, I made out the brief note without much trouble. It stated that the rebels of the mainland were troublesome again and we were instructed to go forth and subdue them.

Brid was delighted at the prospect of proving himself again. I, on the other hand, had many concerns. From the overview given me by Brid earlier, these "rebels" were various groups who had refused to submit to Minos' allies who had taken the Mycenean capital. They had been invaded at the same time Keftui had been conquered, and the Myceneans had fought valiantly also. They, however, fell for no tricks and have maintained control of the countryside by using brilliant hit and run tactics.

Brid knew that word was sent to Kho-An-Sa that the rebels had become a serious threat. But he did not know that we arrived under the pretense of giving aid to take the Blade of Shai and king Minos' life. And so I was in a predicament. The blade was not in my possession and Minos was still alive. Though Kho-An-Sa was not due back for several moons, I did not know if I could afford to go off to war. I did know though, that I could not aid the invaders here or on the mainland against the innocent natives.

After reading the note, I feigned enthusiasm before Brid and

## SHADES OF MEMNON II

excused myself for the day. As I walked back to my quarters, I wondered what I should do. To decline the chance to prove myself would arouse suspicion, but to aid a war against a blameless people was out of the question. I walked into my quarters and lay down upon the couch, my mind weighed down by indecision. My eyes had closed for only moments when I heard a familiar voice quite near me.

"I am here," the voice said.

Opening my eyes, I sat up quickly. There standing before me was the missing Anu, but looking much different from the last time I saw him. Now vibrantly healthy, wearing a robe of deep purple, Hra-Twa stood proud and regal. With a small, elaborately carved staff in his hand, he looked like the paintings I had seen of his folk since childhood.

"Hra-Twa!" I cried.

"Shush!" he said, putting a finger to his lips." Quietly, my friend. No one must know I am here."

"But where have you been?" I asked in a whisper. "Why did you leave? What have you been doing?"

"I have been healing, my friend," he replied calmly. "Certain rituals and purifications had to be performed, else I would be no good to you."

A great smile broke across my face.

"Then you are the one I was sent for! You are who Kam-Atef meant!"

Hra-Twa leaned upon his cane, brushing off his robe nonchalantly.

"Of course I am," he replied. "Why ever did you doubt it?"

"Oh, Hra-Twa..." I said in relief. "It is good to see you."

"It seems our destinies have become intertwined, my friend," Hra-Twa said. "Now then, tell me your story so that I shall know how to assist you."

I told Hra-Twa the full tale from my first meeting with Kho-An-Sa up to the current situation there in Keftui. He listened intently to every word, nodding his head at key points.

"Well now," he began. "The first thing to do is to find out what your Mut spoke about."

"How are we to do that," I asked.

"Stand up," he replied. "And you will see."

I stood up before him and he began to dance again. As he whirled around me in a circle, I could feel the life force extending from his body, enveloping me once again. But this time there were noticeable touches and probings in certain places.

"Whoa!" I exclaimed, as the force touched my privates,

"Sorry, my friend, " Hra-Twa replied, as he kept dancing. "I must check everywhere. You'll thank me later."

After long minutes of dancing and subjecting my body to these invisible touches, Hra-Twa stopped and looked up at me.

"Well," he began, "the good news is that the influences of Nala are almost gone. This woman Maa-Ra is very good for you..."

"And the bad news?"

"The bad news is that Kho-An-Sa laid a curse upon you and your weapons. Rather, upon your use of your weapons."

"What do you mean?" I asked.

"I mean, if you keep spilling blood using those blades, the negative spirit of Sekmet will overtake you. You will become Sebau, a servant of Set. It's a very bad thing and very dangerous. Kho-An-Sa must want you very badly."

I sat down heavily upon the coach.

"But the Claws of Sekmet are a part of me. Now you say I can't use them?"

Hra-Twa paced the floor, rubbing his chin with one tiny hand.

"I didn't say that. Pay attention before you weep. Tears are costly. I said you can't make it a habit of spilling blood with them."

I was confused.

"But how am I to use them without spilling blood?"

Hra-Twa grinned widely.

"Let an Anu expert handle that. Now to the other immediate problem. Lets see what the Voice of the Deity has to say about your latest assignment."

Hra-Twa reached into his robe and pulled out a handful of small shiny pebbles. Kneeling down, he shook them up in both hands and cast them upon the floor. When they tumbled to a standstill, I noticed small engravings etched upon them.

"I carved this batch myself," said Hra-Twa, gazing upon the pebbles. "It is a very powerful oracle."

He studied the pebbles for a few moments, then he looked up at me.

"The Voice of the Deity says that you should go. Go to Mycenea.

SHADES OF MEMNON II

It will be the key to your destiny in this land."

"Well..." I replied, "I will do as you advise. But what about my weapons?"

"I'll figure something out. Meanwhile try not to fight anyone."

"But I'm going to a war..." I lamented.

"You're the general, let someone else fight. Right now I must be leaving to find a solution for you."

"Go? Where?" I asked. "Wait!"

"When you need me, go off alone. I'll show up."

"But...I..."

"Why look," Hra-Twa said, pointing at a nearby table, "nicely decorated."

"What?" I said, turning my head. "What's nicely decorated?" When I turned back again, Hra-Twa was gone.

Within two days Brid and I organized 4000 warriors and outfitted two warships and once again I found myself sailing to an unknown land. After a day and a night, the mainland of Mycenea appeared upon the horizon, and few hours later we docked in the ports of this renowned city.

As we disembarked, I noticed that the architecture looked similar to that of Keftui, but with a sternness, a seriousness that the island structures lacked. The street were laid out plainly and the entire atmosphere was cold and unfeeling. Even the two emissaries who greeted us had stuffy, businesslike demeanors as they conducted Brid and I to waiting chariots. We rode through the city at a brisk gallop, finally stopping before a large, boxlike building painted gray.

As soon as I stepped inside I heard a hideous scream. Brid and I stopped and looked at each other, while the emissaries seemed not to hear anything. They led us to the room from which the screaming emanated and motioned for us to enter.

The first thing we saw was a large man with his back to us. The screaming came from a small Tamahu man, who was being held down on his knees by several warriors. The torturer turned around when he heard us come in, revealing his victim's viciously cut up face. I wanted to turn my head, but found myself strangely compelled to look. Chunks of flesh hung off his jaws and chin, revealing white bone where the flesh once lay. Gripping a bloody dagger, the torturer acknowledged us with a nod.

"Greetings," he said. "You have come just in time to see this spy executed. I will be with you momentarily."

With the words barely from his lips, the big man raised the knife high, plunging it deep into his kneeling victim's chest. The man screamed once, then slumped over immediately, dead.

"Take this trash away," said the big man as he wiped off his knife with a rag and sheathed it in is belt. Then he strolled over to a big table, beckoning us to join him. The large map was laid out, which the man poked with one long finger.

"You see this?" he asked, indicating a small section of the map. "This is my kingdom. The rest of it belongs to the enemy. Now what do you plan to do about it?"

Brid and I looked at each other. I had no idea we were speaking to the king. He was dressed in the common battle gear of all the other warriors, with no signs of regal trappings.

"I am Melanaus," the man said. "king of a dwindling nation. You must be Memnon, son of Memnon of Troy, Minos new general."

I nodded and bowed slightly.

"And this is Brid," I replied. "My...advisor. We will do what we can."

"Oh, I'm afraid I'll need more than that. I need these rebels crushed. If you can't do that, then you may as well go back home."

"We will dispatch our greatest, out elite warriors," Brid replied. "We will find these rebels and destroy them."

"That's what I want to hear," cried Melanaus. "Now go do it!"

We left the war room of Melanaus to gather our forces from the ships. Brid was eager to begin marching that very day, but I needed time to formulate a plan. After finding lodging for our warriors, I chose seven of the elite Kushites, all masters of Pan-Kau-Rau-Shen, to accompany me on a "search mission" to locate the enemy. My real intentions were something else entirely.

I told Brid that we would be back in five days and assigned him to stay with Melanaus to formulate an attack plan. I was pleased that he reluctantly obeyed, because if he hadn't I would have had to kill him. The warriors and I left the city of Mycenea, heading for the outlands controlled by the rebels. When we stopped to rest that evening before a small fire, I took my life in my hands and told the men my real intentions.

"Men," I began," we will fight for the tyrant Minos no more."

## SHADES OF MEMNON II

They looked at me with a mix of surprise and suspicion.

"What do you mean?" one asked.

"Now fellows, you know that I am a stranger to your lands and I have no ties to you or yours. I could join Minos and his people in their tyranny, but I choose to go the other way. Join me and your people will soon be free."

The men looked at each other. Suspicion still ruled their expressions as they whispered for a few moments. When the next one spoke up, I recognized him as the warrior who had won the contest at Minos feast.

"But what of our children? We elite guards must give over two captives. They will surely die."

"No they will not," I replied. "Because I know where they are."

The looks of suspicion turned into utter astonishment.

"And I know how to get them."

I took a stick and scratched in the dirt a map to the island where the children were kept. I outlined the defenses there and the small number of warriors watching over the captives. The men believed me because what I told them matched rumors they had heard for years.

"Why are you doing this," a warrior asked.

I looked into the eyes of each of them before I spoke.

"I have a loved one held captive far away from here. She and I are being abused just as you and yours are. My wish is to see justice done."

"When do we go?" one warrior asked.

"First we need advice from a friend, then we need a small ship. Wait here."

Night had fallen, so I lit a small torch and wandered away from the campsite. When I could no longer see the men, I stopped and leaned against a tree. Looking up at the stars, I tapped my foot. A moment later Hra-Twa stepped forth from the shadows.

"It is a good night for plotting rebellion, eh?" the Anu said with a smile.

"A very good night indeed," I replied. "But where do I go from here Hra-Twa ?"

"You follow him," Hra-Twa said, extending his hand to his right.

Suddenly a man emerged from behind a tree. He was a tall Tamahu with long black hair and piercing gray eyes. Stepping forward, he extended his hand.

"I am Persus," he said. "Leader of the Mycenean rebellion."

When glowing Aten rose high the next morning, we were sailing aboard a ship provided by Persus to the island of the captives.

The craft was not large and besides the crew of 12, carried only 29 warriors. Hra-Twa, myself, the seven Keftuans, Persus and 19 of his men. A mere handful, sailing to change the destinies of two nations.

Persus men, excellent sailors and disciplined warriors, were a mix of Tamahus and Kushites who seemed in all respects to be equal. They told me that their people were a mix of both races, who had come together ages ago and forged a nation peacefully. Now they fought together against other Tamahu from the north, who were attempting to impose a new and unequal order. In return for their assistance, we promised to help them throw off the yoke of the invaders in their land.

My curiosities about Persus and the Myceneans answered, I turned my attentions toward Hra-Twa. I was pleased that he had not disappeared and took the opportunity to engage him in intense conversation. We spoke of many things as we bobbed upon the waters of the Great Green that day, including his solution to the problem of my weapons.

"Well my friend," Hra-Twa explained. "I found no way to lift the curse from your blades, but there may be a way to turn it to your advantage."

"How could a curse be turned to my advantage?" I asked.

"Listen now," the Anu continued. "Kho-An-Sa applied this curse during the forging process, when he locked it in along with your blood. It is designed to warp the life force, so I believe that we can use it to cut the life force, the Rau, emanating from others, instead of cutting the flesh itself."

"What are you saying?" I asked.

Hra-Twa grinned broadly.

"I'm saying that you are in just the right place, at just the right time, to learn to use your blades on a higher level."

Hra-Twa called out to Persus and the Keftuan warriors. They joined us and discussed my predicament for a good while. All agreed that Hra-Twa's plan may work.

"Persus is a master of the long sword, renowned and feared throughout the northern lands." said Hra-Twa, motioning toward the rebel leader.

"When this is over," said Persus, "I will teach you all I know. Only very precise swordsmanship can make this thing work."

## SHADES OF MEMNON II

Then two of the Keftuan warriors stepped forward. One was the warrior who had performed at Minos feast.

"I am called Hu-Nak," he said. Then he pointed to the man next to him. "This is Pan-Shu. We will teach you the ways of Pan-Kau-Ra-Shen, the secrets of pneuma, the hardening of the life force."

"And I will show you the secret places of the body where the Rau emerges," said Hra-Twa. "But first let us retrieve these children."

It took only a day to find the island we searched for. I remembered the maps Brid showed me in detail and led the sailors directly to it. Midway between Keftui and the mainland, it was surrounded by larger islands that effectively shielded it from detection. I also remembered Brid's description of the tall tower used to look out upon the sea. It loomed before us now as we came near the island.

From the information I gathered, it was not wise to approach by day, so we skirted around another island until we were out of site of the watchers in the tower. There we waited until nightfall, then packed rope, tools, weapons and warriors into several small boats and rowed quietly. Upon sliding onto the beach behind the tower, we lit small torches and struck out for a group of hills in the distance. Somewhere among them was the prison compound which housed the captives and the 50 or so guards who watched over them.

As we crept over the beach, I noticed deep impressions in the sand. Some of us stepped into them and had to raise our legs high to step back out. I started to notice a definite pattern to the impressions when Hra-Twa called us to a halt.

"What is it?" I asked.

Bending over, Hra-Twa examined the impressions closely.

"What do you think these are Memna-un?" he said.

"I don't know..." I replied.

Hra-Twa looked up, his face showing grave concern.

"I now understand how they control thousands of captives with only 50 men," Hra-Twa said. "These are footprints."

Startled by his words, all of us bent down, shining our torches upon the impressions. Indeed they were footprints, with clear toe and heel impressions, but they were 10 times the size of a normal man's.

"There is a dangerous creature here," said Hra-Twa. "A giant of monstrous proportions. Before we can get those captives, we will need to deal with him."

I agreed. And I knew we had to do it stealthily, or the compound would be alerted and the lives of the captives put in danger. Looking around for a place to hide and plan, I spied three large rocks in the distance which formed a crude shelter. Beckoning the men to follow, I walked over to them.

There we settled down, putting out our torches for fear of being detected, to discuss this matter.

"I have heard of such creatures, but have never wished to see one," said Persus. "They say that it is impossible to kill them."

"I too have heard of them," added Hra-Twa. "I have never seen one either, but I know how they are created..."

"How?" I asked.

"It takes a twisted, spiteful mortal to become one," Hra-Twa explained, "who makes a deal with the powers of evil to gain physical size to match his delusions of self importance."

"And they only have one eye..." added Persus.

"That is because they only see life one way," said Hra-Twa. "Their way. Make no mistake friends, this thing will have to be dealt with harshly."

I considered the size of the footprints and how many men we might lose fighting the thing. After a battle with this creature, there may not be enough of us alive to rescue the children. Glancing around at the boulders around us, I hit upon a bold idea.

"Persus, you know the nature of these waters," I said. "Are steep drop-offs common along these beaches?"

"Usually, yes," he replied. "And powerful undertows."

"And when do the tides come in?" I asked.

"Near day break," Persus answered. "High tide should come in with the light. But why do you ask?"

I told them all my plan and we agreed that it was worth trying. First two warriors were sent up and down the beach to act as lookouts. Then Persus and I took oars from a boat and probed the waters until we found a steep drop-off point. Next we selected a huge boulder and rolled it to the edge of the water.

Chipping a deep groove around it with bronze hammers, we slipped a stout rope into the impression, tied it, and rolled the boulder into the water near the drop-off point. Pulling a length of the rope out onto the beach, we then fashioned a huge noose and covered it over with sand. Then we sat down to wait.

## SHADES OF MEMNON II

When the first light of Aten crept over the horizon, we heard a shout from one of the men sent out on watch. Suddenly he appeared, running toward us in a near panic. There was no need for him to report, for we saw the creature pursuing him immediately. It was indeed 10 times the size of a man, looming over the beach taller than many trees further inland.

Covered with thick matted hair, it indeed had a single eye in the middle of its forehead. A huge club fashioned from the trunk of a tree was slung over it's shoulder and fangs longer than my arms jutted from its mouth. Looking down contemptuously, the monster surveyed the tiny men scampering before it. As it gripped the shaft of it's huge weapon threateningly, the look on its face told me it intended to kill us all.

SHADES OF MEMNON II

# CHAPTER 4: "A RAZOR SHARP REPAST"

The creature ran forward with it's club raised high, and we scattered before it like mice. I had no choice now but to draw both my blades, silently praying for my Mut's forgiveness.

The club came down, missing the men it had aimed for, but causing sand to burst high into the air. Taking advantage of this momentary distraction, Persus called to his archers and a dozen arrows flew through the air, only to bounce off the giants skin with little effect.

"Keep shooting," shouted Persus.

As the archers fired volley after volley, the Keftuans were standing in a circle, breathing loudly in the rhythms I had heard at Minos feast, building the force of their "pneuma. Suddenly Hu-Nak and another warrior broke off and ran towards the giant. Seeing them coming, he swung his club down, smashing Hu-Nak into the sand like a nail driven swiftly through wood. The other warrior charged on and leapt into the air, landing a vicious kick on the top of the giant's foot.

The creature doubled over in pain, dropping his club as he seized his aching foot. Then the rest of the Keftuans, heartened by the proof that the creature could be hurt, ran forward and rained terrible blows upon it's feet and legs. As they attacked from the front, Persus archers shot at the creature's neck and head from the rear, causing monster to twist back and forth from one attack to the other, writhing in pain and confusion.

I looked at the jewels carved upon my sword. The blood red gem glowed with inner fire, indicating that this was a creature born of the negative aspects of Herukhuti. Walking toward the creature, I chanted the hekau of that deity and there was an immediate effect on the giant.

Dropping the club, it held it's head in it's hands and stumbled about. Seeing this opening, the men redoubled their furious attack, but again the effects on the giant's body were negligible.

Persus, pulling back to study the waters washing upon the beach, shouted to me over the sounds of the battle.

"Memna-un! The tide comes, we must get him to the noose!"

I sprang forward and shouted at the warriors, telling them all to pull back. Then I ran up to the creature and jabbed deeply into the side of it's foot with my long claw. Howling in pain and fury, and truly hurt for the first time in the battle, the giant lurched toward me with his hands extended. Swiftly ducking his crushing fingers, I took off toward the

## SHADES OF MEMNON II

hidden noose.

"Hurry Memna-un," cried Persus. "The tide is coming in now!"

Ahead I saw the rope, slowly pulling free from the sand, heading for the open sea. Soon the tide would pull the rock from the ledge and our chance to be rid of the giant would be lost. Hesitating briefly, I jumped up and down to taunt the creature further, while chanting to keep him disoriented. Blundering after me in a disoriented rage, he failed to notice when his foot fell into the trap. Sheathing my weapons quickly, I dove for the rope and pulled with all my strength.

The circle of rope slid up the giant's foot, snapping tightly around his huge ankle. Realizing he had been tricked, he shook his fist and bent to free himself, but it was too late. A large wave dashed against the shore, snatching his leg forward, sending him reeling upon his back. As a second wave dragged him into the water, the creature gazed at me with bitter hatred and spat into the sand before me. Then a third wave came and he was swept away, gone beneath the waters without a trace.

We stood on the shore for long moments, watching Aten reflect upon the green waters. Persus put his hand upon my shoulder, giving me a grim nod of approval. We had done what had to be done.

"How deep are these drop-offs, Persus?" I asked.

"Hundreds of cubits," he replied. "Sometimes thousands."

Turning to leave, we found Hu-Nak digging his way out of the sand. His great control of the inner force had protected him. We could now attack the compound at full strength.

Gathering up our tools and weapons, we hurried towards the hills. We had planned to attack under the cover of darkness, but the giant had taken that chance away from us. Now our only hope lay in swiftness, surprise and subterfuge.

The hills were thick with trees that shielded our movements as we stealthily made our way. Within minutes we spied the compound in the distance. Sitting atop the highest hill in the vicinity, it was surrounded by a defensive wall that would be difficult to scale without detection. Our only choice was to gain entrance by trickery.

Choosing the youngest of the Keftuan warriors, I tied his hands loosely, put a noose around his neck and placed the rope in the hands of Persus.

'Go to the gate and tell them you have a new prisoner," I explained. "If they give you any trouble, the passwords are "Minos Speaks." Once inside, take out the gate keepers as quietly as you can and let us in."

Persus nodded, then he and the "prisoner" made their way up the hill toward the gate. We were too far away to hear what was said, but words were exchanged with the lookout. Then the huge doors swung open and they walked inside.

As we waited in hiding, I worried about the coming battle. This was my first time leading a group of warriors on a mission of life and death and the responsibility was overwhelming. Though I was sure we were doing the right thing, I wondered how we should proceed in the battle, so I asked Hra-Twa to consult the oracle.

He produced the pebbles, cast them onto the ground and gazed at them for a moment. Then he looked up with a grim expression.

"The Voice of the Deity says that the men you go forth to battle will have to be dealt with harshly," explained Hra-Twa. "Mercy is a virtue that is loved by the just, but I wouldn't suggest it in this case."

I fully understood what Hra-Twa meant. Brid had informed me that the policy in case this island were invaded was to kill all prisoners instantly. I could not let that happen. If one innocent child died as a result of our actions, I would live in grief of it all my days. The men who guarded these young captives, I grimly decided, would today have join their ancestors.

Suddenly the doors of the gate swung open and Persus appeared where the lookout once stood, beckoning us forward. As we ran up the hill, I instructed the men to find the warriors barracks immediately and let no one leave it alive. When we ran inside there were several bodies lying about, but the compound was quiet and still. Persus and the young warrior had done their work well, giving us the chance to get into position.

In the distance there were several buildings of various sizes and shapes. We broke off into small groups to find the warriors quarters. Peaking into the window of one of the buildings, I saw rows of youngsters sleeping on beds of filthy hay. One little girl was awake and saw me peaking in. Startled, she opened her mouth to scream.

"Shhhh!" I whispered. "Do not be afraid. We have come to take you home. Get the others up and be prepared to flee."

She nodded and smiled, then began to shake awake the others around her. I looked over my shoulder to find the Myceneans surrounding a large gray building, notching arrows and peaking into the windows. They had found the warriors barracks.

## SHADES OF MEMNON II

Positioning archers at the two exits of the building, we threw torches through the windows and waited. Shouts and screams were heard as they detected the fire and ran for the doors. When they emerged the archers were waiting, ruthlessly cutting them down one after the other.

Some saw what was happening and leapt from the windows, weapons in hand to defend themselves. These were met by the Keftuan warriors, by Persus and by me. Hra-Twa was nowhere to be seen.

As we engaged the enemy I noticed that Persus was indeed a great swordsman. Any warrior he confronted was halted by a net of metal woven by his sword, while the Mycenean cut and stabbed his opponents at will. My own sword work was slow and awkward in comparison and Persus cut down many of my opponents for me.

Far from being ashamed, I was glad for his assistance, for each time one of my blades sank into an enemy, I felt a familiar rush of emotion that I now knew was caused by the curse upon my weapons. It was a tingling sensation that rushed up my arm each time fresh blood soaked my blade, accompanied by a heady mix of pleasure and my conscious anxiety about it. I knew I would indeed become a monster if I continued down this course.

The piles of bodies grew until no more opponents stood before us. Except for a few last groans of death, everything was silent. Panting and huffing from the exertion of the fight, we looked up to see thousands of children surrounding us, waiting fearfully for our next move.

Suddenly two small children burst from the crowd. Shouting with glee, they ran into the arms of two Keftuans who greeted them with tear-filled eyes. Then a loud cheer rose up from all the children and they rushed in to embrace us.

Barely did we have time to sheath our weapons before we were engulfed by young bodies, nearly knocking us over in their enthusiasm. I personally hugged hundreds of children, who acted as if no one had held them in all their lives.

It pained me to think that they had to witness the slaughter we were forced into to save them, thus adding more trauma to already tortured little lives. But when I saw Hra-Twa being held aloft by a crowd of laughing youngsters, I knew that despite the killing, we had done a great thing that day.

We left the island the next day with seven prisoners and 300 children crammed onto the small Mycenean vessel. The prisoners included three men from the lookout tower, who, after witnessing the fate of their comrades, came down immediately to surrender.

The other four were nursemaids we found cowering inside one of the buildings. They would be held by Persus rebels until hostilities had ceased.

The children aboard were carefully chosen for their family ties with high ranking Kushite warriors in the Keftuan army. It was our intention to offer them as evidence that it was at last safe to rebel. The rest of the children we were forced to leave behind for lack of space, but several of the Keftuan warriors remained to assure that they would be safe until Persus could send more ships. We had now but to put into action my next bold plan—the subduing of the Tamahus in Minos army and the taking of Mycenea.

After arriving at the Mycenean rebels secret docking place, Persus left to gather his forces for the taking of the city. The plan was to start the rebellion amongst the Keftuan Kushites and raise much commotion. Then, when their forces gathered to crush the Kushites, Persus forces would descend, attacking from all sides. With the help of the common folk that he was sure would rally to our assistance, Persus was confident that we could defeat the enemy and take back Mycenea.

We bid good-bye and headed in opposite directions, me with Hra-Twa, the three remaining Keftuans, 20 of Persus Myceneans and the 300 children, while Persus left with the prisoners and a small group of messengers.

It was with great caution that we approached the vicinity of the city until we found a sufficient hideaway in a very large cave. There we left the children in the care of Hra-Twa and the Myceneans, while the Keftuans and I made rapidly for the city.

When we arrived in Mycenea we rushed immediately to the palace and the war room of King Melanaus. There, hovering over the war table, stood the king and Brid. They turned to us when we rushed in, eager to hear our report.

"Where are the other warriors?" Brid asked. "You took seven with you and return with only three..."

I pretended to be very angry.

"I had to kill two of the dogs," I cried. "Once outside the city, they attempted to assassinate me. Two escaped, no doubt to join with the enemy."

## SHADES OF MEMNON II

Brid and Melanaus looked at each other, surprised.

"Only these three remained loyal to me," I added, pointing to Hu-Nak and the other Keftuans. "Brid, step forward!"

Brid approached me with a bewildered look upon his face.

"Why did you not know about an alliance between the local rebels and some of the Kushites in your army?"

"Well, I..." Brid began.

"Silence" I screamed. "Just as I suspected. Your intelligence is weak, man. You know not what goes on in your own army. Be grateful that I don't strike you dead where you stand."

I berated Brid for a few moments more. Melanaus looked on with a concerned expression.

"Now Brid," I said , "this is what you will do if you value your life: I want all high ranking Kushites brought to the southern edge of the city. There I will personally administer a test of loyalty. Any of them found wanting will be killed instantly. Do you understand."

"Yes, my general," Brid replied. "I will see to it immediately."

"And Brid, " I added. "You will disarm all but a few essential Tamahus and all of the army's Kushites, until I find out just what is going on."

Brid nodded and left with great haste. I had no doubt that he would carry out my orders to the letter. Then I turned towards Melanaus.

"Now then, good king," I exclaimed. "Let us make a plan to finally crush these rebels."

Melanaus grasped my shoulder, nodding his head respectfully.

"It is time someone competent took over the army of Minos," he said. "I've waited years for that fat pig to send me assistance of substance. How ironic that it turns out to be a Kushite."

Though I yearned to knock a few teeth from the head of this cruel and racially prejudiced monarch, I ignored his last remark to concentrate on his battle plans. For hours we poured over the city's defenses and the capabilities of his army. By the time he was finished, I knew enough about his forces to practically defeat them myself.

We finished late in the evening and sat sharing a flask of wine when Brid entered and reported that all was in readiness for my "loyalty test."

"Fine," I said with a satisfied smile. "We will begin first thing tomorrow. I shall soon find out who is loyal to whom."

"Here, here," exclaimed Melanaus, clinking his cup to mine.

"Here, here indeed," I thought, gazing at the doomed king over the edge of my cup. "Here, here indeed..."

The next morning we stood at the southern edge of the city, not very far away from the cave where the rescued children waited. A long line of Kushite warriors stood before me, each bound by their wrists. Beside me stood Brid and the few guards he had allowed to keep their weapons. The first in line was a rather dignified looking old warrior who looked like he had seen many years of combat. I called for him to step forward.

"State your name, man" I said coldly.

"I am Tu-Ka-Na," the man replied. "Captain of the Kushite forces of Minos army."

I looked him up and down, then glanced over at Brid.

"Tu-Ka-Na I have been informed that you were at one time involved in an uprising against the majesty of the great Aten, King Minos II, Pa of the current king."

The captain shook head.

"That was in my checkered youth," he replied. "I am loyal to the house of Minos now..."

"We shall see," I cried, seizing him by the arm. "Come with me."

Whipping out my dagger, I dragged the old warrior into the forest. I continued to menace and ill treat him until we were out of sight of Brid and the guards. Then I gave him the respect he deserved.

"GrandPa," I began, using the normal Kushite designation for an male elder as I sheathed my dagger, "forgive me for my affront to you. All will be revealed soon."

Tu-Ka-Na looked confused but was too astonished to say anything. Minutes later were before the entrance to the cave and I called out the predetermined password. It was repeated and we walked into a cavern filled with Keftuan children. Tu-Ka-Na nearly slipped to the floor in surprise.

"By the sash of the Goddess!" he exclaimed.

"Who is kin to grand old Tu-Ka-Na?" I asked loudly, cutting the bonds from his wrists.

Six screaming children came running from the crowd and leapt upon the old warrior, who let out a loud exclamation as he embraced his own grandchildren. He hugged them for long moments before finally looking up. Profuse tears ran from his eyes.

"What?" he asked. "What is this?"

SHADES OF MEMNON II

"Tu-Ka-Na," I said. "All of your children have been freed. It is time to overthrow the tyranny of Minos."

He looked at me in disbelief as I described to him how we had rescued the children and planned to defeat the enemy. I knew that he would not have believed me if proof had not been wriggling in his arms. I asked him if we could count upon his support.

"Yes," he cried. "A million times yes!"

I returned Tu-Ka-Na back to the holding spot. Brid looked at the old man and turned toward me.

"Whatever you did to him you did it well," Brid whispered. "I see the old man has been crying. Is he loyal or not?"

"Oh, yes, he's loyal," I said, nodding. "He is loyal to the end."

And thus I interviewed 150 men that day, all captains of the half of Minos army who fought ever against their will. To a man they secretly pledged to support my plan and to pass the word about the children. They were all so happy about their loved ones that each came back crying or with drying tears upon their faces. This so impressed Brid that he kept inquiring about my interrogation techniques. I told him that all would soon be revealed to his utmost satisfaction.

It was late evening when we went back to the city. After another session in the war room with Melanaus, the king and I quit to go to our separate quarters for the night. But I did not go to my quarters at all. Instead I met Hu-Nak, and we stole into the room where Brid had stored all the arms, stacked them into boxes and secretly distributed them amongst the Kushite warriors.

No one knew what we were doing, as we wheeled the boxes atop a small cart into the warriors quarters, pretending to hand out marching rations as I had told each captain we would. Though it was all subterfuge, we were indeed handing out a meal— a razor sharp repast that would be the last these invaders would ever eat.

After hiding the rest of the weapons so that most Tamahu warriors would be defenseless, Hu-Nak and I retired to my quarters to await the next phase of the plan. Thinking of nothing better to do until the appropriate time, we both went to sleep until we were awakened by loud knocking on the door.

I strolled to the entrance, while Hu-Nak stood stealthily beside it holding a stone vase. Opening the door, I spied my good assistant Brid. He was in a state of utter panic.

"Memnon," he cried. "The Kushite warriors somehow got their

weapons. They have fallen upon the others fiercely and have killed fully half our Tamahus."

"Come in Brid," I said.

He stepped inside my door with a puzzled look upon his face.

"Memnon, you were right," he cried. "They are allied with the rebels. But...but how can you be so calm?"

"Because I planned it," I replied.

An astonished look flashed across Brid's face, then his hand shot quickly for his sword. But before he could pull it, the stone vase in Hu-Nak's hands came down upon his skull. He crumpled to the floor, senseless.

The sounds of fighting exploded nearby as we tied Brid hand and foot and tucked him into a corner of my quarters. It was now time to give Persus the signal.

Hu-Nak seized a bowl of pitch, a bow and several arrows. Then, peering into the hallway and finding it empty, we dashed down the hall and up a staircase. Swiftly we ran up several flights to the top, where I seized a torch and kicked the wooden door open.

Emerging upon the roof of the palace, we looked around at the city. Flames and fighting were breaking out in all directions. The rebellion was going fully as planned.

Hu-Nak dipped an arrow into the pitch, I lit it and he shot it as high as he could. Then we fired and shot three more and waited. A moment later we saw identical signals from Persus' forces positioned at the edge of the city. It would not be long before they arrived.

Meanwhile my plans continued to progress, as I saw hundreds of King Melanaus' warriors streaming towards the palace. Shouts and oaths filled the air, along with the sound of clashing metal. In the distance war horns bellowed, calling more of Melanaus' warriors to subdue the raging Keftuans.

Now the fighting grew hotter, and from what I could see, the forces of King Melanaus were getting the worst of it. Several times I saw the elite Pan-Kau-Ra-Shen warriors rush forward, mowing down dozens with their bare hands. But thousands more of the enemy were pouring into the area and I prayed for speedy assistance from Persus. Even the mighty wielders of "pnuema" could not last long against such odds.

Hu-Nak was agitated.

"I should be down there with my brethren," he cried.

## SHADES OF MEMNON II

"Patience, my friend," I replied. "Soon we will be in the thick of it. Let us first see that the battle is well orchestrated."

We both scanned the sky until we saw the signal we had been looking for. In each of the four corners of the city, we saw a huge fire blaze to life. It was the signal that Persus and his rebels were about to descend from the four directions.

"Now," I cried, turning to Hu-Nak, "is the time!"

"Finally!" he cried.

We raced down the stairs and leapt into the fray. All over the palace, the Keftuan guests had turned the place into a bloody battlefield. I had never seen such furious fighting. After years of pent up frustration over their children and the tyranny they endured, they at last were able to wreck their vengeance. And a terrible vengeance it was.

But as the fighting continued, I could see that our forces were being pushed back due to the sheer numbers that had joined against us. Melanaus army still streamed into the courtyards and avenues of the palace, while we were already surrounded by an ocean of them. Just as things looked the worst for us, I heard cries from the rear of their forces.

"For Mycenea! For Freedom!"

The rebels of Persus had finally arrived and were attacking from the rear on all sides. With wild cheers, we attacked with renewed vigor as the enemy turned much of their attention to the larger forces behind them.

I saw many of the Keftuan elite actually tear men asunder, so furious were their attacks. It became so bad that no warrior among the enemy would willingly fight them and had to be prodded by swordpoint by superiors.

So between the terror of the practitioners of Pan-Kau-Ra-Shen, the valiant and vengeful efforts of their brethren and the powerful swordsmanship of Persus rebels, we slowly began to get the upper hand.

All through the night we fought, the piles of dead growing higher and higher. Most of the fallen though, were the forces of King Melanaus.

As the light of day grew across the city, untold numbers of the common folk joined the battle on our side. Just as Persus had said, the people assisted in beating down the oppressors when they saw that their chance had come.

When this dawned upon the forces of Melanaus, most of his army tried to flee. But there was no escaping the vengeance of the angered populace. Thousands of his warriors died in the street, cut down by the picks, hoes and axes of the common folk.

At one point Persus and I were battling side by side when a loud voice rang out and the warriors engaging us stepped aside. There King Melanaus appeared. Tattered and bleeding, his face was livid with rage.

"You curs!" he screamed, waving his sword . "You have betrayed me and destroyed my kingdom. But before I see it taken I shall know that you both are in your graves!"

I stepped forward to see if the king could make good his boast, but Persus put his hand upon my shoulder.

"He has ruined my land for years, Memna-un," the rebel leader said coldly. "Let me mete out the justice that all Mycenea has longed for."

Nodding, I stepped back as Persus leapt forward. His sword met the king's blade in a flash of sparks and they had at it. Faster sometimes than my eye could follow, they parried, blocked and clashed. Both were master swordsmen, rivals and leaders with a long history of hatred between them. All nearby fighting ceased as we watched the outcome of this inevitable conflict.

For long minutes they raged in the courtyard, fairly even in skill and determination, but in the end it was the abundance of emotion that King Melanaus brought to the fight that proved to be his undoing.

After a particularly biting taunt tossed out by Persus about his manhood and ability to rule, and a well placed nick upon his thigh to back it up, the king went mad and rushed forward with his guard down. Persus sidestepped gracefully, then ran his sword beneath the king's arm, piercing the monarch's heart.

As his body fell the Mycenean rebels and Keftuans shouted for joy, while the remaining forces of Melanaus dropped their weapons. The battle for Mycenea was over.

We had little time for celebration after the battle though, because the fighting was not nearly done. After assigning some of his forces to oversee the cleanup activities, Persus and I turned our attentions towards reconquering Keftui. We dispatched several ships to retrieve the children and their guardians from the island, then we filled the Keftuan vessels from stem to stern with Myceneans and Keftuan Kushites.

What few Tamahus were left from Keftui were imprisoned with the exception of Brid, who I brought along in bonds. I had other plans for him.

## SHADES OF MEMNON II

After a night of well deserved rest, we sailed with haste to Keftui. Not knowing if any of Melanaus' forces had escaped to tell the tale, we thought the sooner we got there, the better would be our advantage. After much discussion during the two-day voyage, we hit upon a plan to facilitate the defeat of Minos forces.

It was simple, direct and designed to arouse the fervor of the Kushite warriors still under Minos sway as well as the general population. Though it would involve some risk to some of the children we had rescued, we were sure it would bring a swift end to the conflict with a minimum loss of life. A consultation with Hra-Twa and his oracle confirmed the plan's validity, though the Anu did tell me to beware the unexpected in the coming conflict.

When we arrived at the docks of Keftui, we first secured the area, sweeping it of all Tamahu guards and dock patrols. Then the Kushite warriors formed several long war columns. Inside the protection of these columns we arranged several hundred rescued children and began out march through the streets.

Everywhere we went there were two reactions: the population of Kushites went wild to see their children free and Kushite warriors fell upon their Tamahu comrades immediately. After killing them, the warriors would join us in our march.

In district after district, we swept through like a sickle, hacking down the small Tamahu forces as we went. I knew that word had probably gotten to Minos and that he was no doubt mustering his forces to stop us. But he would be too late. Our marchers had grown by the thousands and Persus' Myceneans where positioning themselves to launch a surprise attack.

After hours of marching, we arrived at the main road leading to the palace compound. Thousands of Kushite warriors had heard about us and rushed out, eager to finally join the fight for their nation. Many of them greeted their own children and the mood was almost festive, until we saw thousands of Minos' forces streaming from the palace to challenge us.

I ordered the children sent to the back of the line, for the final battle was about to begin. As we watched the enemy ahead, a warrior in fine and regal trappings rode forth in a chariot. I stepped forward to hear his message.

"The great Aten, King Minos," he began haughtily, "demands that you surrender immediately and give over the children which he rightfully owns."

I drew my long claw and waved it in the air.

"You tell that pig of a swine king that we demand his surrender—and submission to prosecution for crimes he and his family have committed upon the people of Keftui. We will never surrender—and furthermore—the only thing we will give over will be a length of sharp blade to penetrate the thick of his voluminous rump!"

At the end of my speech thousands of men at my back cheered and raised their weapons. The rider looked at me with disgust, pulled the reigns of his horse and trotted back to his battle line. There he engaged a group of people in intense conversation before throwing up his hands in resignation. Then the people he had been talking to mounted chariots and trotted out to meet us.

As they came closer I recognized one of them. It was Maa-Ra, accompanied by several other high-ranking mixed breed men and women. Finally they stopped before me, their faces bearing pleading expressions.

"Greeting, Memnon," said Maa-Ra.

"Maa-Ra!" I exclaimed. "What are you doing here?"

"I have come along with these others to negotiate a peaceful ending to this conflict..."

"There can be no "peaceful ending," I replied, "until the tyrant gives up his rule."

"But Memnon...you know he will not willingly do that," Maa-Ra pleaded. "There will be much blood spilled...Perhaps you could give back some of the children as a token of peace?"

This last suggestion totally incensed me and I looked around at those Maa-Ra had beside her. These must be the "unexpected players" Hra-Twa had warned me about. All were high officials I had seen before, who treated their Kushite cousins as lower beings. It finally dawned upon me what they had come out for and my eyes narrowed into slits of anger at the thought of it.

"I see it all now," I replied. "The only "blood spilled" you mixed breeds are worried about is your own. You are afraid of the retribution to be brought against you by the populace for your collaboration, afraid to lose your cushy positions in the corrupt pecking order of this regime. Is this not so?"

Maa-Ra and the rest of them bowed their heads.

"Well," I continued, "if you wish to avoid retribution, get down off

## SHADES OF MEMNON II

those chariots and join us. Show us who you stand with."

Again the men and women before me bowed their heads in shame. I shook my head in disgust.

"No?" I asked sullenly. "Then I suggest you leave the field, Maa-Ra."

Maa-Ra and the rest of her mixed breed cohorts turned and trotted back, disappearing behind the lines of the enemy army. They had chosen sides and shown to all present what their ultimate alliances were. I was saddened because of what she and I had shared and the assistance she had given to me, but there could be no middle ground in this conflict.

Both armies now faced each other just a few hundred cubits away. Archers on both sides notched arrows. Chariot horses stamped hooves in anticipation. The leader of Minos forces and I eyed each other menacingly, until he broke the tension with a yank of his horse's reigns. As his chariot surged forward, his forces followed close behind.

Drawing my blades, I leapt forward also, with thousands of vengeful Keftuans at my back. A great battle cry went up from both sides as we rushed toward the final conflict.

SHADES OF MEMNON II

# CHAPTER 5: "THE GODDESS BE WITH YOU AGAIN"

An unforgettable noise filled the air as thousands of warriors clashed sword to sword, shield to shield and bone to bone. Dodging the long spear leveled at my chest by the enemy leader, I hacked the blade of the weapon to the ground, then cut it's bearer down from his speeding chariot. A quick stroke of my short Claw as he hit the ground insured that he would never rise again.

As I looked up from my fallen opponent an arrow sliced through the air, barely missing my head. Another nicked my shoulder, then a Keftuan shield appeared, blocking several more arrows that would have surely hit me.

I looked up the arm of the shield bearer to find Hu-Nak smiling grimly. Another shield-bearing warrior stood beside him.

"Careful, Memnon," he said. "You have been chosen as a special target for the archers. Fight on, we will protect you."

I nodded in thanks, then we plunged into combat once again.

We made a powerful team, Hu-Nak, his comrade and I. First they dashed into the enemy with the force of their "pneuma" and shields to disorient them, then I waded in with the Claws of Sekmet, striking the enemy down while they protected me from projectiles. Soon others among our forces noticed this powerful tactic and the enemy was beset with hundreds of these three pronged engines of destruction.

The Keftuan Kushites fought with the ferocity of panthers, especially those who had just met their returned children. As for the Tamahus in the defense of Minos, they were taken aback by the bloodthirstiness of their former slaves. Too long had they been accustomed to commanding docile Kushites who bowed their heads and meekly obeyed. Now the seeds they had sown grew back as sharp bronze blades and the respect the Kushites taught them was for many their very last lesson.

The fighting had become so chaotic that I sent orders for the children to be taken far away to safety. Moments afterwards, as I stood over my latest fallen foe, a runner came with a message that chilled my blood.

"Great Memnon," he cried gravely. "The children are in danger!"

I immediately broke from the front line and raced back to the rear. It was then that I saw how we had been out maneuvered.

A thick wall of enemy warriors had sneaked up to our rear and were engaging our forces there. Beyond them lay the bodies of the warriors

## SHADES OF MEMNON II

sent to escort the children. Further on I saw the youngsters themselves—racing down the avenue with a force of Minos warriors in hot pursuit. The only reason they had not been overtaken was because of their speedy determination to remain free and because of the brave civilians who leaped out by the dozens to assist them.

But the unorganized commoners proved only momentary distractions as the better equipped and trained warriors cut them down and continued their pursuit. I had no doubt that the civilians could eventually overwhelm the few hundred warriors that pursued the innocents, as they had done in Mycenea, but they needed the strength of numbers and there simply was not time to gather them.

With a cry of anger and frustration, I dashed into the line of enemy warriors, hacking away with such violence that a swath was cut through them. Immediately I leapt through it, followed by dozens of other warriors, determined not to let the children fall into the hands of the enemy.

But though we ran with gravest haste, it was clear that we would arrive too late.

The Tamahu warriors were only a few cubits from the slowest of the children. Some of them had their hands extended to catch them, while others brandished weapons with the clear intention of murder.

I cursed aloud a thousand times as I ran, silently condemning myself to whatever fate the parents of these children would mete out to me. Then suddenly there was a mighty roar ahead, causing the warriors chasing the children to hesitate. Then a dense hail of arrows sliced into their flank.

A score or more fell dead or dying as a second volley cut into them. Then a horde of warriors, Kushite and Tamahu, emerged from an adjacent avenue and smashed into their surprised ranks. Fighting furiously, they wrecked havoc among the enemy with spears and flashing blades. There amidst the attackers stood Persus, chopping the enemy down without mercy. The children were saved.

As the children ran on to safety, what was left of the warriors who had chased them turned from the terrible blades of Persus and the Myceneans to retreat— directly into the path of the Pas of the innocents they had threatened. What took place next was an example of the terrible carnage that is best meted out to such cowards. It will suffice to say that none of those who threatened the children lived to see any of their own again.

As we fought side by side dispatching the rest of this lot, Persus informed me that his forces were attacking from all sides. After running to the front lines we saw that the forces of Minos were indeed besieged from the front and rear and that their flanks were being chewed to bits by Mycenean archers.

Their defeat was eminent and we had them on the run. And just as we expected, the Kushite population had now organized and were assisting us; ambushing the enemy on the streets, alleys and avenues. Soon Minos rule would be a memory, but the fat tyrant himself had to be called to account. We had only now to take the palace.

I had Brid brought forth to accompany us, then I organized a few hundred warriors, including Persus, Hu-Nak and more elites. After dispatching several parties to cut off possible escape routes, the bulk of us took off up the avenue and through the inner courts.

A few palace loyalists tried to oppose us, but we made short work of them and burst into the palace. There we were cheered by the Kushite servants, while Tamahu and mixed blood officials ran from us screaming. We harassed none of them, though. We had come for the king.

As we approached the throne room, dozens of Minos elites ran to meet us. But after a short, hot battle they lay dead before the huge door. Stepping over their bodies, we threw the portal open to behold the throne room.

It was filled with officials of Minos court, who immediately pled not to be hurt, offering us chests of jewels and deeds to their stolen property. Some even pushed forth their daughters, but we ignored them all and marched up to the throne. There sat King Minos, shaking in fear, his face dripping with tears. I stepped back and let Hu-Nak speak for his people.

"Minos!," he cried bitterly. "Generations ago we opened our arms to your people in friendship and your grandPa took advantage of it to grind us underfoot. Now our once peaceful land has been bathed in blood and it is all the fault of your people. But now your reign is over and we will have justice for all the innocents you killed for sport and gave to that creature in the labyrinth. Also for all the little boy children, Kushite and Tamahu, who were delivered to serve your perverted lusts!"

Hu-Nak had been slowly climbing the stairs as he confronted the king. Now he pointed directly into Minos face.

SHADES OF MEMNON II

"We demand no less than your life as justice. Only blood will satisfy our need for retribution. Afterwards we will be lenient with those of your family and court and send them away with their lives. If you have any honor, any loyalty to those who have been loyal to you, take out your dagger and do it yourself. We wish not to soil our hands with the likes of you."

Loud cheers went up from the warriors behind me as Minos took out his dagger. He looked at it for a moment, then tossed it away, burying his face in hands.

"I can't do it," he cried, sobbing pathetically. "I can't, I can't, I caaaan't!"

Brid, who had been standing nearby watching, screamed out.

"Let me do it!"

Everyone turned to look at him.

"I'll kill the weeping cur for you! Let me do it!"

I nodded at Persus and he cut Brid loose. Eyeing Minos hatefully, he rubbed his wrists where he'd been bound. Persus pulled his own sword and handed it to him.

"Be my guest," the Mycenean said with a wave of his hand.

Brid hefted the sword and smiled malevolently. At last he would have his revenge for the abuse he had taken and I would keep my vow never to kill for Kho-An-Sa. Just as I had planned.

The throne room was silent. Hu-Nak came back and stood beside me to witness the execution. Brid walked up the steps to the throne slowly, savoring the fear in the face of the whimpering king. Suddenly a woman broke from the crowd and bound up the steps, blocking Brid from the throne. It was Maa-Ra.

"Wait," she cried. "Wait! How can you call yourselves men of justice? You would kill a king without even a trial?"

Brid's face twisted into a mask of terrible rage.

"Move woman!" he screamed.

"How can you do this?" Maa-Ra continued, ignoring Brid. "Memnon, you have only been here a short while, how do you know Minos truly deserves death?"

I could not believe what I was hearing. I had been sent to die myself on a whim by this evil king. So had many others. Maa-Ra and everyone here knew this for fact. Why was she protecting him?

"Maa-Ra," I replied. "This man deserves death a million times over. What has he promised you?"

# CHAPTER 5: "THE GODDESS BE WITH YOU AGAIN"

Maa-Ra looked down at her feet. Once again I had seen through her deceptions. For a long moment she looked at the floor.

"Treasure," she replied finally. "Treasure in the labyrinth. He promised us a way to get it without facing the creature..."

"To Hades with a treasure," screamed Brid, raising the sword menacingly and pointing accusingly at Maa-Ra. "This is typical of you half breeds! You grovel for the sake of your masters, eat the leavings off their table and keep your faces firmly planted up Tamahu rears while pretending to be better than your darker cousins! I hate Kushites, but I despise you most of all!"

"Brid, No!" I screamed, but he ignored me, bringing the razor sharp blade down in a glittering arc. A sickening chopping noise filled the air and Maa-Ra's head rolled down the steps. As her body fell he turned to Minos, who was nearly fainting from fright.

"Now for you!" Brid screamed, stabbing Minos straight through the heart. Blood spurted from the dying king's mouth as Brid twisted the blade. Then he withdrew the sword and walked down the stairs with a look of utter satisfaction. He handed the blade back to Persus and turned to address us all.

"It is done," he said. "I care not what you do to me. I have been avenged."

Several men came forth and took Brid away as I stood staring at the bloody scene before me. The body of Minos was slumped over in the throne and Maa-Ra's headless form lay prostrate across the stairs. I had no feelings for the dead king, but Maa-Ra's fate saddened me. Why could she not cleave to the people of her Pa? Why did she succumb to the seduction of greed and position?

I looked over at the members of Minos court, who stood there shaking in their shoes. They did not know what their fate would be.

Hu-Nak and a group of warriors walked up to them and took everything of value from their persons. Then Hu-Nak pointed towards the entrance to the throne room.

"Go and get your belongings," he said. "You will leave our land right now!"

Days later all hostilities had ceased and Hra-Twa, Persus, Hu-Nak and I stood on the shore of a newly freed Keftui. The sea before us was filled with ships as the last of the Tamahus floated away from the island

SHADES OF MEMNON II

nation. With them went most of the mixed breeds, who couldn't stand the thought of living as equals with the Kushite majority and rightfully feared retribution. The war for freedom had been won. Now the time had come for peace.

The time had also come for me to deal with the curse upon my weapons and the effect it was having upon me. My body was fairly abuzz with negative emotions after the wars for Mycenea and Keftui. All the blood spilled across my blades had just the effect upon me that Hra-Twa said it would: I was plagued with violent dreams, harsh impulses and fits of needless aggression. Hra-Twa said I needed to be purified and conducted a ritual to do so.

After cleansing myself with a fast of fresh water and special plants, Hra-Twa did a dance similar to the one he had done to examine me earlier. Again I felt the force from his body searching, but this time I felt a sort of suction as he pulled the negative life force from me. When he was finished I felt normal once again.

For more than four moons I underwent the training that Hra-Twa had outlined for me. Invaluable sword fighting lessons were taught to me by Persus, who frequently interrupted work in his own homeland to teach me. As I learned the Mycenean told me much of the history of his land; marvelous tales of how two different races came together in peace, but whose constant battles for survival prevailed upon them to become deadly fighters. As I learned advanced swordsmanship from this noblest of Tamahu warriors, I came to love Persus as a brother.

I also had sessions with Hu-Nak and other Pan-Kau-Ra-Shen warriors, who instructed me in mastering the force of "pneuma," the hardening of the life force. I found some similarities to the training I had earlier when the Rau force was boosted within me.

Both areas of training complemented each other, just as Hra-Twa said they would. I learned to push the Rau force to the edge of my weapons as before, but this time I "hardened" the force until it formed a razor sharp duplicate over the metal. With this I had but to touch the secret areas of the body taught to me by my Anu friend and my opponent would fall before me.

First I tested the technique on doomed food animals, then very carefully on sparring partners. Whether the result was death, maiming or paralysis was a matter of my choosing, based upon the area I cut and how deeply I sliced into the channels of their life force. We had turned the curse placed upon my blades into a unique fighting instrument, that in the years to come would be legend.

I found other skilled women who kept me strong, but none quite as skilled as Maa-Ra, who I thought of often. One day I was coming from a session with one of them, my body bursting with vibrant force of life, when the chance finally came to test my new abilities.

One of the elite warriors, a good friend of Hu-Nak's, ran up to me as I walked back to my quarters. The message he relayed was most distressing.

"Great Memnon," he cried. "Come quick! Hu-Nak has fallen into the labyrinth!"

We ran with great haste to the throne room. On the way the fellow, whose name was Utau, told me that he and Hu-Nak had been examining the throne, when he accidentally touched the knob that opened up the trap to the labyrinth. Hu-Nak was standing there and disappeared immediately.

"Please help him, Memnon," he cried. "You are the only one to ever emerge alive. Only you can retrieve him."

We burst into the throne room and ran to the dark pit.

I could not hold back a slight shudder as I remembered my own experience. I had no wish to see the creature that dwelled there again and had planned to explore the labyrinth for the treasure and Blade of Shai after the monster inside had starved to death. But Hu-Nak was my teacher and valued comrade, so there was nothing else I could do now but prepare to plunge into it again.

"I'm coming too," said Utau. "It is my fault that he fell into this insidious trap."

"No Utau," I said. "I want you to find Hra-Twa and Persus. Gather a force of warriors and find the subterranean door to this infernal place. If we are still alive we will be waiting. If we are dead... find that beast and avenge us."

"Yes, great Memnon," said Utau reluctantly. "May the Goddess be with you again."

I steadied myself for a moment, then stepped off into the dark void. Once again I found myself sliding down the dark winding chute. But this time I was ready and landed on my feet. The horrid odor assailed my senses again as I called out Hu-Nak's name. Far in the distance I heard him call back, and I was relieved to have come in time.

SHADES OF MEMNON II

Running toward the sound of his voice, I continuously called out to him. I knew that the commotion would bring forth the monster that lived here, but it was only a matter of time before we would be forced to confront it regardless. Better it be soon, I thought, before we are overcome with hunger and exhaustion.

Hu-Nak's voice sounded closer and closer, but I had no sure way of knowing if the twist and turns in this infernal place would let us come together. I kept running, hoping against hope that I would reach him soon, when suddenly the air was split by that terrible and familiar bellow. The bull creature was stalking one of us.

I heard the bellow again, followed by an oath from the throat of Hu-Nak. The creature had found him. I ran around corner after corner, hoping the next chamber would lead me to him. Then another bellow rang out, followed by a loud thump, more oaths and this time curses from Hu-Nak. He was now fighting the creature.

I ran frantically now. Though Hu-Nak was a seasoned warrior of Pan-Kau-Ra-Shen, I doubted if even he could long withstand the ferocious bull creature alone

The sounds of the fight then became louder and louder. I had no doubt that Hu-Nak was giving a good account of himself, but it was only a matter of time.

I ran with desperate speed, but still I could not find them. Suddenly I skirted a corner and spied a familiar sight. It was the area where I had escaped the creature before, with the makeshift ladder still protruding from the wall. Snatching up a nearby spear, I dashed to it and began to scale.

Once again I sprung to the edge of the wall from the topmost spear. Standing up, I scanned the area and spotted Hu-Nak and the creature, just in time to see a terrible sight. The beast clutched Hu-Nak in its huge hairy claws, then threw him against the wall like a small doll. Hu-Nak fell limp.

Poising the spear to throw, I ran toward the chamber in which they fought. In a moment I was standing on the wall right above the monster's head. It had bent down and was in the process of tearing off Hu-Nak's clothing. I yelled and leaped upon it's back, plunging the spear into the side of it's bulky neck.

Roaring terribly, it rose to it's feet, shaking it's giant head and pounding it's hairy fists onto my back. But I kept stabbing the spear despite the pain, determined to make it turn away from my comrade.

# CHAPTER 5: "THE GODDESS BE WITH YOU AGAIN"

The creature finally stopped pounding at me, then backed away from my fallen friend. As it stumbled backwards I thought it was about to fall, but instead the wily creature backed up rapidly, dashing me against the wall. I fell from its back in a daze.

As I lay there the creature snatched up its great war ax, which it had tossed aside to molest Hu-Nak, and turned to do me in. Quickly thinking of a sly ploy, I placed my hands upon my Claws and pretended to have lost my senses. Then it raised the giant ax high and brought it down. But I was not there when it landed. Rolling aside quickly, I sprang to my feet, unsheathing The Claws of Sekmet. Then it was that all the tricks taught to me by Hra-Twa, Persus and the others came to bear.

Dancing around the creature with my blades whirring, I cut at every place Hra-Twa taught me, inflicting such utter devastation upon the beast that it dropped the ax and fell to it's hairy knees. As it cried out in bitter anguish, I paused to glance at the hilt of my long Claw. The light red jewel blazed brightly, indicating that this creature was a negative manifestation of the power of Heru. Chanting the hekau of that deity, I continued slashing away until the beast's body broke down, falling like a sack of grain.

Hurt and confused, the monster looked at itself for signs of physical injury. Seeing none only added to its frustration as it breathed a last long sigh and collapsed before me. As it's eyes rolled and fixed into the final stare of death, it did not understand what truly killed it.

I was standing above the creature, swords still poised for any sign of movement, when Hu-Nak's voice broke the silence.

"By all the lords and deities," he exclaimed. "That feat will live in legend for all eternity."

"Hu-Nak," I cried, sheathing my weapons. "Are you all right, man?"

He pulled himself to a sitting position.

"I will live. And I will tell all I have witnessed here, if we ever get out of this place."

"We'll get out," I replied. "I will get us back to my ladder and we will leave this place..."

He seized my hand.

"But Memnon, what of the treasure? What of the knife you seek?"

"Are you up to searching for that knife?" I asked.

"Get me to my feet," Hu-Nak replied.

## SHADES OF MEMNON II

I helped him up. He stood still for a moment, then walked around. Next he stretched his arms. Then he smiled confidently.

"Let us go and find that treasure," he said, pulling a knife from his waistband. "But first we shall take a trophy."

Minutes later we made our way back to the chamber of my ladder, where we striped clothing off of the dead and tied together makeshift rope for climbing and carrying our "trophy." I had protested, but Hu-Nak insisted on carving the bull creature's head from its carcass and bringing it along as proof of my victory. After binding it to his back, we climbed up the ladder. After making the leap to the top, I pulled up Hu-Nak's spear and the head, then he leapt to join me.

We were scanning the labyrinth as far as we could see, when Hu-Nak spotted a twinkle in the distance. It was as good a start as any, so we made our way towards it.

Long minutes later, and after several harrowing leaps from wall to wall, we stood over the chamber that had obviously been the bull creature's nest. Piles of hay lay all about and the horrid odor was especially strong here. Looking closely, we saw the source of the twinkle that Hu-Nak noticed. There were shiny items beneath the straw.

After wedging the spear into the wall as I had done that first time, Hu-Nak tied the rope to it and we descended. The head we left on top as we explored the home of it's owner.

When our feet landed upon the straw, a clatter came from some-where beneath it. Bending down, I lifted a section of the straw, revealing gleaming slabs of gold and bronze cut into the shape of ox hides. Kicking the straw aside, we saw that the floor was covered with the things. Leaping together, Hu-Nak and I slapped hands in joy. We had at last found the treasure.

As Hu-Nak uncovered more of the precious metal, I explored further. Noticing a pronounced bulge, I nudged aside the straw covering it. It was a golden chest.

Upon it was the insignia of the family of Minos. Opening it up, I spied a scroll bound with a piece of leather. I snatched it up and beneath it lay a beautifully crafted knife. Upon it was the inscription of the deity of destiny. I had found the Blade of Shai.

I picked it up and tucked it into my belt. Unrolling the scroll, I found it filled with the writing of the Tamahus, which I knew very little of. What I could make out seemed to be telling a strange story. I called out to Hu-Nak.

"What have you found?" he asked, coming to look over my shoulder.

"I found the blade I seek," I replied. "And this strange scroll..."

"Let me see that," Hu-Nak said, peering over my shoulder.

He scanned the content for long moments, his face growing more astonished as he read.

"By the lords!" he exclaimed. "Do you know what this is, Memnon?"

"Why, no..." I replied.

"Why my friend, this is a diary of the first King Minos!"

"The first King Minos?"

"Yes," exclaimed Hu-Nak. "No one knew what became of him. One day he just disappeared and his son, the Pa of the Minos you knew, took his place."

"And so what happened?" I asked.

"Well, this account tells of how the king made a pact with dark forces to take control of Keftui, but the price was his humanity."

"And his fate?" I asked.

Hu-Nak looked at me for a long moment.

"His fate Memnon? You just killed him!"

I was speechless for several moments. It seems the family of Minos was cursed from the start. For a hundred years their first king lived as a monster, sitting in his own filth atop a treasure he could no longer use.

"Come Hu-Nak," I said. "Let us leave this cursed place."

We pulled up one golden slab, took the scroll and Blade of Shai and made our way back to the exit of the labyrinth. There was the huge door as I remembered and we climbed down and sat beside it to wait. Hours went by, and just as I began considering another horrendous climb up the narrow chute, the great door began to open.

Several torches appeared, then I heard the voice of Hra-Twa.

"Memna-un," he cried, stepping forward. "Sorry for the lateness. I assume there is a dead monster hereabouts?"

I rushed to embrace my little friend as Hu-Nak hefted the huge head for all to see. Gasps of amazement turned to questions as we made our way through the subterranean halls back to the surface. Persus

SHADES OF MEMNON II

beamed with pride as Hu-Nak recounted my killing of the bull monster and everyone marveled at the solving of the mystery of the first King Minos. They made plans to come back for the treasure and then wall off the accursed labyrinth, thus putting an end to the works of the Minos family forever.

I stayed and learned in Keftui for two more moons, until one day a runner came bursting into a dinner shared by Persus, Hra-Twa and myself and several others. He scanned the dining chamber until his eyes rested upon me.

"The ship of Kho-An-Sa has docked," he said. "The dock guards will not let any disembark as you instructed, great Memnon. But Kho-An-Sa demands the return of his "servant.""

"Thank you," I replied. "My friends it seems the day has come that I knew must come. Is everything in readiness?"

"Yes," replied Hu-Nak, "all is ready."

After many tearful good-byes, I came to the one that threatened to tear my heart apart. I embraced Hra-Twa and said farewell. His first reply was a laugh and a wink. Then he spoke up cheerfully.

"Why this is no good-bye, my friend," he exclaimed. "Where you go, I go. The Voice of the Deity says that our destinies are entwined."

"But how?" I asked.

"Just go off alone, my friend," he replied. "I will be there."

An hour later I was dragged roughly down the dock to the ship of Kho-An-Sa. Hu-Nak and a few other warriors pushed me roughly down upon the planks, tossing a sack containing the Blade of Shai and my weapons next to me. Kho-An-Sa stared down from the deck of the ship.

"Here is your precious servant, magician," Hu-Nak said scornfully. "We Kushites run this place again and we have no need of spies. We have no wish to make an enemy of you, so we did not kill him. Take him and leave this place!"

Kho-An-Sa sent two warriors down to get me. Once on board he looked me up and down and cut the bonds around my wrists.

"I see you did not fare well during this visit," said Kho-An-Sa. "Did you accomplish anything?"

I reached into the bag and produced the Blade of Shai. He immediately snatched it from me, his face glowing with pleasure.

"Ahhh!" Kho-An-Sa exclaimed. "So you have the blade!"

"And Minos is dead," I said. "But not by my hand."

Kho-An-Sa looked up at me.

"It matters not, as long as the fat pig is with his ancestors. The blade is what I really wanted. Now we can go on to other plans."

"How is Neftiji?" I asked.

"Your sister is fine," Kho-An-Sa replied. "You may have her back after you successfully perform this last task."

"What?" I cried in astonishment.

"You may have her back and be free to leave if you wish, after this assignment."

I looked at the magician suspiciously.

"What is this task?" I asked.

Kho-An-Sa held the knife up to the light of a torch.

"Oh, just a theft..."

"A theft of what?"

"I want you to steal a necklace..."

"A necklace?"

"Yes a necklace," he replied. "From the neck of the second of Kamit, the beloved skilled scribe Ra-Nefer."

Days later I sat in my quarters aboard the sailing ship, thinking intensely about what Kho-An-Sa had requested. I heard a noise and looked up. There standing before me was Hra-Twa.

"My friend," I said in a whisper. "What took you so long?"

"I have been observing those aboard this ship," he replied.

"It is a very interesting vessel."

I told Hra-Twa everything: How Kho-An-Sa requested that I join the Medjay warriors of Kamit and work my way up to a post in the palace of the Shekem. Then, for reasons he would not reveal, he would have me steal the necklace of Ra-Nefer, the second most beloved of Kamit. And I must cut the necklace loose with the Blade of Shai.

Hra-Twa listened carefully, then took out his pebbles and cast them upon the floor. He looked at them carefully for a few minutes, his brow wrinkled in concentration. Finally he looked up at me.

"The Voice of the Deity says that you should go to Kamit," he said. "We'll have to do another reading later about the theft."

I nodded and looked into Hra-Twa's eyes.

"What of the Medjay warriors," I asked.

SHADES OF MEMNON II

Hra-Twa smiled as if he knew more than he was telling.

"The Medjay?" he replied. "Memna-un, your destiny lies with the Medjay."

# CHAPTER 5: "THE GODDESS BE WITH YOU AGAIN"

SHADES OF MEMNON II

*"What Dreaming Memnon Wakes And Sings*
*Of Miracles On Mercury?"*
*Don Marquis, "Dreams And Dust" - 1917*

# CHAPTER 6: "WE ARE MEDJAY"

The small drinking house in which I sat was smelly, dimly lit and filled with unsavory characters. I had been told that it was a favored meeting place for the worst outlaws, thieves and assassins and it surely looked it. As I sipped from a tall mug of the terrible local wine, I glanced over at the rough looking crew of Shashu sitting at a nearby table. They had looked me over suspiciously when I walked in. I think they suspected I was Medjay.

It had been a full moon since I left my beloved comrades in Keftui and sailed to this land of the northern Shasu aboard Kho-An-Sa's ship. After putting ashore at Canaan days ago, I received final instructions from the magician and traveled by caravan to this destination.

It was a small trading village in Djahy, nominally under the jurisdiction of Kamit, but in reality untamed territory claimed by several ruthless warlords and their hired killers. Just the type of situation that the battle loving Medjay thrived in. And so I sat down to wait; my back against the wall, my hands filled with badly fermented wine and my eyes upon eight men who looked as if they would rob their closest kin.

It had been mid-afternoon when I arrived. Now the orb of Aten drifted close to the horizon and my patience was beginning to thin. Just as I began contemplating giving up for the day, a chariot halted before the open door of the drinking house. I noted it's familiar markings and the two Kushite riders who dismounted.

Speaking to each other in the thick accent of upper Kamit, the two men strolled through the entrance and I immediately recognized them as Medjay. Not only did they enter with the traditional swagger and audacity that these warriors were known for, but they possessed the thick, muscular frames, tightly braided hair and blue-black skin that always made pure blood Medjay stand out. With their traditional weapons of battle axes, throwing darts and small shields, the men were classic examples of these proud warriors. As they walked in and approached the drinkmaster's bar, I realized that they were more than just companions. The two Medjay were identical twins.

"Drinkmaster!" one of the twins shouted, "Bring us wine to wash down the dust of this stinking territory!"

"Make it a tall drink man," shouted the other, "our thirst is large and the dust of this place is thick and sour."

## SHADES OF MEMNON II

I noticed the group I had been observing. They became very tense and agitated as the Medjay walked in. A couple were slowly reaching for weapons. Suddenly it dawned upon me what was taking place. I pulled the flask of wine closer and snatched a candle from a shelf along the wall.

The Medjay stood next to a table, their heads thrown back, gulping down the wine they had been served. As one of them drained his cup, his gaze skirted over to the table of men I had been observing. Locking eyes with one of them, he pulled the cup down from his lips.

"What are you looking at, sand-dweller?" the Medjay shouted boldly.

Suddenly the men leapt to their feet, shoving aside their table. Three of them rose with bows and arrows poised, while the others pulled swords and daggers.

"We are looking at a Medjay dog that we have been sent to kill!" one of them shouted back in rough Kamitian.

The other patrons in the drinking house quickly vacated, then the attackers looked threateningly my way. But I had no intention of letting my Medjay contacts be killed before I had a chance to talk to them. Leaning the flask of wine over slightly, I lit it with the candle and tossed the liquid as it burst into flames. The flaming wine splashed upon the archers, who stood conveniently close together, their eyes locked on the Medjay.

Immediately their garments caught fire. Screaming in fear and surprise, their arrows flew into the air erratically. This was all the chance the Medjay needed. Moving with blinding speed, they seized some of the razor sharp darts hanging from their belts and cast them with uncanny accuracy. Two of the archers fell dead immediately, the blades of the darts buried deeply between their eyes. The other warriors leapt forward, brandishing their weapons as the third archer fell writhing to the floor, his body engulfed in flames. I was glad I found a use for that terrible wine.

Four of the remaining attackers charged the Medjay, while one broke off and headed towards me. He was a large Shashu with a pointy beard, an evil grin and a curiously curved sword and dagger. I armed myself to match him and the battle was on.

He lunged with the dagger as I twisted away, flicking my own short blade across the top of his hand. Suddenly his weapon fell as he lost control of his fingers. Confused, the Shasu hesitated as he examined his newly crippled limb. Then he looked up at me, his face livid with rage, swinging his sword in a sweeping arc. I blocked it easily, flicked my dagger across the wrist of his other arm and watched as the sword too fell from his grasp.

There he stood before me, his uncontrollable hands quivering at his sides. Upon his face was a fearful and confused expression. No blood leaked from his body where I had cut off the flow of his life force and he could not understand what I had done to him. Smiling grimly, I brought my long Claw up to his throat, nicked a few beard hairs and pointed towards the exit. Realizing that I offered him his life, he turned and fled the building. I turned to leap forward and assist the two Medjay, but I could see they needed no help.

Two of the attacking warriors lay dead at their feet. The other two they battered against a wall, using the astonishing fighting style that made the Medjay feared the world over. Almost faster than the eye could see, the Medjay's feet repeatedly smashed into their attacker's chests, groins and throats, pinning them against the wall with every blow. Bones snapped with every strike, until the Medjay finally ceased kicking. Then both men slumped to the floor, bloody, broken and very much dead.

Carefully surveying the scene, the twins backed up and lifted their flasks of wine. As they gulped down their drinks, the remaining archer tried to creep by. Horribly burned, he groaned in pain as he crawled towards the exit. With one hand clutching their cups, the twins glanced at the archer, then at one another with a raised eyebrow. Nodding in agreement, each pulled a dart and cast it into the neck of the dying archer. He fell flat as they drained the last of their wine.

"Ahhh," exclaimed one of the twins, pulling the cup down from his mouth. "This swill tastes good today, eh Ka-Sah?"

"Are you mad Pa-Sah?" his brother replied. "This swill is horrid!"

Simultaneously, they slammed down their cups and turned towards me.

"What say you warrior," Ka-Sah exclaimed. "Is it good swill or bad?"

I shouted to the drinkmaster, who was peaking out from behind a fallen table.

"Drinkmaster," I exclaimed. "Bring us all another round."

SHADES OF MEMNON II

Then I turned to my new associates with a smile.

"Let us drink more of it, my friends. Bellies filled with wine seldom fret over the quality of the taste.

We drank heartily for a while, as I informed my new companions about my intention to join the Medjay. They were very grateful for the assistance I had given them and offered to help me. But first they were required to finish their rounds and invited me to accompany them. So we left the drinking house and patrolled the streets for the protection of the businesses that were important to Kamit.

At the other drinking houses, market places and roadside check points there were more unsavory characters whose hatred for the Medjay was apparent. But word of what happened in the drink house had obviously preceded us, and met no more challenges. Along the way we met some two dozen other Medjay and set out for the local Kamitic fort.

After a day's journey into the western region of Djahy, we arrived at a tall, foreboding structure situated along the main trade route into the Valley of the Two Lands. With tall lookout towers placed to monitor the four directions and thick fortified walls slanted inward for easy defense, it was an impressive outpost of Kamit's power.

After resting in the sleeping quarters of the warriors, I was taken before the chief of the fort, a gruff, pipe smoking elder named Rau Mu. In a small dark room he conducted the interview for my induction into the Medjay.

"It is true that we know of the woman Meri-Ta," said Rau Mu as he paced the floor before me. "And we are well aware of the glory of Memnon of Troy. But how do we know that you are truly their son? We thought your family all dead..."

"No," I replied. "I and my sister survived. I escaped, but she is still being held. It is my hope to one day lead warriors to retake her."

Rau Mu stopped pacing and looked into my eyes.

"It is commendable that you wish to retrieve your sister and avenge the death of your Mut," he admonished. "But you must know that service with the Medjay is for the good of all of Kamit and the glory of the ancestors, not for personal vendettas."

"I understand," I replied.

"Do you really? asked Rau Mu. "Would you be willing to put service in the ranks of the Medjay above your own agenda?"

I lowered my head and thought for a moment.

"I would," I replied. "Because one day the Medjay and people of Kamit will have to face the evil ones who captured us. I would only ask to be in the vanguard of that battle."

Rau Mu gazed at me intently for a moment more. Then he walked to the door and opened it.

"Ka-Sah! Pa-Sah! he called out. "Come here."

The two twins filed in and stood before the elder warrior.

"Will you two sponsor this one, who calls himself the son of Memnon of Troy, for induction into the ranks of the Medjay?"

The twins looked at each other. It was no small thing Rau Mu asked of them. If they agreed, they would be responsible for my training as an inductee. They would also be required to kill me if I dishonored the Medjay.

"Yes, chief Rau Mu," they exclaimed in unison.

"He saved our lives," added Pa-Sah. "We will train him as a brother-in-arms for the sake of Kamit."

Rau-Mu nodded.

"Very well then. For now we will consider you an inductee. Because of the descriptions given to me of your fighting abilities, I believe you are who you say you are. When my investigations are complete and they prove this, you can begin the initiation into the ranks of the Medjay."

During the next few days, word was sent out for any who had knowledge of the Port Mistress Meri-Ta and her family to report to Rau Mu. Luckily, several Medjay had been transferred to Djahy from the area near my home. Some recognized me and this satisfied Rau Mu. Ka-Sah and Pa-Sah began to prepare for my initiation.

I wondered greatly about what would happen, for the Medjay initiations were a closely guarded secret, which none dared divulge on pain of death. The only thing known by the common folk of Kamit is that not all come through the rites alive or with minds intact. When I asked Pa- Sah and Ka-Sah what would take place, they would only tell me that I would be tested for courage, conviction and brotherhood.

I remained at the fort for half a moon while the twins planned for my initiation. Though I was not allowed to participate in anything, I was encouraged to watch everything.

Each day the fort was alive with activity: There was much sparring and practicing as the Medjay performed the foot fighting arts that made

SHADES OF MEMNON II

them famous.

Each morning as Aten rose, the grounds of the fort were filled with warriors going through their drills.  It was an astonishing sight to see: With hundreds of warriors in battle formation, a drill commander would toss a small, heavy ball to the man at the end of the front row. That  man would catch and balance the ball on  the top of his foot,  then toss it up and kick it to the next man. The next would catch it and do the same, and so on down the line.

Meanwhile, the drill commander would keep tossing balls, which would be kicked down the line, until there was a ball for each of the warriors. With their legs spinning and flashing at incredible speeds, the warriors would kick the balls back and forth down the line until the commander called for a halt.  Each morning I watched the Medjay perform this amazing feat of precision, for up to two hours at a time. Never did I see a ball fall to the ground before the time to stop was called.

Next they would use the same balls for dart practice.  Two  warriors would face one another, up to 40 cubits away.  Each held a ball and had rows of darts wound around their chests or waists.  The warriors would then throw the balls to each other, simultaneously pulling a dart and throwing it into the approaching sphere.

I was speechless at  the level of trust that each warrior gave to the other.  For to miss an approaching ball would almost certainly mean hitting your comrade with a razor sharp dart.  But these Medjay, unerring as a diving bird of prey,  never seemed to miss.  And they were as fast as vipers, for when the balls were plucked from the air, they would some-times have up to four darts imbedded in them.

I saw the same superior speed and precision in the wielding of other weapons. Though swords of the type I wielded were known to them, the Medjay preferred the traditional Kushite weapons, especially spears and axes, for close combat.

Many were the wondrous feats performed by these warriors and I marveled at the inhuman level of the skills they constantly exhibited. I longed to learn, to participate, but they would  not let me.  Even so, I was very happy, for I was at last surrounded by my people's greatest warriors, witnessing the fighting arts that kept Kamit free for hundreds of years. I longed to go through the initiation so that I could become one of them.

That time finally came one early morning when I was shaken awake in my bed by Ka-Sah and Pa-Sah. Peeling my eyes open, I found that the light of day had not yet arrived and the other men in the barracks still asleep.

"Come, Memna-un," whispered one of the twins. "The time has come for your first test."

I rose up from my bed and reached for my clothing and weapons, but the twins pulled me away, insisting that I leave them. I was loath, of course, to leave my weapons behind, but after assuring me that the captain of the barracks would look after them, I reluctantly agreed. The twins were themselves unarmed, except for a small dagger at their waist, and each wore only a small loincloth of tanned skin. Both carried bags and water flasks slung over their shoulders.

I was given an identical loincloth, dagger and water flask, and, after donning them, accompanied the twins to the front gate. There a wagon and driver awaited. As the first rays of light appeared, we sped away from the fort.

We traveled for several hours to the south and east, on bumpy old roads long fallen into disrepair. At last we came to the end of an over-grown, barren highway and stopped. Before us lay a vast savanna, filled with antelope, hyena and other wild creatures. We disembarked and the wagon turned back. As we watched it disappear in the distance, I looked at the twins inquisitively.

"Fear not, Memna-un," Pa-Sah said with a nod. "All of your questions shall now be answered."

Ka-Sah lifted his bag and turned it over. Several items fell to the ground. A length of rope, cooking utensils and several strange objects that I had never seen before. Ka-Sah picked one of them up and held it before me.

"This, my friend is a sacred object," he said. "The Setjet..."

The object was like nothing I had ever imagined. It had an oblong shape with rounded points at the ends and a handle in the middle. It seemed to be made of bronze and was inscribed with strange markings. Ka-Sah handed it to me and I held it by the handle, flipping it over in my hands. I could not fathom what the purpose of it could be.

"What is it for?" I asked.

"It is used to test our warriors for courage," Pa-Sah said. "We use it to acquire our lion's teeth, the greatest possession of a Medjay warrior."

They both pointed to necklaces I had only casually noticed before.

SHADES OF MEMNON II

Pa-Sah's string had three large, chunky teeth hanging from it. Ka-Sah's necklace had only two. Pa-Sah took the Setjet from my hand, gesturing with it as he explained.

"This Setjet paralyzes a lion," he explained. "You shove it into the great cat's mouth..."

"Shove it... into the lion's mouth..." I repeated in disbelief.

"Then, you turn it upwards and it locks the jaws."

"Turn it up..." I repeated "Lock jaws..."

"Yes, and then he is immobile and you can cut loose a tooth. Understand?"

I was speechless. No wonder many who go through the Medjay initiation never make it out alive.

"You are making fun of me, no? I asked.

The twins glanced at each other, then back at me.

"We do not joke about such things," replied Pa-Sah. "Every five or six years, we Medjay come back to the wild to get another tooth. This year Ka-Sah has chosen to earn his third. He will show you how it is done."

Ka-Sah nodded and walked towards me. Placing his hand upon my shoulder, he gazed into my eyes.

"I will show you the way," he said. "Have you the courage to see it through?"

What they asked of me did not seem possible. Shoving a hand into a lion's mouth was the act of a fool or of a man with a level of courage I did not understand. Since both twins still possessed their hands, I could only conclude that they were the latter. I knew I would do anything to earn the respect of such men, but first I required council. I returned Ka-Sah's gaze and spoke up.

"Give me a few moments alone," I replied. "Then I will give you my answer..."

Both twins nodded and sat upon the ground. Ka-Sah began checking the rope from his bag, while Pa-Sah picked up a flat stone and raked it across the blade of his dagger. I walked for a while, observing the beautiful savanna and the animals bounding to and fro. I came to a hill and walked to it's far side, out of sight of my Medjay comrades. Then I called Hra-Twa's name and sat down at the foot of the hill.

Suddenly my little Anu friend appeared, strolling towards me from around the hill. Smiling broadly, he sat down on the grass beside me.

"Greetings, Memna-un" he said cheerfully.

"Greetings, Hra-Twa. "I have need of your skills..."

I told him of the initiation practice and he listened intently, nodding intermittently. He pursed his lips as I explained my fear of being killed in this initiation and therefore unable to save Neftiji or find my Pa. At last he pulled out his pebbles and cast them upon the ground. After reading them intently for a few moments, he looked up.

"Fear not Memna-un," he said. "The Voice of the Deity has spoken: Good tidings are in the air for this venture. The men you are with will not allow you to be killed as long as you show the bravery you have exhibited thus far. It is important for your future that you go through with this initiation."

I nodded, looking back the way I had come with renewed conviction. When I turned back toward Hra-Twa, I found that he had disappeared once again.

"Thank you my friend," I spoke into the wind. "Once again you have given me the wisdom I require to go on."

I trotted back and rejoined my companions, who were sitting patiently just as I had left them. They looked up inquisitively as I stood before them.

"I am ready my comrades," I said. "Let us find those lions."

Hours later we lay in the tall grass, observing a group of lions in the distance. The twins had explained the procedure to me completely, and though it seemed sound, our chances of being killed or maimed were still quite high. But, here we lay, upwind of the beasts to avoid detection, awaiting our chance to catch a full grown lion.

Presently a herd of gazelle appeared and the lions bolted upright, noting their chance for a quick meal. Several females slunk towards the herd to begin the hunt, leaving a few others behind to tend the young cubs that scampered to and fro. They also left two huge, woolly manned males, who sat regally watching the females hunt. Our objective was to get one of the males.

Ka-Sah and I crept closer, while Pa-Sah slowly circled to the east of the pride. When he was in place, Ka-Sah threw stones and got the attention of one of the protective males, who slowly stalked away from the others to investigate the movements in the grass.

Pa-Sah maintained his position as his twin and I tossed stones one after another, which the lion mistook for small game scampering to escape. When he was lured far enough away from the others, Pa-Sah's hand signal waved us forward. The crucial time had come.

Ka-Sah and I followed behind the lion, who was now a considerable distance from his peers, following the trail of female mating scent laid down by Pa-Sah from a vial he brought for just that purpose. We were close enough now to clearly see the beast. With it's head down, tail flicking to and fro, and male member clearly erect, it anticipated a female in heat at the end of the scent trail. And, just as the twins had said, it did not make a sound for fear of luring it's male rival.

I looked back at the other lions in the distance. They were circling the area curiously, looking for their missing comrade. Ka-Sah noted this also and pulled me close for a cautious whisper.

"This must be done very quickly and carefully, Memna-un," he said. "Else we will have more than one lion to contend with. Keep an eye upon them."

I nodded and watched as Ka-Sah stalked ahead of me. Suddenly he let forth a loud whistle and rose to his feet. The rope, now tied into a lasso, was whirling above his head. A return whistle came from Pa-Sah, then both men stood up in the tall grass, whirling their lassos overhead. Pa-Sah flicked the lasso, snaring one of the startled lion's front legs. At first it tried to yank loose, then, with a mighty roar, charged it's captor. But before it took five steps, Ka-Sah's rope had snared a rear leg and snatched it from under him.

Now roaring furiously, the lion struggled against its bonds as the twins dragged it further away. Coming to a thick tree, Pa-Sah wrapped his rope around the trunk and tied it there. Ka-Sah coiled his end until he was quite close to the beast, then he handed the rope to me. Reaching into his bag, he pulled out a tiny flask and the tool for paralyzing the lion.

"Keep the beast off balance," he instructed. "I will get that tooth..."

Perspiration streamed from my body as I held onto the rope, continuously yanking the lion's rear foot, while Pa-Sah jerked the beast's front leg. His end though, was secured by a tree, while I had no such leverage. My arms strained painfully against the struggles of the great cat.

Ka-Sah approached the lion cautiously. Though Pa-Sah and I jerked it repeatedly, it's free front claw flailed dangerously, ready to rend flesh and break bone. But Ka-Sah had clearly done this before and stood over the beast looking for an opening. After a few moments one came and he seized the lion by the mane, yanked it's head back, and shoved the instrument into the huge toothy maw.  Before the sharp fanged mouth could snap shut, he turned the tool up, locking the beast's jaws into a wide gape.  It's struggles immediately ceased and it grew silent.

I was amazed at what I had just witnessed. Ka-Sah displayed absolutely no fear during the whole procedure. With a rock steady hand, he uncorked the small flask, pouring the liquid it contained down the lion's throat. Within moments, the beast's eyes closed and it's breathing became slow and deep. It was sound asleep.

The twins nodded to each other and Ka-Sah pulled his dagger from his belt.  Choosing a large front tooth, he began to carve it from the lion's mouth.

I observed Ka-Sah's triumph, a smile beginning to spread across my face, when suddenly I heard something behind me and turned around. There, a short distance away, stood the other male lion. It was even larger than the one we had caught and eyed the scene well before letting forth a tremendous, earsplitting roar.  The twins looked up, their faces gravely concerned.  Then Ka-Sah shouted out to me.

"Memna-un. Save yourself! Drop the rope and flee!"

I looked around quickly.  There was nowhere to go.  Flat savanna surrounded us and the nearby trees were not steep enough to keep the lion down.  It was possible that two of us could get away while the beast tore the other to bits, but the thought of that I could not bear. I had to stop the lion, or one or more of us would surely die.

I dropped the rope as the lion poised to charge. Ka-Sah's bag was before me, so I reached into it and seized another Setjet, just as the lion sprang forward. A quick glance behind revealed the twins rushing forward with their daggers drawn, but the lion would get to me first.

As the beast drew near I crouched down,  concentrating upon the Rau in my center, trying hard to remember all I had been taught. When the lion leaped, I waited until the huge weight of the beast descended upon me, then focused the Rau into my arms and seized it by it's hairy mane. Letting the force of it's own bulk carry it, I rolled with the beast, swinging it over onto it's back. Rolling over quickly as we both hit the ground, I swung the Setjet directly into it's mouth and twisted my wrist. The lion was paralyzed.

All was silent for long moments.  Only the loud panting of the still lion and my own breathing could be heard.  A bird of prey screeched

SHADES OF MEMNON II

high in the air. Then the twins spoke up.

"By all the Neteru, Memna-un," declared Pa-Sah, "we have never seen the likes of this..."

"To catch a lion, alive, alone and without a rope..." Ka-Sah added. "you truly are the son of a mighty one...the seed of a valiant one..."

Ka-Sah poured some of the liquid down the beast's throat and it fell fast asleep. I took out my dagger and cut loose a large, pointy front tooth. Both twins continued to gaze at me in amazement as we untied the first lion and removed the instruments from the mouths of both sleeping beasts.

"Come," said Ka-Sah. "You have passed this first test beyond our wildest hopes Memna-un. Let us leave this place."

When we arrived at the fort, the twins relayed what had happened. I was congratulated and slapped upon the back by many Medjay warriors. Then they took me to the yard in the center of the camp and locked me inside a wooden box.

I was left there in total darkness and instructed to hold the lion's tooth. Time went by. I received no food and little water for what seemed like days and no one would answer or acknowledge my many calls. Then the drumming began.

It was a strange rhythm that I had never heard, surrounding my cage for hour after hour without let. When I slept the sound of the drums continued, when I awoke the drums were still there. The beat pounded into my head relentlessly and I began to see strange visions.

In my mind there were small prey animals being chased by large predators and I found my point of view blended with that of the creatures being hunted. Feelings of helplessness and terror reigned as I found myself threatened by sharp fangs and talons.

And the drums continued.

I was a small bird on the run from a fearsome hawk; a tiny hare scampering from the fangs of a hungry jackal; a small fish staring into the jaws of a larger one; a young antelope being overcome by a swift savanna cat.

Over and over, my consciousness jumped from one doomed creature to the next, leaping on just as I would be caught and the end about to come.

And the drums continued.

At first I was overwhelmed by the terror, and battered myself against the box in utter panic. Raw fear and the need to escape threatened to overcome me as my body shook and I beat the walls until my fists bled. The panic continued until a tingle in the palm of my hand made me pause.

I looked down and opened my fist. There was the lion's tooth, soaked in my own blood and glowing with a pulsating orange light. In the distance I heard voices rise in a sudden shout, as the orange light flared, sending a rush of force through my entire being.

Suddenly I felt strengthened. Shaking my head as if I possessed a woolly mane, I fought against the fearful images and shouted in bitter defiance:

"I AM NOT PREY!!!!"

Somewhere nearby the shouts of many men seemed to answer my own, then the images began to change: No longer was I a small creature being chased. I was now a large predator, filled with strength and conviction. But my role was not chasing the weak and small, but protecting and defending my territory:

I was a lone male lion attacking a pack of thieving hyenas; a bull elephant charging a roguish rival stalking the females of my herd; a hippo with young, rushing to attack a sneaking crocodile; a raging bull charging down a sneaking savanna cat.

And the drums continued.

Suddenly I knew that my prison could not hold me, for I was a predator and no one could keep me caged. Rushing the wall with all my strength I battered against it until the wood began to crack. I kicked and kicked until the walls began to split.

And the drums continued.

When my foot broke through I heard the roar of a many men, urging me on, beckoning me forth. Then the images of animals disappeared. In their stead came visions of Ka-Sah, Pa-Sah and other Medjay I had met, along with many others that I never known. Flashing through my mind, they greeted me by the thousands. An endless array of warriors, all urging me on, welcoming me and greeting me as if I was known. Suddenly I realized that I was seeing every Medjay warrior that had ever lived, and that they were accepting me as one of own.

An indescribable feeling of joy and brotherhood permeated my entire being. I had to leave the cage so that I could join them, nothing could stand in my way. I kicked the walls again until the wood parted further, then tore through with my bleeding hands and stepped out into

SHADES OF MEMNON II

the cool night air.

Then the drumming ceased.

Gradually my eyes became accustomed to the light and I saw hundreds of torches blazing all around. A circle of drummers surrounded me, each with his magical instrument perched between his legs. Beyond the drummers stood every Medjay at the fort, a torch in one hand and their lion tooth necklaces in the other. The strange orange glow surrounded their teeth also, pulsating in time with my own.

I lifted the bloody hand containing my tooth as a cheer went up from the crowd. Then I scanned the faces of the brethren before me and I knew. The secret of the invincible Medjay was at last revealed to me.

"BROTHERS!! I shouted, clutching the tooth close to my heart.

"WE ARE THE LION! WE ARE THE PROTECTOR!!! WE ARE MEDJAY!!!

A roar that shook the very clouds was my answer and the drums began to beat again. Then we danced a great war dance, long into the night, celebrating the birth of a Medjay lion.

SHADES OF MEMNON II

# CHAPTER 7: "THE SPIRIT OF THE LION"

For five moons I dwelled in great happiness at the fort, learning the ways of the Medjay and sharing in the Spirit of the Lion. I found that it was that spirit, the Medjay's own deity called Apademak, that made all things possible for these great warriors. Each day began with a prayer and ritual to the Great Protector, Apademak, whose might all Medjay shared in to destroy evil and uphold Maat.

It was through the power of Apademak, activated through the rituals of the lion teeth, that allowed the Medjay to attain the astonishing skills I had noted. And now that I was initiated, I too shared in these gifts, which included access to the skills of Medjay Shepsu, enhanced senses akin to a hunting lion and a natural affinity for their sacred fighting art, called Kupigana Ngumi.

And I learned another amazing thing as I worked the rituals of Apademak while holding the Claws of Sekmet: Through signs and visions, I sensed that the deity of my blades, the lioness Sekmet, slayer of monsters, was somehow related to Apademak.

When I brought this up to elder Rau-Mu, he confirmed it, saying that long ago, before the Kushites who make up the Medjay split from the Kushites who became Kamitians, the two Neters were enshrined together, as mates. During the many conversations we had on the subject, the elder noted that I might personally signify the final reunion of these two Kushite groups.

My role, Rau-Mu said, could be very important, for despite reuniting centuries ago to cast off the Hyksos oppressors, the two groups still harbored some suspicion and distrust toward each other.

I was amazed and overwhelmed by this revelation. To be sure I checked with Hra-Twa and his oracle. The Voice of the Deity confirmed it: I was following in my Pa's footsteps as a uniter of Kushite people.

Another thing that I learned about the Medjay was that they too had the knowledge of empowering Rau through the intimate union of man and woman. Indeed, Medjay warriors were required to be mated with a Medjay woman or one who had gone through the initiation process of Medjay females.

Twice every moon the wives and sisters of the warriors paid a visit to the fort. It was during one of these visits that I met the woman who would become the strength of my own life. Her name was Sha-Sah, older sister of Ka-Sah and Pa-Sah.

## SHADES OF MEMNON II

I first saw her one early morning during my second moon at the fort. Along with hundreds of other Medjay women, she walked through the gate of the fort bearing a large basket upon her head. Tall and graceful like a gazelle, her strong, shapely frame was wrapped in a vibrant blue robe that accented her ebony skin magnificently. Her hair was cropped short, and even from afar I detected an almost regal air about her. She was accompanied by Su-ta and A-ka-ti, the wives of my two friends.

Kneeling carefully, the women removed the heavy burdens from their heads and rushed toward us. I stood aside, watching as the twins embraced their loved ones.

They introduced me and I was embraced also, then we sat down to get acquainted. After hearing news of their home nome, the twins gave gifts to their women, receiving the contents of the baskets in return. Our mouths watered at the sight of the fruit and breads, great changes from the fort fare of beef and plain vegetables. They also brought clothing and crafts, which had the twins beaming with pride over the skills of their women.

Looking on as they enjoyed their families, my mind wandered, conjuring images of Neftiji and my parents. I must have looked quite sad, for soon I felt a tap on the leg. I looked up to find Sha-Sah gazing at me.

"Why are you so sad, warrior?" she asked.

"I have loved ones as well," I sighed. "But they have been... taken from me..."

She looked into my eyes with great compassion.

"A wife?" she asked.

"No," I replied, "My sister...my parents..."

Reaching into the basket she had brought, she produced a large ripe melon.

"Here," she said, offering it to me. "Take it."

Pa-Sah stopped talking to Su-ta and shot a glance our way.

"Wait!" he cried. "That's my melon!"

"You'll have to share it Pa-Sah," his sister scolded. "Don't be selfish, now."

Pa-Sah sighed, throwing up his hands in resignation. I accepted the melon and thanked her, then took out a dagger and sliced it. As we all sat eating, Sha-Sah and I caught each others eyes frequently.

After a night with their women I noticed vigor among the men surpassing that which I had witnessed before. During the morning drills, when we all kicked the rubber ball, I found I could not keep up. It became so apparent that the drill commander excused me from practice.

"You need a woman," he whispered as I walked past him.

Indeed he was right. I had not been empowered by a union with a skilled woman for several moons. Though I used my weapons very little in practice among with Medjay, I could feel the difference when I picked them up. I applied the breathing methods I had been taught and made sure to stick to a vegetable diet, but slowly and surely, I was getting weaker.

As I strolled to the sidelines to watch the drills go on, I noticed the visiting women on the other side of the fort engaged in a ritual with much drumming and dancing. Intrigued, and since I could not keep up with the men, I strolled over to observe them.

Their dance was quite vigorous, consisting of foot stamping, pelvic thrusts and whirling motions. Each sequence ended with a wave towards the men across the fort and a deep, sensuous moan. After observing them carefully, it became clear to me. They were ritually sending power to their men.

As I continued watching, spellbound with wonder, I felt the presence of someone close by. Turning to look, I saw Sha-Sah, half observing the ritual, half curiously eyeing me.

"Greetings, sister," I said. "Why are you not in this ritual?"

"I have no man," she replied, "to do ritual for."

Then I noticed her staring at my hand.

"Where did you get that ring?" she asked.

"It was given to me by the Anu," I replied. "Why do you ask?"

Reaching into her robe, Sha-Sah drew forth a long cord. At the end of it was a medallion. When she brought it up to my face, I saw a design identical to my ring. Right down to the panther's head and changing expressions.

I looked up at her in utter amazement.

"Years ago," she explained, "as a small child, I was taken away by the Anu. They taught me many things..."

"And the medallion?" I asked.

Sha-Sah looked up at me intensely. Tears began streaming from her eyes.

"Oh, I had given up hope..."

"Hope for what?"

"They told me that when I meet the man whose ring matches this medallion, that we would belong together..."

I was stunned. No words would come from my mouth. Seizing Sha-Sah by the hand, I began to walk, dragging her along.

"Where are we going?" she cried.

I did not answer as I led her far to the rear of the fort, away from all other eyes. Rounding a small supply house, I shouted for my Anu friend.

"Hra-Twa!" I cried. "Hra-Twa! Hra-Twa appear before me!"

Suddenly he was there, strolling from around the supply house.

"Ahh," he said. "I see you two have met."

Sha-Sah's eyes grew large and she fell down upon one knee, bowing her head.

"Hra-Twa what is going on here?" I asked forcefully.

"You have found your wife," the Anu answered. "That's what is going on..."

"But...but...I don't need a wife...don't want a wife.." I replied.

Hra-Twa smiled.

"You'll want her," he shot back. "She has been trained and prepared for you."

Slapping a hand across my forehead, I pointed accusingly at my Anu friend.

"You knew about this all along, didn't you?

"I knew it was going to happen," he replied. "Didn't know exactly when..."

He walked over to Sha-Sah, laying a gentle hand upon her head.

"Get up my child," he said.

Sha-Sah stood, a broad smile spreading across her face. Her eyes were liquid pools as she looked up into mine..

"No!" I cried. "Oh, no!"

"Oh, yes," said Hra-Twa, matter-of-factly.

"But...but what about Neftiji? I must find my Pa..."

"And you can only do this if you remain strong, Memna-un. "The oracles have confirmed it. She is the one."

"What is going on here? I asked, raising my hands to the skies.

"Memna-un," began Hra-Twa, "do you think that all that has

happened to you has been by chance? No, I say. We Anu have watched over your family for many years. You will fulfill your destiny. This woman has been trained to help you do it."

I walked over to Sha-Sah and gently took her hand in mine.

"Sister, are they making you do this against your will?'

"No, Memna-un, no," she replied. "I have seen some of the future. Terrible times are ahead for the world and we will need champions to defend those who are for right. I agreed of my own free will."

I was still confused. Things seemed to be happening that I had no control over. I felt like a puppet in my on life.

"Fear not, Memna-un," said Hra-Twa. "There is a way to consult those closest to you so that you can see what they have to offer in this matter."

Hra-Twa disappeared behind the side of the building, returning moments later with an urn filled with water. Placing it upon the ground, he began to dance and chant around it. When the water began to tremble, he reached into his robe and produced a small silver seed. This he dropped into the urn and a silver mist rose.

"Come, Memna-un," he said. "Greet your Mut, Meri-Ta."

I walked over and peered into the urn. There was the face of my Mut, looking much as she appeared when I had seen her in Ausar's realm before. Smiling at me warmly, she began to speak.

"My son," she began, "I have been watching you from this place..."

"Oh, Meri-Ta..." I said.

"Hush, now, child," she replied, "we do not have much time."

"I am listening, Mut..."

"This Sha-Sah is a good and powerful woman. I agree with Hra-Twa. If you would remain strong and uphold right, you need her. It is up to you, but know that your union would have my blessings. Farewell."

"Yes, Mut..." I said.

Suddenly the mists swirled again and the face of Kam-Atef appeared. Nodding, he flicked his long tongue as he greeted me.

"Greetings, Memna-un," he cried.

"Kam-Atef," I answered. "Oh great serpent, so much has happened..."

"I have been kept aware by Hra-Twa," he replied. "Listen now for we must be quick. Those who could hear our exchange are lurking not far away. You must accept this woman Sha-Sah. She can help you to accomplish your goals."

"Yes, great serpent..." I replied.

"And the other issue, that of your mission for Kho-An-Sa. Do not do as he asks. When you can arrange an audience, go to Ra-Nefer and explain the situation. Just be careful how you approach him and be sure that the two of you are alone..."

"But what of Neftiji? I cried. "If I don't do it, then Kho-An-Sa will never set her free..."

"Fear not Memna-un," the great serpent replied, "Hra-Twa will find a way to retrieve her. Trust in him. Do not try to contact me again until he tells you, for the danger is too great and you are not yet ready to face the forces that could descend upon you. Be strong, little warrior. Farewell."

The image disappeared from the urn. The mist swirled above it for a moment more, then drifted away with the wind.

I stood above the urn for long moments, my mind reeling from what just occurred. Suddenly I heard a gruff voice shouting at me.

"Here now!" it cried. "What are you two doing behind this store house?"

I turned to see a drill commander, his arms filled with practice balls, emerging from the supply house. Sha-Sah stood nearby, but Hra-Twa was nowhere to be found. A sly smile appeared on the commander's face as he looked us over.

"If you want to do what I think you want to do," he said, "why not go to the marriage house? It's more comfortable."

I started to open my mouth, but Sha-Sah covered it with a warm soft hand.

"Thank you, brother, " she replied. "I believe we will do just that."

Then she took me by the hand, this time pulling me along. Presently we came to the large building that I had noticed couples disappearing into when the wives visited. Outside it was painted the drab brown of the entire fort, but when we went inside the halls were awash in vibrant green and yellow. Sweet sandalwood incense burned everywhere, while soothing music came from an unknown source.

A kindly Mut elder greeted us as we passed the check in table, handing Sha-Sah a key and blanket and giving us both a playful wink.

Sha-Sah led me to a door near the end of a long hall. With a quick twist of the key she opened it and we stepped inside. The room was large and beautiful, with a shallow pool of steaming water surrounded by a large bed and two couches. Sha-Sah lit a stalk of incense and turned towards me with a sensuous smile.

"I have wanted so long to come here," she said, "I have waited all my life for you..."

Untying her robe with the pull of a string, she dropped it to the floor. I wore only a loincloth, the standard for warrior practice, which she untied and plucked easily from my body. Taking my hand again, she led me into the pool of water.

Laying within reach was a sweet smelling cake of soap, which we used to wash each other's bodies. Like all Medjay I had seen, she was endowed with a tight, muscular build that rippled beneath smooth dark skin. But unlike the Medjay men I spared with, she was soft, curvaceous and inviting.

I embraced her and she melted into my arms, covering my face with kisses. Then she wrapped her arms around my neck and her legs around mine.

The moment our bodies united I felt a surge of life force such I had never felt before. I closed my eyes from the intensity and when I opened them, I found Sha-Sah's head engulfed by a glowing halo. Flowing from the middle of her forehead, it churned with all the colors of the rainbow.

Tilting her head back, she spoke words of power that scorched the air as they left her lips. Suddenly our bodies rose from the water as if lifted by an unseen hands. Then, still united, we floated over to the bed, landing gently upon the soft cushions, her body atop mine.

Sha-Sah's eyes were like flames as she quivered and cried out.

"I am yours Memna un! I am yours!"

With that, my body felt as if it were covered by a blanket of power. Every pore of my skin seemed to stretch and contract and an almost unbearable pleasure washed over me. Looking down into my eyes, Sha-Sah worked a hand sign in the air near her breasts.

"I am for you and I shall prove it!"

Seizing my hand, she pulled it towards her heaving breasts until my ring touched the medallion swinging there. Like a burst of lightning, a flash of light appeared above us. Within it I could see Sekmet and Apademak, tangled together as we were in intimate embrace. Roaring with pleasure, the lion deities seemed overjoyed at being together after all the years that had passed. Suddenly the image of Sekmet emerged from the vision and descended into Sha-Sah, while the image of

SHADES OF MEMNON II

Apademak descended upon me.

Strange words that I cannot recall emerged from our mouths as we conversed in the language of the deities. No longer where we mortal beings, but the Neteru themselves, united through human hosts. As my mortal mind gave way to the personality of the deity, I accepted that Sha-Sah was correct: we indeed belonged together, and in ways I would spend a lifetime learning.

We made the wedding announcement the following day.

The twins and their wives were overjoyed when they heard of our plans. But preparations were cut short due to an urgent message from Kamit: We were being called up for an impending conflict.

The assembly was near the front gate of the fort. There Rau-Mu strolled back and forth, a scroll held tightly in his hands, as he waited for all to appear. At last he scanned the warriors and women before him and began to read.

"There is a nest of vipers to the south and east of Kamit," he shouted. "For too long has this nest been left to thrive. Now the nest has grown and it's poisonous dwellers threaten to turn towards Kamit. This we cannot allow, so we will destroy them in their lairs. The name of the nest is Petra!"

I nodded grimly, remembering the state of Petra, with it's Kushite population ground under foot by strange foreigners. I also remembered Hazz, my noble friend, to whom I made an oath to return and free his people. Now that my chance to do so had arrived, I stepped forward.

"I know much of Petra," I shouted up to Rau-Mu. "I wish to make my knowledge known for use in the coming battle."

"Ahh, Memna-un," replied Rau-Mu. "You shall get your chance. For we leave shortly for Kamit, to gather for the coming conflict. There you can address the great Shekem himself, for Ra Mesh is eager to meet you."

Several days later, most Medjay at the fort set out on the march for Kamit. I would have liked to speak to Sha-Sah before leaving, but the women had left days earlier. Still, my body was abuzz with the power she had given me during our time together

and I felt as if I alone could defeat an army.

Three day later we reached the Desher Sea, where several ships awaited. There we met more warriors: Medjay, Kamitic rank enlisted and mercenaries. There were thousands of them. This was indeed to be a major assault.

After sailing for a day, we docked at the port town of Kuser in the region of Sewew and marched to the local fort. There we gathered, along with thousands more from the western regions to await the arrival of our king, the Strong Heru, Shekem Ur Shekem, Ra Mesh III.

For two days we waited, milling about in the yard of the fort, sparing and playing games. Then, on the morning of the third day, the trumpets blared and the drums began to beat. Shekem Ra Mesh was coming.

Leaping to our feet, we gathered into formation as the great gate opened. First came the drummers, fifers and trumpeters, playing a martial tune. Behind them the flag bearers marched, carrying the banners of the 42 Nome's of the Two Lands. Then the honor guard of the king filed in, gleaming and glittering as the rays of Aten struck their golden corslets, silver spears and sickle swords. Then came the fine chariots of the royal archers, and finally the chariot of the Shekem himself, with the magnificent royal lion trotting beside it.

There, standing tall and regal in the chariot platform, stood the king of Kamit. His blue war crown shined to a high polish and his corselet, collar, belt and apron gleaming of jewel encrusted silver. He looked as regal as I had ever imagined.

Pulling his chariot to a halt before us, the Shekem scanned the ranks before disembarking. Immediately his honor guard drew into formation around him and the royal lion, coal black and larger than any I had ever seen before, also drew close to his side. Patting the huge beast upon it's hairy mane, he drew his assistant close and whispered briefly into his ear.

The assistant immediately turned towards the assembled masses.

"The Shekem will now survey the warriors! If there are any spies or those with ill will towards Kamit, I suggest you come forward now! You will be permitted to leave in peace."

I looked at Pah-Sah and Ka-Sah, who stood beside me on either side. They did not look at me, but stared ahead as if awaiting a command. I opened my mouth to speak, then thought better of it, continuing to stare ahead myself.

"Again I ask: come forth, those of you with ill will towards Kamit," beckoned the king's assistant, "you will be granted mercy and safe passage away!"

SHADES OF MEMNON II

There was complete quiet. No one moved from the crowd. The assistant shook his head sadly, then bowed to the king and stepped aside.

Then Shekem Ra Mesh stepped forward, beckoning his great lion to follow. First he walked toward the rank enlisted, conscripts from the various Nome's. All stood still and at attention, as he and the lion walked past. The Shekem stopped several times, talking to men at random, while the great lion sniffed each warrior.

After long minutes, they were done with the ranks of the enlisted and the Shekem turned towards the mercenaries. These were men from the countries surrounding Kamit, renowned for great fighting skills, but who fought for profit alone. I had heard that there were frequent problems with men such as these. Many thought it a bad idea to employ them at all.

I watched as the Shekem strolled down their lines, stopping more frequently than he had done before. Suddenly the lion at his side roared before a Tamahu mercenary wearing a horned helmet. A chilling scream emerged from his throat as he reached for his weapon, but before he had a chance to draw it razor-like claws and long sharp teeth had sunk into him. In a heartbeat he was torn to ribbons.

I was horrified. Why would the Shekem allow a warrior to be killed who had come to fight for him? While all eyes were upon the cruel spectacle before us, I nudged Pah-Sah.

"He was given a chance," my friend said. "He should have taken it..."

Suddenly another scream emerged from the ranks of the warriors. A second mercenary, this time a Tehenu, had fallen under the claws of the lion. I pulled Ka-Sah close, demanding to know what was going on.

"The royal lion," he answered, "has great magic. It can read what is in a man's heart. They should have left when he gave them the chance."

Three more northern mercenaries and another Tehenu went down beneath the claws of the lion before another Tamahu broke from the crowd and attempted to flee. Pushing desperately past those closest to him, he broke into a fast sprint toward the front gate.

But the gaze of Shekem Ra Mesh followed him, and in an awesome display of his legendary might, our king tilted his head and spoke a word of power. Like a flash of lightning, a line of bright red flame leaped from the serpentine Uraeus upon his brow, engulfing the fleeing traitor in a ball of fire.

Screaming in mortal anguish, the mercenary stopped in his tracks, his arms flailing as he tried to fight the flames. He took two more steps, his legs quivering beneath him, then his body simply fell where he stood. I noted that he did not fall forward, but collapsed straight down upon his shoes, as if his bones had been plucked from his body. All that was left of him was an eerie lump, resembling a pile of crushed fruit. Smoke rose from the remains.

All was deathly quiet for long moments. I nudged Pah-Sah, looking at him inquisitively once again.

"His bones have been burned up within him," my friend whispered in awe.

Finally the king broke the silence, calling for his assistant once again. After speaking to the Shekem briefly, the assistant turned towards the ranks of the mercenaries.

"All mercenaries are hereby ordered to stand down," he shouted. "To avoid more bloodshed you are all dismissed."

A loud groan went up among the foreigners. Many had come a long way for the campaign and would now go home with nothing. Their murmurs grew louder as the king and his assistant spoke again.

"Enough," cried the assistant turning toward the crowd. "Those mercenaries who wish to engage in this campaign, you can receive an audience later. Except you northerners and Tehenu. You are all permanently dismissed."

The mercenaries broke formation, many preparing to leave. Some men from the eastern lands wanted to stay, and approached the Shekem's assistant to schedule audiences. The Tamahu and Tenehu all sulked away, bitterness in their eyes.

Next the Shekem inspected the Medjay.

He and the lion moved quickly through our ranks with no incidents. Looking each in the eye and nodding, the Shekem seemed satisfied with us all. I understood his confidence, for no initiated Medjay was ever known to betray Kamit. It was, in fact, nearly unthinkable.

After surveying us all, the Shekem called Rau-Mu to the side, speaking to him briefly. Finally the elder bowed, then came over to address me.

"The Shekem will speak to you, Memna-un," Rau-Mu said.

Strolling forth from the crowd, I approached my king. Many warriors watched with great interest, for it was an honor indeed to receive a private audience with the king.

"Anecht Hrak" I said, greeting my king in the traditional manner as I fell to one knee and bowed my head.

"Stand before me warrior," he replied.

I was a bit taller than the Shekem, but we were built very similarly. His face had the look of northern Kamitic stock: straight nose, high cheek bones and hazel brown eyes. His jet black skin, and his thin, yet muscular frame indicated that he might be the product of mixed Kushite blood.

"Greetings, Memna-un," he said.

"Great Shekem," I replied, "my life is yours to command..."

"Come," he said, "join me."

We walked into a nearby tent set up for the king. There his attendants awaited with flasks of wine. After pouring us two goblets, the king dismissed them. Eyeing me up and down intensely, he handed me my drink.

"So," he began, "you are the son of the great Memnon of Troy?"

"Yes, Shekem," I replied, "I am indeed."

"You know, it is said that your Pa could have taken the throne of Kamit..."

"I have heard that spoken, yes, Shekem."

The king gazed at me over his goblet.

"Tell me, younger Memnon," he asked, "do you have political aspirations?"

I was very surprised. What my king suggested was the farthest thing from my mind.

"Why no, Shekem," I replied. "My Pa did not wish this, and neither do I..."

We sipped the wine in silence for a few moments. Then the Shekem motioned towards two couches.

"I believe you," he said as we were seated. "I have heard amazing things about you. Things that rival the tales of your Pa. Please, tell me your story."

I told the Shekem everything that had happened since the day Kho-An-Sa first appeared, except for the mission against Ra Nefer. He was greatly intrigued.

"So," the Shekem replied as I finished. "Quite a tale. You have received many rare gifts, especially the strengthening process you underwent at Petra, which is usually reserved only for kings."

"I realize this, Shekem," I replied. "It is all at the disposal of Kamit."

The Shekem nodded.

"Very good, Memna-un. Now I have someone I want you to meet..."

He clapped his hands and a servant appeared.

"Bring forth our guest," he ordered.

The man disappeared, only to come back a moment later accompanied by another. He then bowed and left the new man alone with us.

"Greetings Shekem Ra-Mesh," the man said, bending his knee.

The king nodded and gestured toward me.

"Step forward, Ul-lal, there is someone I would like you to meet."

I stepped forward also. As we bowed to one another, I noticed something familiar about him. He was definitely an eastern Kushite, as his straight hair and sharp features denoted. But there was something else intriguing that I could not quite place.

"Greetings Ul-lal," I said. "I am Memna-un."

His hands went up to the sides of his face as his eyes grew large.

"I am the brother of Hazz!" he cried. "My brother spoke of you often!"

Indeed it was true. The familiarity I sensed was his resemblance to his brother.

"Yes," I replied. "I see...how is your brother?"

Ul-lal lowered his eyes, shaking his head sadly.

"Alas, I do not know. He was alive when I left."

"Ul-lal's story is much of the reason we embark upon this campaign, Memna-un," said the Shekem, motioning toward the easterner. "Tell him Ul-lal."

Ul-lal nodded and began to relay his tale: It seems that since I had left Petra, the place had become a hotbed of activity. The invaders had been preparing for a major campaign, rumored to be an attack upon Kamit. Knowing that if the enemy somehow overwhelmed the Two Lands, their chances of ever being free were reduced, Hazz, Ul-lal and others decided to act. Ul-lal left his brother behind to organize an uprising, while he and others escaped through hidden tunnels beneath Petra.

"Where are the others?" I asked.

"Alas," Ul-lal said sadly. "I am the only one left. The others never made it from the tunnels..."

SHADES OF MEMNON II

"What happened?"

"When the invaders found out that there were secret tunnels," replied Ul-lal grimly, "they blocked all entrances they found and placed emissaries inside to dissuade us."

"Emissaries?"

"Ifrits," Ul-lal shuddered. "Desert dwelling beasts from our worst legends. We thought of them only as myths, but somehow the enemy has summoned them. My companions sent me ahead as they engaged the beasts. I heard their death cries as I escaped."

Tears filled Ul-lal's eyes as he became overwhelmed with grief. I placed my hand upon one shoulder to give him comfort. The king did the same upon his other.

"Be at peace warrior," said the Shekem. "You have done well to bring this news to us. We shall destroy those who have enslaved your people, along with these beasts you describe. The sacrifices of your companions shall not be in vain."

"Indeed," I added, pulling my flashing blades before him. "I know of ways to deal with such creatures. The Claws of Sekmet shall avenge your friends, Ul-lal."

*"Aias Rages With His Polished Spear,*
*And Memnon Lusts for Blood."*
*Alkman, Greek Poet,700 BC*

SHADES OF MEMNON II

## CHAPTER 8: "ENEMIES BY OUR BLOOD"

The desert's night air was cool as we marched in silence under the quarter full moon. No torches were allowed as Ul-lal led us stealthily toward the entrance to the secret tunnels leading beneath Petra. Behind Rau-Mu and I marched a full column of the Kings Braves: 300 seasoned Medjay, hand-picked by the Shekem, in full war accouterments. Along with us were 200 asses, their jaws tied shut for silence, bearing weapons to outfit Petra's Kushite rebellion.

The hill of rocks loomed ahead, just as described by our eastern guide, who by leading us back into tunnels filled with beasts from his worst nightmares, was proving his valor beyond any doubt. I was very proud of Ul-lal, the brother of my old friend Hazz.

This encounter with the beasts though, would be different. For after consulting with Ul-lal about the nature of these creatures, and confirming the findings with Hra-Twa's oracle, I had discerned the nature of these "Ifrits." With that knowledge I had given the men special training and devised a very special surprise for the beasts.

Finally, after a full two days of marching, we arrived at the foot of the hill of rocks, five or six miles southwest of Petra. Ul-lal led us up the paths until we came to a giant white stone standing flush against the side of a cliff. Here he lit a torch and slid his hand along the side of the stone. After a moment he emitted a grunt of satisfaction and stepped back.

Immediately the stone slid aside, revealing cleverly constructed hinges attached to the cliff and a sophisticated spring system to move it. After marveling at the workmanship and ancient look of the construction, we pushed the stone door open wide, revealing a dark foreboding tunnel.

Ul-lal peered into the chasm before us with a shudder, then, with a deep breath, bravely step inside. I followed closely, my weapons drawn, as other torches flared to light behind us. Then we began our descent into the secret tunnels beneath Petra.

For nearly an hour we heard or saw nothing, save the torchlight flickering against the craggy gray walls of the tunnel, which was about three times the height of a man and broad enough for six walking abreast. This is the formation Ra Mau instructed the men to take, keeping the beasts of burden and their precious cargo safely flanked.

Following a set of chalk markings placed by Ul-lal during his escape, we trekked through miles of tunnels before we finally heard strange sounds.

## SHADES OF MEMNON II

At first it was very faint, similar to the noises made by clicking insects. But as we came nearer, the sound became more distinct. It was a scraping noise, described by our guide as the claws of the monsters hitting against the hard stone floor. Then an awful odor assailed our noses, causing some warriors to visibly retch.

"The Ifrits..." said Ul-lal fearfully, "are near."

The tunnel widened into a large rock chamber with pointed stones jutting from the ceiling and floor. It was here that Ul-lal said that his party was attacked, and we did not have long to wait before dark shadows began to appear. Taking no chances, Rau-Mu ordered the men to get ready. The terrible odor was nearly overpowering as we got into formation for battle.

Spears with torches attached were extended high overhead, revealing hundreds of loathsome creatures milling about the cavern. About half the height of a man, the beasts had frog-like heads containing rows of razor sharp teeth. Their bodies, muscular, slate gray and coated with a putrid slime, were supported by short, thick legs. Long, spider like arms jutted from their midsections, with elbows that they used to walk about, while their legs served only as anchors.

Their misshapen forms were a most unnerving sight, but the most fearsome thing about them was their claws. Long, curved and razor sharp, they resembled three sickle swords attached to gnarled hairy palms. According to the legends, these claws were for digging and the slime upon their bodies for slipping quickly beneath the desert sand. There they awaited their hapless victims, who are pulled down into sandy traps and shredded to bits for food.

Looking at the expressions of the Medjay around me, I could tell that even these hardened warriors never imagined such fearsome opponents. It was apparent that the instructions and training I gave them would not be enough. To save lives due to doubt and hesitation, it had to be proven that these beasts could fall to men.

I thought for a moment, then quickly whispered a plan to Rau-Mu. After surveying the troops himself, he nodded his approval.

Pushing past the shield bearers, I walked out before the troops alone. The creatures stood motionless, as if awaiting some command, as I beat my chest and paced back and forth between the lines. Pointing at individual creatures accusingly, then down before me forcefully, I hoped the beasts were intelligent enough to realize what I wanted.

After several moments they seemed to get the message, as their crowd parted and there emerged an especially fearsome specimen. Considerably larger than the rest of them, it had marks of healed over wounds gouged into its hide and one claw broken into a craggy, serrated shape deadlier looking than the norm.

With it's red eyes burning intensely, the creature shuffled forward and began its attack. Barely was I able to bring up my blades before the deadly claws swept toward my midsection. Parrying rapidly, I repelled its claws, causing sparks to fly high into the air.

Shouts of encouragement came from my brethren as I stepped back, glancing at the jewels in the hilts of my blades. Just as I had expected, the dark, blood red ruby glowed with a dark light, indicating that these beasts were creatures of pure low evil, the very brood and children of Set.

I was about to start chanting the mantra that would deal with this beast properly, when the monster burst into a desperate frenzy, attacking me with a ferociousness that I could barely withstand. Somehow it knew that the light spelled doom and wanted to kill me before I could take advantage of the information.

Swinging it's claws in from both directions, they locked against my blades as I blocked. As we strained against one another face to face, I smelled its putridness and was very nearly undone. It occurred to me that this odor was a potent weapon that would render me senseless if I stayed too close. So, in an act of desperation, I lifted my knee to my chest and booted the beast viciously in the face. As it reeled back head over heels, I turned and caught a much needed breath.

Rolling to it's feet, the creature shook its ugly head and turned back quickly to reengage me. But by then it was much too late. I chanted and it became disoriented. Then, flashing down with the speed of a viper, my blade cut the life point upon it's neck.

Jerking it's head in agony, it swept at me with a claw. This I sliced at also, then I stepped back to watch the effect.

There it stood before me, its head cocked to one side , leaning upon it's one useful elbow while the other arm lay motionless. Deciding to put it out of it's misery, I slashed two more life points upon it's throat and it fell down dead before me.

The Medjay cheered enthusiastically, while the legions of Ifrit roared in anger, dashing their claws against the stone floor. Stamping my

SHADES OF MEMNON II

foot upon the body of their dead companion, I pointed a blade at them defiantly.

"Come you slimy beasts," I shouted, "let there be an end to this! Now!"

A war cry went up from the ranks of the Medjay as they advanced to join the battle, while the Ifrits surged forward to the attack. What happened next made me proud to be a Medjay and would be the source of boastful tales for generations.

The shield bearers led boldly, deflecting the claws of the beasts and battering them back into utter confusion. Then warriors behind them rose up on the shoulders of others, showering razor sharp darts dipped in a concoction of lotus and sage oils, down into the slimy hides of the Ifrits.

With no protection against the uncommon accuracy of the Medjay, or from the blessed oils of Ausar set loose in the streams of their blood, dozens of creatures fell immediately. Scores more followed after a second and a third volley, leaving only a few dozen beasts alive.

Then the spear fighters had their turn. Held in reserve until now, they leaped over the bent backs of the darters, used the up turned shields of the shield-bearers for spring boards and came down burying their blades in the breasts of the Ifrits. Led by Ka-Sah and Pa-Sah, they chanted words I had taught them to disorient the beasts, but the amazing skills they fought with were all their own.

Churning forward in a beautiful dance of precisely paced destruction, the Medjay moved in rhythmic unison. Each seemed to sense the exact movement of the other, as they battered the beasts with their flashing footwork and cut them down with lightening fast spearplay. It was a complete slaughter. And though there were a few serious injuries, not a single Medjay brethren lost his life.

Ul-lal, who helped dispatch some of the beasts himself, stood leaning upon a spear, catching his breath. At first he had a look of utter satisfaction and then, gazing at the warriors around him, great bewilderment.

"By the Deities," he exclaimed. "You Medjay are the heartiest fighters I have ever seen. You know no fear."

"We are the lions of Kamit," I replied. "We are not prey."

"I do believe we could free my people with this group alone..." he added.

"Oh, no," I replied. "It will take much more than this. Many more Medjay will come, and the Shekem will be there with them, you'll see."

We counted nearly 400 dead Ifrits. Some warriors sliced off claws and kept them as trophies. Then we cared for the injured and continued on our way.

As we wound our way through the tunnels we spotted a few more straggling Ifrits, but they scampered away at the sight of us. After an hour or so, we came to another wide area. Here Ul-lal pointed to a small tunnel.

"This passage," he said, "emerges near the region of the city where the slaves are kept. Since most adult males are used for this function, we should set up for weapons distribution here."

Ra-Mau agreed and instructed warriors to bring forth the beasts of burden and begin unloading weapons. Our next task was to contact Hazz.

"My brother comes and stands near the secret opening twice a day, awaiting my return," said Ul-lal. "That is if nothing has happened to him since I left. Come, I will show you."

Rau-Mu and I accompanied Ul-lal down the tunnel, which was only wide enough for one man at a time. After ascending slightly, we found ourselves in a broader chamber where we could all stand together. Once again Ul-lal pushed a stone before us and it sprang slightly open.

We found ourselves peaking out into a garden. Tall flowers and bushes were cleverly arranged around it, concealing the portal from the outside, but allowing us to peer through to observe the scene.

The garden went on for several hundred cubits. Then a paved walk way was laid out before it. On the other side of the walk stood a large white building.

"There is where the slaves go to receive assignments," said Ul-lal. "We can arm most of the rebellion from right here."

"And how is it that your brother comes to be here twice a day without drawing suspicion?" Rau-Mu asked.

Ul-lal smiled.

"Simple," he replied. "he is the gardener."

When we first peered from the portal the light of day was fading, so, Ul-lal told us, we would have to await the morning before Hazz would appear. And so we bunked down inside the tunnels, posted guards for the night and rested.

I was awakened hours later by the sound of voices. Sitting up, I saw Ul-lal and Rau-Mu speaking to someone through the opening.

Looking over their shoulders when they heard me stir, they beckoned me over excitedly.

"Greetings, Memnon," a familiar voice said as I came near. "It is good to see you again."

Peering through the opening, I spied my old friend Hazz. His smile was as warm as I remembered.

"Hazz," I said, "it is good to see you also."

"I see you have come back to keep your promise."

"Indeed I have, my friend," I replied. "How go the preparations for your rebellion?"

"Well. As well as can be expected. We were beginning to wonder if any got through. We have heard of what goes on in the tunnels..."

"We took care of that problem on the way here," I replied. "Thanks to the bravery of your brother. We are all very proud of him."

"As am I," Hazz replied, shifting his eyes to his brother. "As am I."

Quickly Hazz told us of their plans for rebellion: Under the noses of the invaders they had developed a sophisticated system of messaging and secret meetings. Plans for sabotage and sneak attacks had already been made, needing only weapons to carry them through. And since we had brought them, there was left only to devise a way to distribute them. After much debate, Hazz hit upon a plan.

"Look, my friends, he began, "I am the gardener here. Very frequently I receive requests for flowers to be clipped and sent to the wives and concubines of the invaders."

"And so?" I asked.

"And so," Hazz replied. "It is the slaves who pick up these flowers and deliver them."

"Ah," said Ul-lal," I see where you are going..."

Rau-Mu and I looked at each other, puzzled.

"Don't you see?" Ul-lal began. "My brother will hand out flower bundles..."

"With weapons concealed inside," ended Hazz with a smile.

We had one week before the Shekem would lead an attack upon Petra as planned. During this time we handed Hazz thousands of weapons, which he bundled with flowers and secretly distributed to members of the rebellion. While we waited, some Medjay became restless and amused themselves by hunting Ifrits in the tunnels. Rau-Mu approved, for he wanted to see an end put to every one of these loathsome creatures.

Finally the morning came which we were all waiting for. Trumpets blared and much commotion could be seen as we peered through the crack in the opening. Hazz appeared and confirmed it.

"The army of Kamit is massing in the desert before Petra," he said excitedly. "Our rebels are ready to go upon your words, Rau-Mu."

The elder warrior looked at me.

"Memna-un, are you ready to slay these vipers?"

I tapped the hilts of my blades, smiling grimly.

"Let us drive them back to where they came from," I replied, "or bury them under the desert sand."

Rau-Mu shouted to a warrior behind us.

"Tell the men the time has come!"

Then he looked at Hazz through the crack in the rock.

"Do it Hazz," he said. "It is time to hit them now."

Hazz nodded.

"I shall meet you at the appointed spot near the gates. May the deities be with you!"

Moments later fire broke out in the building across from the garden. Then groups of men came running from the doors, fighting furiously. Rau-Mu looked at Ul-lal, pulling a sickle sword from his belt.

"Open it Ul-lal," he cried. "Let's do this!"

Ul-lal touched the stone before us and it sprang open wide. Rau-Mu and I pushed it further and climbed out onto the ground. The fighting was quite hot before the building, but it was only a matter of time before the enemy saw us emerging. Rau-Mu noted this and shouted for haste among the Medjay.

"Out, out, hurry, hurry," he cried as they emerged, "faster."

Just as we feared, a Tamahu warrior fighting rebels looked over at us. His eyes widened in surprise, then he broke off and ran back into the building. Moments later, he and dozens of his comrades emerged and started running towards us.

"How may are out?" I shouted to Rau-Mu, my eyes locked upon the approaching enemy.

"About half," he replied. "You must hold them off Memna-un."

With a great war cry, I and the Medjay who had emerged ran out to meet the approaching enemy. Swords clashed and shields resounded as hot fighting ensued.

But these warriors were no match for the Medjay, whose rhythmic

SHADES OF MEMNON II

footwork mowed them down in short order. After hacking down their forces, we met the rebels on the walkway and introduced ourselves. The rest of the Medjay emerged, then we gathered to plot our strategy.

The word was that the enemy was in a state of confusion, with half their forces engaging the rebels all over the city and half massing to defend against the approaching army led by the Shekem Ur Shekem.

Our appointed task was to open the front gates in order to end the conflict quickly. Otherwise, due to the tall stone cliffs flanking the only one road leading in, only a long siege could bring about victory. This we could not allow. At all costs, the gates of Petra had to be opened.

As fires of sabotage and vicious fighting raged around us, we ran toward the gateway to the city. A few token forces of the enemy tried to engage us, but we rolled over them like a wave. There simply were none among them who could stand up to the Medjay.

Finally we arrived at the gate, where the determined rebels engaged in desperate battles with the enemy. We joined them in this fight as grateful cries of joy went up among the Petrans. Looking around, I saw mostly Tamahu enemies, but other members of the strange serpent worshipping coalition fought against us too.

There were the strange men from far eastern Kun-Lun, home of Sung Li, who increased my Rau and strengthened my bones. There were Shashus and other easterners, as well as the mysterious red skinned warriors with feathered headgear I had noted on my last visit to Petra.

Questions about the origins of these strange people burned in my mind now as they did then. But, now, just as then, the time was not right to pursue them. Putting these thoughts aside, I plunged into the battle, for the time was only right to kill them.

After an hour of furious fighting, we finally succeeded in taking the gate tower. Rau-Mu decided to stay behind to guide the fight to keep it, instructing me to take the outer gates.

Looking back, I saw thousands of fresh enemy warriors converging upon the scene. Odds even the Medjay could not long last against. The gates would have to be opened quickly for the Kamitic forces or all would be lost. As it was, many Medjay would lose their lives defending what we had already been taken.

Clasping Rau-Mu's hand briefly, I shouted for half the Medjay to follow and rushed through the gate as they raised it.

In the distance I could see the two outer gates, nestled between the steep walls of the mountains. Beyond them, on the sands of the desert before Petra, the forces of Kamit were massed.

Behind me, I heard shouts and curses as the Medjay holding the gate tower came under attack. Focusing on the task at hand, I urged the men on to greater speed as we ran down the road. Within moments we were rushing upon the first gate, taking the warriors manning it completely by surprise.

Because it was designed to ward off attack from without, Medjay archers cut down many before they knew what hit them. Then we swarmed over the building, killed those inside and raised the heavy door.

Once again we left a force to hold what we had taken, then rushed on to take the next gate.

I noted that the forces of Kamit were already starting their siege, exchanging arrows with the gate's defenders. Preoccupied, these gate protectors would be taken unawares also, leaving the opening for the Kamitic forces free and clear.

But as we neared this final obstacle, a shadow fell across our path. Looking up, the warriors around me gasped in astonishment.

"A skyboat!" someone exclaimed.

Indeed it was a skyboat, similar in design to the one I had seen on the island of the Ka. Something told me though, that it did not contain friendly Anu.

As I and the rest of the Medjay stood in awe, a familiar voice rang out near me. It was Hra-Twa.

"Memna-un," said my little Anu friend desperately, "you cannot stand against the occupants of that vessel. Quit standing there and take the other gate. The Shekem is your only hope."

I was totally surprised. Hra-Twa had never come to me on the field of battle. Something very dire was about to take place.

"Half you men take that gate," I shouted, "go, go, go!"

I was left with perhaps 40 warriors, including Ka-Sah and Pa-Sah, who stood ever by my side. The sky-boat landed before us and the door began to open.

"Memna-un," cried Hra-Twa, "don't do it."

"I have no choice my friend," I replied coolly. "I cannot allow them to attack us from the rear. Better to face them now."

Hra-Twa stepped into a shadow and was gone, as the door to the sky-boat completely opened. Out stepped several Tamahu warriors

## SHADES OF MEMNON II

wearing attire I had never seen. Their silver corselets wrapped in black sashes immediately caught my eye, along with strange headgear topped by stiff, upright horsehair. All of them carried exquisite long swords of very fine workmanship and brightly colored, thick round shields.

A column of 50 or so emerged, placing themselves into battle formation to the left and right of the sky-boat. Then out stepped two strange Tamahus unlike any I had ever seen.

Both were as tall than I, unarmed and wearing long white robes and elegant jewelry. With circular green wreaths wrapped around their heads, they stood with a haughty, arrogant air. But the most striking thing was their golden colored hair and strangely glowing complexions.

As these two stood motionless, from behind them stepped a man that I did recognize. It was the yellow-haired warrior that I had seen when I last visited Petra. The one who had wanted my head. Dressed similar to the two shining ones beside him, he was armed with a long gleaming spear and two swords.

His eyes swept the scene for a moment, finally settling upon me. Then he handed the spear to one of the shining ones and strode toward me, a bitter sneer spreading across his face.

"Greeting, Memnon the younger," he said in broken Kamitian.

"Who are you?" I asked, stepping forward myself.

"Who am I? he answered with a evil grin. "Why, I am your death man. I am Aias, son of Achilles."

Then it dawned upon me. I had heard that my Pa's great rival in the battle of Troy was a warrior named Achilles. They said it was he who defeated my Pa and killed him. But I knew now that my Pa was alive.

"Your Pa was the only man to ever humble mine, younger Memnon," said Aias. "We are enemies by our blood, you and I, and I have vowed to kill you. Revenge has already been taken against your sister..."

"What?" I shouted. "What have you done to my sister?"

Aias replied coldly.

"Oh, Memnon, the bitterness in your voice. You sister means all to you, doesn't she? Well, you shall go to your grave without knowing her fate. Let me tell you though: it is far, far worse than death."

The tone of his taunts chilled me, as a blood red haze of anger appeared before my eyes. I had been taught never to battle this way though, and breathed deeply for a moment to calm myself. Hefting my

Claws, I took a step closer to my enemy.

"I hope the life behind you has been fulfilling, Aias" I said grimly. "For the path that lies ahead of you is short. Pray to whatever deity comforts you, for my sister shall be avenged this moment!"

"Really, Memnon," he spat. "I think not, for my Myrmidon warriors, who I inherited from my Pa, are mightier than your Medjay dogs. And I am superior to you. I shall earn my place among the immortals of Mt. Olympus by taking your head."

"We shall see," I shot back, signaling the men behind me. "Medjay, attack!"

A shower of Medjay darts flew into the ranks of the Myrmidons, but most were deflected by the enemy's round shields. Then a furious battle began.

Aias rushed forward, long and short blades in hand, and we went blow for blow for what seemed like endless moments. It was a lightning fast dance of death that did not allow me to even observe how the rest of the warriors were doing.

Aias' reflexes were unusually fast, requiring me to call upon every ounce of skill just to hold him at bay. All the while he wore a hateful sneer as he gazed into my eyes and taunted me.

"Ah ha," he growled, "you cannot long stand against me. I shall prove to these witnesses from Olympus that I deserve the place once set aside for my Pa. A place that your Pa wrongly stole from him!"

I knew nothing of what Aias spoke of, but I did notice that when he opened his mouth, his sword play became a little slower.

I decided to play upon this to put an end to him.

"Your Pa was a swine, Aias," I sneered, recalling tales I had heard of the Trojan conflict. "It is said he raped the dead upon the battlefield, that he lusted for his young male opponents..."

Aias face turned bright red. Shaking with anger, he screamed hatefully.

"My Pa was the mightiest warrior, the most valiant warrior before Troy," he cried. "I'll gut you for that, you Kushite dog!"

As Aias continued to rant in anger, I noticed his short sword extending a bit far, lingering a bit long when he jabbed. So in a desperate gamble, I dropped my long claw, seized his wrist and pulled him to me. Simultaneously I deflected his other blade, then swung the edge of my own up to his throat. He was completely taken by surprise.

"Go ahead," he said, "Kill me. Kill me with your enchanted blade. Do it."

I obliged him immediately, pulling the edge of my short claw across the lifeline near his throat. His eyes rolled back and he fell down at my feet. Looking up, I spied the two strange "witnesses" at the skyboat looking at one another, clearly shocked. The one with the spear started towards me, but was pulled back by the other. Then both stood still, continuing to look on silently.

I lifted my foot to stamp Aias' hateful face, hoping to taunt the glowing strangers into battle, when a Myrmidon leaped to engage me. Though I would have preferred to settle things with the two others, I had no choice but to engage him.

This time I could observe the battlefield, for though he was a great swordsman, my present opponent was much slower than Aias. Glancing around between blows, I noted for the first time the skill of these warriors called Myrmidons.

Besides my own brethren and the Pan-Kau-Rau-Shen warriors of Keftui, these men were the most astonishing fighters I had ever seen. They too moved in uncommon unison, while superb swordplay, meshed with a bit of Pan-Kau-Ra-Shen, made their defenses nearly impenetrable. I wondered though, were they had acquired the knowledge, as I had been told Pan-Kau-Rau-Shen was a Kushite art. Though their skills was not on the level of my Keftuan comrades, they indeed knew enough to be quite deadly.

Many men fell on both sides, each group giving as good as it got. Even Pa-Sah and Ka-Sah, the very best of the Medjay spear-fighters, were hard pressed to ward off the swordplay of these northerners. It was something I had never expected to see, but Medjay and Myrmidon seemed nearly evenly matched.

But I did not have long to contemplate the nature of these Myrmidons, due to the strange behavior of the one I was engaging. I caught him peering over my shoulder several times, which I first took as a trick to get my guard down. Then a reflection upon his shining corselet gave me warning. Someone was sneaking upon me from behind.

Ducking quickly, I saw a shining spear surging past where my back would have been, plunging into the body of the warrior I was fighting. Rolling to the side, I sprang to my feet to discover the identity of this craven assassin. It was Aias.

"Damn you, Memnon!" he cried, pulling his spear from the body of his dying comrade. "I will get you yet! I swear I will!"

I knew not how Aias yet lived, but I leaped forward to see that his next death would be permanent. Then suddenly a roar came from the direction of the gate. Glancing over my shoulder, I saw the chariot of the Shekem hurtling towards us.

Men were falling before his uraeus' flame like grass before a sickle, while others were being torn to bits by the furious royal lion. Fresh Medjay accompanied them, mowing down all who stood in their way. The Medjay with me let forth a loud cheer.

Aias looked on fearfully as the Shekem and his warriors approached, then questioningly he glanced towards his two strange companions. Shaking their heads, the two walked back into the sky-boat. Then Aias called to his warriors.

"Myrmidon, retreat," he shouted, "back to the ship! Back to the ship!"

I lunged for the son of Achilles, but he pushed one of his own men upon my blade and scampered back to the skyboat. His Myrmidon broke off from the Medjay and followed, a few valiantly selling their lives to hold us back as the others escaped. As the Shekem's chariot pulled up beside me, the skyboat rose and took off into the air.

The Shekem and I watched it disappear into the distance, then he addressed me loudly.

"Greetings, Memna-un!" he exclaimed. "Who was that?"

"Anetch Hrak, great Ra Mesh," I said, bending upon one knee. "It was a mortal enemy, Shekem. An enemy by the blood."

The Shekem nodded.

"I see," he replied. "I assume the other gates has been opened?"

"Yes, Shekem," I answered.

"Then let us take this place and return it to its rightful owners."

The face of my sister suddenly appeared before me. Momentarily, I hesitated.

"Memna-un?" the Shekem said with concern.

"Yes, Shekem," I answered, resuming my composure. "Let us take this city back."

We passed back through the first outer gate, then through the main gate of the city, to find savage fighting raging all around us. Though the Medjay there were hard pressed, they had managed to hold on and

SHADES OF MEMNON II

shouted with joy at the sight of the Shekem.

Then hordes of fresh Kamitic warriors poured through, beating the enemy back from the gates. Led by the king, they combined with the forces of the rebellion and fought the invaders furiously in every corner of the city.

As in past rebellions I had witnessed, the common folk joined in, giving the invaders no where to run or hide. With the Kamitic army and the entire city against them, the Servants of the Serpents were immediately on the defensive. Within a few hours they were suing for peace.

That night, as we watched the prisoners bound and in procession before us, burning questions about my sister, my Pa, and the strange "witnesses" accompanying Aias distracted me. The Shekem noticed this and looked at me with great concern. Pulling me aside, he placed his hand upon my shoulder.

"Fear not, Memna-un," he said. "Whatever concerns you, I pledge the resources of Kamit to help you solve it. For now be at peace, for when we return you will receive great honors for what you have done here."

For three weeks more we remained, helping the native Petrans to rebuild and reclaim their city. The Shekem was asked to sit in judgment upon the invaders, who had committed murder and other atrocities as they lorded over the captured people. The populace, insisting upon swift redress, drafted all officials who had not been killed to join the king of Kamit in this task. Hazz and Ul-lal, as leaders of the rebellion, were themselves called upon and eagerly took up this duty.

The justice they dispensed was harsh, as many were condemned and killed on the spot. But the crimes the invaders committed justified it. As I had seen in the visions revealed to me by Kam-Atef, this coalition had a love for human sacrifice. And as testimonies of hundreds of torture victims and thousands of witnesses confirmed, they had shed much blood in Petra.

As I watched justice being served for the sake of this city, I thirsted for the same for my family. I had told no one about what Aias had said to me, torn as I was between honoring my pledge to the Medjay and leaving so that I could seek out personal vengeance. For if what Aias spoke was the truth, Kho-An-Sa had lied to me when he said that Neftiji would not be harmed. Even at the cost of my own life, the magician must be made to pay.

# CHAPTER 8: "ENEMIES BY OUR BLOOD"

SHADES OF MEMNON II

*"The Ethiopes, who are divided in two,
the most remote of men:
Some where Helios (the sun) sets, others where he rises..."* - Hesiod.

# CHAPTER 9: "INVADERS FROM THE NORTH BEWARE"

We were greeted in the city of Waset by throngs of swarming Kamitians, all cheering the victory at Petra and praising the Shekem and his warriors. Streams of colored papyrus rained down and beautiful dancers cast flowers in our path as I rode in the Shekem's chariot alongside him; a great honor that few earned during the entire history of the Two Lands. Aten shined brighter than I had ever seen as we proceeded down the crowded avenues.

But though the day was bright, my heart was heavy. It was all I could do to manage a smile as we continued the procession toward the Temple of the Neteru. I felt as I had for weeks: Longing to leap from the chariot, run to discover the fate of my sister and take my vengeance upon Kho-An-Sa. But I stood stern for the sake of the Shekem, reluctantly remaining by his side.

Finally we arrived at the temple complex where we were to consecrate the spoils of the war to the deities. To participate in this ritual, the Shekem had chosen a group of us who had distinguished ourselves in battle. These included elder Rau Mu, Pa-Sah and Ka-Sah, myself and several others.

Stepping down from the chariots, we were greeted by the priests who were to prepare us for coming onto holy ground. It was then that I at last saw Ra Nefer, Grand Vizier, Second of Kamit, and the man from whom I had been sent to steal.

Just as described by the evil magician, Ra Nefer was short and thin. What wasn't described was his wise and patient manner and easy, disarming smile. Along with the traditional white robe of Kamitic priesthood, he wore a golden necklace glittering with all the gems of the Neteru. This was the item that Kho-An-Sa craved to possess.

After receiving the honored greetings from the rest of us, Ra Nefer bowed to the king, then stepped aside with him to speak alone. After a few moments, Ra Mesh beckoned me to join them.

"This is Memna-un, the younger," he said proudly. "The one you have been hearing about."

"Word has come to us," said Ra Nefer, "from as far away as Keftui of your exploits, young Atef. You follow in the footsteps of your Pa well. We are all very proud of you."

SHADES OF MEMNON II

"Thank you elder," I replied. "I only hope to continue to serve my people."

Ra Nefer and the Shekem looked at one another, smiling.

"He is much like his Pa in his humbleness," declared Ra Nefer to the Shekem.

"You knew him?" I asked.

"I and many others in the priesthood. There was a time when we may have placed the crown of Kamit upon his head."

I stood speechless.

"But we will speak of that later, as well as many other things, Memna-un. Now for the presentation before the Neteru."

A group of lower priests lifted the bags and boxes of booty we had taken from the campaign and carried them into the temple complex. Led by the Shekem, we proceeded behind them until we found ourselves before a large bathing pool. Here we disrobed and filed into the cool, sweet smelling waters. After our purifying bath, we dried and donned white robes handed to us by the priests.

Continuing on, we passed the outer walls, entering sections of the temple seen rarely by laypersons. Tall torches burned in the long halls, their flickering lights revealing rare paintings and carvings depicting the most sacred Kamitian traditions. These artistic displays were obviously designed to inspire respect for our traditions, and they accomplished that task quite well.

Finally we arrived in the section devoted to Amen, most high and creator of all. Here we were led into a chamber furnished with cushions, where we were seated. Then the Shekem Ur Shekem disappeared into a small doorway behind dark curtains. This was the Holy of Holies, the inner sanctum where only kings were allowed.

The priests who attended us began playing their sacred flutes and sistrums, then we lowered our heads to rest them with Amen.

For a long time my mind fought against calming, struggling as it was with the fate of my sister and Pa. But after a time the soothing melodies penetrated my ka and I found myself floating. Floating in a dark place of total peace where I felt strangely at home. I do not know how long it lasted, but too soon it seemed, the tinkle of bells awakened us.

Looking up, we spied Shekem Ra Mesh standing before us. Exuding a tranquillity that I had never observed in anyone, he seemed to fairly float on air. It stood to reason, I thought, that Kamit's great warrior, who must constantly concern himself with war, would need to find total peace at times. This he apparently cultivated in the Holy of Holies of Amen.

"Come warriors," he addressed us soothingly. "It is time to pay homage to Herukhuti."

Rising, we followed the Shekem and other priests from the chamber. Strolling down the long halls again, we passed briefly beneath an area open to the skies. To my surprise it had grown quite dark, and stars sparkled down upon us. Since we had arrived here during late afternoon, our rest with Amen must have lasted much longer than I suspected.

After a few moments we came to an large entrance covered with paintings and flanked by statues of the Neter of justice and righteous aggression, Herukhuti. As it was the moon of his dominion, we would hold a ritual devoting the spoils we had taken from the invaders of Petra to him.

We were led into a torch lit chamber painted purple and blood red, a huge alter dominating the entire room. As they led us past it, we could see the implements of the Neter displayed prominently: Bronze swords, spears and daggers of recent make, as well as truly ancient weapons like flint blades and throwing sticks. Shards of iron, man made and from the stars, were shaped into hammers and carving tools. And for the deity's consumption, there was strong drink, smoking tobacco, onions, peppers and hot herbs.

Each of us was given a swallow of the strong drink, then mounds of onions and peppers were shoved down our throats. Then the priests pushed us onto the floor and took up their drums. The sounds of the instruments reverberated against the high walls as the ritual began.

As they beat the rhythm of the war deity, Ra Nefer disappeared into a side chamber, stepping forth moments later, arrayed in red and purple war cloth, carrying a large iron sickle sword. The Shekem Ur Shekem, presiding over the scene, was seated upon a large cushion. His head bobbed to the rhythm of the drums, but otherwise he was as tranquil as he had been earlier.

Vigorously performing the dance of the deity, we beat our chests and thrust our hips aggressively to the arouse the force of life within us. Ra Nefer joined at first, swinging the sword and howling war cries. Then he broke from the floor and ran to the alter. There he hunkered over the implements of war, seizing herbs and chewing them vigorously. A few

SHADES OF MEMNON II

moments went by, then he turned toward us as a strange light suddenly appeared, beaming upon the middle of his brow.

I was mystified by this, as the beam came not from the torches around us, but from some unknown source. Eyes closed, Ra Nefer wiggled his head into it vigorously, as if absorbing it into himself. After several moments of this, he raised the sickle sword high above his head.

All drumming ceased and the torches were suddenly extinguished.

The only visible light was that which played upon his brow, which I could now trace to its source in the darkness. Following the luminous beam with my eyes, I saw that it emerged from a small hole cut into the wall. Craning my neck slightly, I saw that it was a shaft of light directly from the moon.

I had heard rumors of this, and here it was before my eyes. The great builders had positioned the temple and cut the shaft to allow only that light to shine in, blocking out all other celestial bodies, purifying the intensity of Herukhuti's moon.

As I stood in awe of this wisdom and ingenuity, Ra Nefer's head rolled from side to side, his body shaking with violent convulsions. Then his eyes went back into his head so that only the whites could be seen and a loud and terrible voice boomed from his throat.

"BRING ME MY SPOILS!" he cried.

The torches were hurriedly relit, then several lower priests appeared bearing the booty we had taken from the invaders of Petra. Gold and silver oxhides were quickly laid out before the possessed priest, as well as mounds of woven items, expensive vessels and works of art.

Reaching down aggressively, he snatched up one of the heavy golden oxhides as if it were mere a toy. Then he struck it with the sickle sword, causing sparks to fly across the room.

"IS THIS ALL YOU HAVE? BRING ME MORE! MORE OF THE WEALTH FROM THOSE WHO WOULD BREAK MY LAWS. "

More booty was brought before him, then a priest appeared with a basket and placed it at his feet. Bending upon one knee, Ra Nefer/ Herukhuti smiled and reached into it. Then up his hand came, clutching the putrefying head of a Myrmidon warrior by it's long yellow hair.

"YES! YES! THIS IS WHAT I WANT! THIS IS THE BOOTY I CRAVE! THE HEADS OF THOSE WHO BREAK THE LAWS OF JUSTICE! "

I looked on in utter surprise. I did not know that the head of a Myrmidon had even been taken, let alone brought here for this ritual.

Glancing around at my Medjay comrades, I found them as taken aback as I was. Then the Neter continued, waving the head in the air vigorously as he spoke.

"FOR THE SAKE OF MY SISTER MAAT, SHE WHO LOVES ALL THINGS AND BALANCES ALL MEASURES, THERE MUST BE JUSTICE! I AM THAT JUSTICE, AND THIS IS THE PRICE THAT MUST BE PAID FOR DISRUPTING MY SISTER'S WORK! SHEKEM UR SHEKEM, COME HERE!"

The king got up from his seat and approached the possessed priest. Ra Nefer/Herukhuti smiled at him.

"RA MESH! YOU ARE ADORED BY HERUKHUTI! I ADORE YOU, FOR YOU ARE A CHILD OF JUSTICE. BUT THERE IS ANOTHER HERE I WANT. ANOTHER HERE WHO NEEDS TO COME TO ME!"

The deity pointed the sickle sword at me.

"IT IS HIM! GIVE HIM TO ME! GIVE HIM TO ME NOW SHEKEM! I KNOW THAT YOU NEED HIM, BUT THE NEED I HAVE IS GREATER! GIVE HIM TO ME, RIGHT NOW!"

The Shekem Ur Shekem nodded and beckoned me over. Standing before him now, the possessed priest seemed as tall as I.

"He is yours Herukhuti," said Ra Mesh, stepping aside. "Do with him as you will."

"COME CLOSER, YOUNGER MEMNON! COME CLOSE AND I WILL MAKE YOU MINE!"

As I stepped closer to Ra Nefer/Herukhuti as he dropped the head to the floor and kicked it away contemptuously. Then, as fast as a viper, he seized me by the neck with the same hand. His grip was like iron and I could smell the putrid odor on his fingers as he lifted me off the floor. Waves of heat, like rays rising off desert sands, emanated from his body as he brandished the sickle sword before my face.

"YOU HAVE BEEN ABUSED YOUNG WARRIOR! ABUSED AND POISONED BY THOSE WHO WOULD BREAK MY LAWS. I SHALL FIX THE POISON NOW!"

With that, the sickle sword came down, slashing a long gash in my chest. Immediately, I felt on fire and all of my limbs became paralyzed. Then a purple mist appeared before my eyes and my mind became a blank. Moments later I felt my feet touch the floor and found myself being held upright by the Shekem.

SHADES OF MEMNON II

"YOUR KA HAS BEEN PURGED OF THE POISONS. YOU CAN NOW USE THE WEAPONS OF MY CHILD SEKMET AS YOU WILL. BUT NOW YOU ARE MINE! LIKE YOUR PA, WHO BE-CAME CONSECRATED TO ME IN A FAR OFF LAND, WHO CALLED UPON ME BY A DIFFERENT NAME, YOU ARE MINE ALSO! DO YOU SWEAR TO WORK FOR ME AND PUNISH THOSE WHO BREAK THE LAWS OF MAAT?"

My mind reeled. The heat in my body still surged.

"Yes," I cried. "Yes I will work for you. I will uphold the laws of Maat forever!"

"HA HA HA HA HA HA! GOOD! GOOD! LET THE INVADERS FROM THE NORTH BEWARE, FOR THE NETER OF JUSTICE HAS A ROVING CHAMPION ONCE AGAIN! YOUR FIRST TASK SHALL BE TO RENDER MY JUDGMENT AGAINST THOSE WHO HAVE ABUSED YOUR FAMILY. AGAINST THE ONE WHO SENT YOU HERE TO DO THE WRONG WHICH YOU REFUSE TO DO! HE AND THE NORTHERNERS WOULD CHASE MAAT FROM THE SURFACE OF THE WORLD. THIS I CAN NOT ALLOW!"

I nodded in agreement, as the deity waved the sword above his head.

SACRIFICE IS WHAT I CRAVE! SACRIFICE! BRING ME THE HANDS THAT THEY HAVE USED TO BREAK MY LAWS MEMNA-UN! BRING ME TOKENS OF THEIR MISUSED MANHOOD FROM WHICH THEY DERIVE THEIR STRENGTH TO DO IT! AND BRING ME THE HEADS THAT THEY USE TO CONTEMPLATE THEIR MISDEEDS! BURN ALL IN FIRE AND SEND THE SMOKE TO ME, THAT I MIGHT SMELL THE SWEET FRAGRANCE OF EVIL BEING DESTROYED! THAT I MIGHT WAFT THE ODOR TO THE NORTH AS WARNING TO THE SERPENT SERVANTS AND THE FALSE DEITIES OF OLYMPUS THAT THEY WILL NEVER GAIN DOMINION OVER KUSHITE LANDS! UNDERSTAND YOU WHAT I WISH, MEMNA-UN?"

"Yes, Herukhuti," I cried, though I shivered at the grisly task he set before me. "Yes I do!"

"THEN DO IT! AFTERWARDS YOU MUST FREE YOUR PA, SO THAT MY GREATEST WARRIORS CAN STAND TOGETHER AGAINST THIS NORTHERN ASSAULT. THESE ARE THE TASKS I SET BEFORE YOU, MEMNA-UN! FROM THIS DAY FORWARD YOU ARE MINE!"

# CHAPTER 9: "INVADERS FROM THE NORTH BEWARE"

The sickle sword descended again, carving a matching gash into the other side of my chest. This time the blood that spurted caught fire before my eyes, burning up into red puffs of smoke. Then both wounds were seared shut by lines of burning flame and I fell senseless into the arms of the Shekem again.

I awoke later with a start, as familiar hands upon my body roused me. Peeling my eyes open, I spied Sha-Sah smiling down at me, rubbing my body with soothing oils. Looking around, I found myself upon a small bed in a humble little room. The simplicity of the furniture and small alters indicated that it was not the temple or palace.

"You are in my room," Sha-Sah said. "My brothers brought you here, to our family compound yesterday."

"I am pleased to be with you again," I said affectionately. "Are we alone?"

"Yes, my betrothed," she replied with a smile. "My brothers have left on an errand."

I sat up and threw my arms around her.

"Good, because I have some things to tell you. But first..."

Pulling her down upon me, I covered her face with kisses. Then we spent a powerful while of pleasure, nearly equal to the very first time. As we lay locked in ecstatic union, the Rau raging between us convinced me once again that Sha-Sah was meant for me.

Afterwards as I held her, my body filled with the power cultivated between us, I decided to tell her the story of my life and how I came to be with the Medjay.

As I informed her of everything, including the plot against Ra Nefer, she listened very intently. Tears came to her eyes when I told her about the plight of my family, but otherwise she was silent. She remained so for long moments after I finished, then suddenly she spoke up.

"It is good that you confided in me, my mate to be," Sha-Sah said. "You know what you must do now don't you?"

"Yes," I replied. "I must go to see Ra Nefer. Perhaps he can tell me more about Kho-An-Sa..."

"And more of your Pa," she added. "Though you have been sanctioned by Herukhuti, you should gain Ra Nefer's wisdom before you seek this justice."

I nodded in agreement, then looked deeply into her eyes.

## SHADES OF MEMNON II

"Sha-Sah," I began, "you know what I must do...afterwards...."

"Yes," she replied. "I do..."

"I may not return..."

Tears welled up in her eyes.

"I understand," she replied. "But I will do rituals to send you strength, to ensure that you come back to me. You must come back to me Memna-un."

Pa-Sah and Ka-Sah soon arrived, and after a long and tearful farewell, I left the compound of my friends and made my way toward the palace. It was well within walking distance, as Medjay settlements were kept close to the seat of power by tradition. As I strolled along the back streets alone with my thoughts, once again a familiar voice rang out nearby.

"Ahh, Memna-un," said Hra-Twa stepping forth from the shadows. "You go to see Ra Nefer?"

"Yes my friend," I replied. "Perhaps he can answer the questions that plague me about Kho-An-Sa. Perhaps even give me the means to defeat him."

"Perhaps he can," said my Anu friend. "But be careful. The oracles predict a dire outcome to this meeting."

I stopped in my tracks.

"Are you saying I should not see him, Hra-Twa?"

"The oracles say you should, but..." he replied. "It is indeed a strange reading..."

"Then I will see him, my friend," I said. "Then that wretch Kho-An-Sa shall pay..."

As I approached the gates of the palace, Hra-Twa stepped away and was gone. The gate keepers all recognized me and let me pass, giving me directions to Ra Nefer's apartments. Darkness began to fall as I passed into the halls of the great palace, where servants lighting torches greeted me by name. No one questioned me about where I was going and for this I was glad. But I was puzzled by my sudden popularity.

Turning down a long hall, I noticed a line of grand paintings upon the wall. They depicted kings and queens through the ages in the act of embracing loyal comrades and bestowing the necklace of Heru upon them. These were the Shemsu Heru, followers of the king, beloved protectors of Kamit who were as highly revered as royalty.

Nearing the end of the hall I spied Queen Nefertari, she who drove the Hyksos invaders from Kamit. Her painting depicted the great queen bestowing the necklace of Heru upon her legendary Medjay husband, Anuk. After walking a few more steps, I stopped dead in my tracks. There before me was a painting of Shekem Ra Mesh III bestowing the necklace of Heru upon a regally arrayed warrior.

The warrior depicted was me.

I was stunned. I had no idea this was being planned. I did not think I had done enough for my people to warrant it. Suddenly a voice spoke up from behind me.

"It is an honor that you and your family have earned."

I turned around suddenly. There I saw Ra Nefer smiling broadly.

"Anetch Hrak," I said, bowing in greeting. "I don't know what to say..."

"Come, Memna-un," the priest said. "I received word that you had come to see me. The Shekem shall join us shortly. It is time we spoke a bit."

I followed Ra Nefer back to his chambers, were we reclined upon sumptuous chairs and began to chat. He told me that the decision was made the day I was chosen by Herukhuti to bestow the honor of Shemsu Heru upon me. It was an honor that was planned for my Pa had he returned from the battle of Troy.

Finally I mustered the strength to tell Ra Nefer about my life for the past three years, including the plot against him by Kho-An-Sa. He nodded as he listened, then placed his hand upon my shoulder as I finished.

"It is right that you came to me with your story," he said. "Kho-An-Sa was once a prized pupil of mine. But he dabbled in forces that were forbidden to those of his rank and became corrupted. He was always jealous of my rank and station, but I am puzzled. He knows that taking my emblem would not earn him my place."

"Then why do you think he wants it?" I asked.

"I don't know...", Ra Nefer replied. "Let me see the weapon he sent with you...this blade of Shai."

Reaching into my belt, where I had been carrying the blade for weeks, I plucked it out. As I held it out toward Ra Nefer, I felt a strange tingling, then a terrible, terrible thing happened.

The knife rose from the palm of my hand and began spinning on it's own. A familiar, malevolent laugh seemed to come from everywhere in the room. Then, before either of us could move, the blade ceased turning and plunged into the chest Vizier Ra Nefer.

## SHADES OF MEMNON II

"Noooooooooo!" I screamed.

His eyes wide open in surprise, Ra Nefer clutched at the handle. But it was too late, for the amount of blood spurting over his fingers indicated that the wound was fatal.

What happened next will forever be etched into my memory as a reminder of Ra Nefer's greatness  As I stood transfixed, too overwhelmed by the horror of the evil magic to even move, Ra Nefer let go of the blade and slowed his breathing.  Then a look of tranquillity washed over him as he accepted his fate.  I will never forget the look he gave me just before his eyes closed forever: It was a look of pure affection and total forgiveness.

But I could not forgive myself.  Kneeling down in grief, I pulled the knife from his body and held him tightly.

"Oh great one, oh great one," I cried.  "I am so sorry."

For long moments I held the limp body of the high priest close to me, tears welling up in my eyes and rolling down my face.  Finally I let him go and stood over him, clutching the bloody blade in my quivering hand and vowing vengeance against Kho-An-Sa.  Suddenly a roaring voice boomed from behind me.

"What is this?!!! What is this?!!!"

Turning around, I found the Shekem Ur Shekem himself, facing me from across the room.  He was accompanied by the royal lion and his eyes blazed with bitter fury.

"I come to explain the great honor we would offer to you and find you in an act of foul murder," he cried.  "Sebau! You shall die right now for this."

"But Shekem," I cried.  "It is not at all as it seems..."

But the king was beyond listening.  Raising his head slightly, he spoke a word of power that seared the very air before him. His uraeus began to glow, then he his lips formed to utter the second word that I had seen lead to instant death.

When the hot blue flame flared, I knew in my heart that my time in this life was at an end.  Thus, it was out of pure instinct alone that I dropped the knife and pulled forth the Claws of Sekmet. I was totally astonished when the beam that emanated from the Shekem's crown struck my blades and dissipated, instead of reducing me instantly to a pile of smoking flesh.

The look upon the Shekem's face indicated that he too was surprised.  Apparently no foeman he turned the deadly light upon lived beyond a heartbeat, yet I stood before him, my blades red hot, but still alive and with all my senses. He frowned and repeated the word of power, but the second beam was deflected also.

"Stand down warrior!" Ra-Mesh roared. "I know not why you still live, but you will be called to account for the crime you have committed this day!"

I looked past the king and out into the hall. No one had come yet, but I heard warriors approaching. Glancing over my shoulder, I spotted an open window. Then I looked at the king and bowed my head in shame.

"Great Shekem," I said. "I will not fight you, but I cannot stay here now. One day I swear to return and find a way to account for what I have done, but now I must depart."

The Shekem's eyes narrowed into angry slits.

"You will come to an account right now!"

He glanced at his tawny companion, then stabbed an angry finger at me. But the lion did not move.

I did not wait for an explanation as to why the deadly beast did not pounce upon me. As the Shekem gazed down at his giant lion in anger and confusion, I snatched up the bloody Blade of Shai, dashed towards the window, and with little regard for the consequences, leapt out into the darkness.

As I hurtled through the air, the voice of Shekem Ra-Mesh rang out in a grim and terrible tone.

"Sebau!" he shouted, "know you that there is a price upon your head!"

I fell two stories, by the will of the deities landing in a soft flower bed. As soon as my feet touched the ground I ran with utmost haste, while behind me the voice of the Shekem boomed accusingly. I will never forget how his words rang in my ears

"Traitor! Sebau! Until the day you are in my grasp you shall know no peace in all creation. The word shall go out to all lands and all nations: Wealth enough for a kingdom in exchange for the head of Memna-un the younger!"

Tears streamed from my eyes as I ran from the presence of my king. Though it was unintentional, I had indeed committed a crime beyond imagining. Because of me the second brightest light in Kamit had been snuffed out. It was only concern for the fate of my sister that kept me

SHADES OF MEMNON II

from going back, from throwing myself down at the feet of the Shekem and all of Kamit to pay for the thing I had caused.

It was for Neftiji that I fled. For Neftiji, for my Pa and for revenge against Kho-An-Sa.

I ran with great haste away from the palace, past the unsuspecting guards and away from the temple complex. Unsure of what route I should take to escape, I found myself fleeing down dark pathways and skirting between houses. Soon I knew, the streets would be filled with warriors, their hearts filled with grief and a great lust to punish the killer of Grand Vizier Ra Nefer. I ran on with out stopping into the night.

For the next several weeks I lived the life of a fugitive, knowing that even my best comrades, Pa-Sah and Ka-Sah, would be honor bound to kill me for disgracing the Medjay and for the death of Ra Nefer. Sha-Sha alone would be able to see into my heart and know that it was not intentional. But I refused to put her into the position of choosing loyalties. With no where else to turn, I had to seek out known criminals, whom I bribed to smuggle me out of Kamit and into Canaan.

And so in tattered disguise, I sailed in leaky boats up the Desher Sea, then took caravans with smugglers across the merchant's highways. All the while I clutched the Blade of Shai, contemplating how I would return it to evil deceiver who had used me.

As for Hra-Twa, he apologized for the vagueness of the oracle reading before my meeting with Ra Nefer and with his characteristic detachment, said that it was my fate. A few times during my flight my Anu friend appeared, each time urging me to contact Sha-Sah, which I refused to do because the oracle indicated that doing so would rend her life apart. Though it also indicated that I needed her, I resolved to face these consequences alone.

Finally I arrived at the port of Canaan and sought out the appointed place that Kho-An-Sa and I had discussed, were he would dock once each full moon and to await me. There I waited the few days until he was due to arrive.

As I stood around in the shadows, wearing a long hooded robe to conceal my features, I heard travelers gossiping about the murder of Ra Nefer of Kamit and of the international manhunt for his killer. I was dismayed indeed when I saw papyrus sheets bearing my name and image being passed around and posted everywhere.

The reward was 50,000 golden oxhides, riches enough to pay an army or to finance a small nation. The announcement was written in a dozen different languages and called for me dead or alive. With a ransom so incredibly high, I knew that it was only a matter of time.

It was too dangerous to roam the docks or to inquire about decent lodging, so I took refuge in an alley filled with derelicts and beggars. There I waited out the days, wrapped in a blanket upon the ground, coming out only at night to seek out Kho-An-Sa's ship.

On the first night of the full moon I spotted a vessel that resembled the one I sought. I watched closely as it's boards were extended to the docks and men began coming and going. Soon it was confirmed when I saw the giant Tamahu Cronn emerge. He was carrying a huge barrel, apparently bringing it to shore to fill with some beverage for the coming journey. After watching him disappear in the distance, I turned to call my Anu friend.

"Hra-Twa!" I cried in a low voice. "Hra-Twa, appear!"

Before I said another word, he stepped forth from the shadows.

Glancing over the docks, his eyes settled upon the ship, then he turned and looked up at me.

"So," he said. "The time has finally come..."

"Indeed it has, my friend," I replied. "Your reading?"

"The oracles say that you must do what Herukhuti has instructed."

I nodded grimly.

"And my sister? Can you make her disappear the way you do? Are you sure you can spirit her away to safety?"

"Yes, I can Memna-un. All I need is a large enough distraction."

I smiled mirthlessly.

"That you shall have, my friend. That you shall have."

Hra-Twa melted away again, as I settled down to rest my head with the Neteru until dawn. At first I breathed and contemplated Amen, in order to clear my thoughts and rest my emotions. Then I paid homage to Herukhuti, whose heat pervaded my body as Aten peaked from the horizon. Then I rested my head with Sekmet, mistress of my blades, as I held my weapons close to my heart. Finally, I prayed to Apademak, power of the Medjay, to grant me the courage and strength of the lion.

At last the rays of Aten beamed down full upon me and I rose to my feet. Checking my weapons, I fingered the dozens of throwing darts wound about my chest, waist and thighs. Then I touched the hilts of my blades, causing surges of Rau to flow to the very edges. I then made my way toward the ship. The time had come at last for retribution.

## SHADES OF MEMNON II

# CHAPTER 10: "ALL OF THESE MEN MUST DIE!"

Filled with the seething power of three Kushite deities of war, I strolled toward the ship of my enemies. My senses were so acute, so heightened by the forces of the Neteru raging within me, that those I passed seemed to move slowly, trapped by limitations of time that no longer confined me.

I climbed the plank and stepped aboard, where two hapless warriors attempted to bar my way, demanding identification and a statement of my business. Casting off my robe, I seized two darts and flicked them, then walked on as the men writhed upon the deck, clawing at the missiles buried in their throats.

Looking across the ship, I spied Kho-An-Sa. With his customary pompous air, he barked at his sailors as they prepared to get underway. Suddenly shouts went up as the dying men were discovered, then Kho-An-Sa turned my way. At first a look of surprise came over him, followed by that dreaded smile that I despised so much.

The hordes of warriors on deck had now spotted me and were gathering to attack. But after a clap of the magician's hands they parted and I walked calmly through their ranks. As I neared the evil magician, I ached to sink a dart into him where he stood, but reluctantly, I held back. First I had to see to my sister.

"Greetings, young panther," the magician said with mock joy. "It seems you have become a man of great renown."

"You lied to me!" I said coldly. "All the time you really wanted Ra Nefer dead..."

Kho-An-Sa nodded.

"Yes, I did, young panther. And you have accomplished it for me. You have my thanks."

"Where is my sister?"

A grin spread across the magician's face.

"Why, she is here, young panther," he replied. "But you cannot have her back yet, for we are not quite done with her."

Several warriors snickered at his last words. Struggling to restrain myself, I shouted threateningly.

"Where is she!"

Kho-An-Sa motioned to his left and two men brought forth Neftiji. I was relieved that she seemed to have her normal senses, but something

SHADES OF MEMNON II

else was amiss. Though she wore a long flowing robe, I could tell that something was not right.

"Oh, Memna," she cried. "Why did you have to come back? I am no good to you anymore...no good to anyone."

It was then, as she bowed her head shamefully, that I realized what was truly the matter. My sister's belly was swollen. Neftiji was with child.

Kho-An-Sa waved his hand at her as he eyed me.

"Oh, don't be angry with me, young panther. This was the only way I could save her life. Aias wanted to kill her immediately."

"Aias," I roared. "What does he have to do with this?"

Kho-An-Sa rubbed his chin.

"It was all for the sake of our coalition, you see. Aias insisted upon his vengeance, and since it was clear that you would never willingly join us...we decided to create a warrior..."

My mind reeled at the horror of what the magician was saying.

"Nooo!" I cried.

"Yes," Kho-An-Sa replied. "She carries Aias' child."

I shook my head as a crushing weight descended upon me. A feeling of failure stronger than I felt about my Mut tightened around my heart.

"No, no, no..." I whispered. "Oh, Neftiji... no."

Seeing how the revelation affected me, Kho-An-Sa continued.

"And since he considered it a shame to deprive the rest of the men after he had his way, Aias then gave her to my warriors. Your good friend Cronn was the first..."

I fell to my knees in grief as the warriors surrounding me laughed uproariously. Neftiji's tearful crying also assailed my ears as Kho-An-Sa went on.

"Of course, Aias insisted she be her true self when she was given to him. So I was forced to lift my spell...she was awake for it all."

A haze of purple and red washed over my eyes and my body throbbed with furious rage. But then I breathed slowly, regaining control of my emotions, as Kho-An-Sa continued his cruel taunting.

"So you see, young panther, your family is ruined. Your sister bears the seed of your family's greatest enemy. Your Pa is forever lost, for even armies from his own fabled land have failed to wrest him from beneath Mount Olympus. And you! You are a disgraced fugitive whose days are numbered. Already you are upon your knees. Lie down and join your Mut! Go on! Join your Mut in death!"

As those last words passed the magician's lips, I heard the sound of a sword scrapping from a scabbard. Pulling my long claw quickly, I pivoted upon my knee, bringing my blade up just in time to block an all too familiar weapon.

Leaping to my feet, I turned to face Cronn. The time had finally come for our final confrontation. Eyeing each other bitterly, we both knew that death alone would end it this time. The other warriors knew this also, and, daring not to interfere, stepped back to observe the battle.

We circled for long silent moments, then Cronn swung his great blade in broad arcs, once again hoping to batter me with his size and sheer strength. Unfortunately for the Tamahu giant, I was a different fighter than I was the last time we had met. This time I battled like a Medjay.

Each time his weapon drew back, I unleashed a furious kick to his belly, staggering the giant and making him wince in pain. After several of these blows he backed off cautiously, finally understanding that the youth he had once intimidated had become a seasoned warrior.

Glancing across the deck, I noted that my sister was gone. The warriors who had held her were looking around in confusion as Kho-An-Sa shouted at them to find her. Giving silent thanks to Hra-Twa for stealing her away, I gazed grimly into Cronn's piercing blue eyes. The time for holding back was now over.

Perhaps sensing that I planned to end it soon, an insidious look appeared on the face of my opponent. Shifting his sword to his left hand, he reached down to his side, bringing forth a device made of rope and several small balls. As he swirled it in a circle above his head, I realized he intended to throw it in an effort to ensnare me.

I ground my teeth angrily. Since it was clear that Cronn's sense of fairness in this fight was now gone, I seized a dart from my own waistbelt and sailed it towards his whirling hand.

The missile hit the mark, the Tamahu screamed in pain and the weapon fell to the deck. Then, his face twisted in a mask of rage, Cronn let forth a animalistic growl and clenched the dart with his teeth. Pulling it from the wound like a dog does a thorn, he spat it out upon the deck. Then he suddenly dropped his sword and fell to his hands and

SHADES OF MEMNON II

knees.

Knowing that the giant was too proud to beg, I could not fathom why he was down on all fours. I was about to admonish him to pick up his weapon and finish the fight, when another animal-like growl emerged from his throat. This time the sound was strangely familiar, and the warriors who stood watching stepped further back, clearly very fearful at what was taking place.

Then, right before my eyes, the giant began to change.

First a covering of thick brown hair crept over his pale skin. Then a ripping noise split the air as the leather tunic around his torso bulged and tore apart. His flesh pulsated and elongated, tearing free from the rest of his clothing. Then his horned helmet fell as his skull changed shape, sprouting ears and a long snout filled with sharp fangs.

A moment later I was amazed at what stood before me. Claws raking the deck, Cronn was now a completely transformed beast. Huge and bulky, with formidable muscles rippling across it's imposing frame, it was like nothing I had ever seen. As it stood up on it's hind legs to tower above me, Kho-An-Sa's taunting voice boomed:

"I know not how you spirited your sister away, but you shall not live to see her again," the magician shouted. "Doom stands before you in the form of the Great Grizzled Bear, deadliest beast of the northlands and totem of Cronn's mighty people. Defeat it if you can!"

Looking up at the fearsome creature, I suddenly realized: This was the beast that assailed the party of Khalibar those long months ago in the deserts near Makka. The thing that had killed camels and horses with one blow and carried strong warriors away into the night.

Pulling my short claw, I circled cautiously, knowing that one swipe from the powerful beast could kill me, too. A glance at the glowing gems in my weapons confirmed what I suspected: Cronn was both turnskin and totem beast, thus empowered by the trickster deity, Sebek and by negative aspects of Heru.

Immediately I began chanting the hekau of both Neters alternately, causing the beast to become immediately disoriented. As it dropped back down to all fours, I continued to chant, predicting a mercifully swift end to the battle. But suddenly I heard another chant, and the beast regained it's composure and stood up again. Glancing across the deck, I spotted Kho-An-Sa. His head held high, the magician uttered counter incantations, negating the power of my own.

This momentary distraction nearly cost me my life, as the bear leapt forward with surprising speed. Leaping aside, I rolled across the deck, springing to my feet and drawing two sharp darts. As it turned for another rush, the missiles sank into it's bulky side, but to absolutely no effect. Without noticing the missiles in it's hide, the bear rushed again, nearly bowling me over with the ferocity of it's attack.

Desperately my mind sought some strategy. The ferocity and sheer bulk of the beast made it hard to get close for an attack, and I was forced to scamper offensively. Knowing nothing of the weaknesses of such a beast, I had to be cautious. Because it was so large, strong and unnaturally fast, even if I dealt it a death blow, it could still kill me before it expired. Without the chants to disorient it, I had to find a way to distract it.

Glancing around quickly, I formulated my plan. Though the creature was controlled by the intelligence of a man, I was counting on the instinct of the beast to accomplish my goal. And so, repeatedly scampering back and forth to taunt it, I lured the beast nearer the crowd of warriors who surrounded us.

After several more near misses, the beast went livid with rage, charging once again. Stepping aside as it slid by, I swiftly kicked it's face, causing it to close it's eyes instinctively. Just as I had planned, the beast blundered into a slow moving warrior, and just as I expected, it's instincts took over and it attacked the man.

The crushing of bones, the taste of the blood and the terrible screams of the warrior distracted the northland creature, giving me just the chance I needed. With a cry so loud that it scattered the sea birds flying overhead, I sprang upon the beast's back. Whirling my long blade once for momentum, I plunged it to the hilt between the beast's shoulder blades, then raked my short claw across the lifeline at it's hairy throat.

Immediately it reared up on it's hind legs again, roaring in mortal agony. Yanking my blade from it's body, I kicked off and whirled backwards, landing on my feet like a cat.

A hush came over the entire deck as the beast staggered in a broken circle. Then it lumbered toward me slowly, claws raised in defiance, bleeding a pool of bright red crimson. I was about to strike again, when suddenly it stopped and dropped to the deck, defeated.

Quivering, shaking, and moaning in agony, the great form changed shape once again. In a moment there lay before me the body of Cronn, naked, in a pool of his own blood.

Stepping forward boldly, I wretched his head up by the hair, and with one stroke of my long claw, severed it from the still quivering body.

A low murmur ran through the crowd as I approached Kho-An-Sa, the head of his great warrior swinging from my fist. With a contemptuous sweep of my hand, I tossed it down at the magician's feet.

"The lion has defeated the bear," I said grimly, "now he shall deal with a lying jackal of a traitor."

Raising my blades, I looked into the eyes of my great enemy. But when I took a step toward the magician, my weapons suddenly became heavy. At first I tried to hold on, but the weight became unbearable and my fingers opened. The Claws of Sekmet fell from my grasp as Kho-An-Sa laughed triumphantly.

"Young fool!" he cried. "It was I who enchanted those weapons! Do you think I would ever allow those blades to be used against me? Do you? Your usefulness to me is now over! It is time for you to die!!!"

With that, the magician's hands flew high into the air and he began chanting the deadly words I heard when I first met him. Suddenly a piercing pain wracked my entire body, centering upon my chest. Looking down, I saw my left breast palpitating unnaturally.

But though the pain threatened to overwhelm me, I was bent upon having justice. Fighting with all my might, I put one tortuous step before the other, determined to rend the life from the magician even as my own heart tore from my body.

Closer and closer I came, my hands straining toward the neck of the chanting magician. Drawing near, I spied a glimmer in Kho-An-Sa's eye that I had never seen before: It was fear. Cold stark fear. But just as my stretching fingers grazed his throat, my quivering legs gave way beneath me.

Slumping to the deck at Kho-An Sa's feet, I rolled over onto my back, expecting to see my heart rise from my body into the hands of the triumphant magician. Instead I was greeted by a powerful vision.

There before me was the image of my betrothed Sha-Sah, hovering in the midst of swirling clouds. Exuding all the power and affection that we had cultivated between us, she gazed down into my eyes.

"Strength, my adored one!" she whispered. "For your heart belongs to me! Hold on to it! Hold it for me and he cannot take it!"

Suddenly my body became flooded with power. A great surge of Rau, centering upon my chest, pulsated within me. Clutching the area above my heart, I felt the bulging and palpitating cease.

Slowly and painfully, I pushed myself to my knees and then to my feet. Looking up defiantly, I saw that the fear had crept back into Kho-

An-Sa's eyes, along with utter surprise at what was taking place before him. Beads of perspiration poured down his face as he recited the chant louder and louder.

Once again I plodded painfully toward him, one hand holding my heart, the other clutched into a defiant fist. Now in an outright panic, the magician's voice became shriller and shriller, higher and higher, as words of power flew furiously from his mouth. The pitch was so sharp that it hurt my ears but I ignored it, reaching into my belt for the razor sharp Blade of Shai.

Kho-An-Sa's eyes widened. Desperately now, he shouted the chant, his voice fairly breaking from the effort, his body quivering and shaking from the strain.

Raising the blade high over my head, I gazed into the face of my hated enemy.

"Shut up!" I shouted, "Shut up! Shut up! Shut up!!!"

Swinging down with all my might, I plunged the blade with every shout, deep into the evil magician's chest.

The chanting immediately ceased, replaced by gurgling, choking noises from my dying enemy's throat. A look of astonishment flashed across Kho-An-Sa's face as thick red blood ran down the blade and over my hand, dripping down onto the deck between us.

Then, slowly, like a falling tree, the killer of my Mut and enslaver of my family fell down dead at my feet.

I stared down at him for long moments before finally looking up. All around me the warriors stood silent. Though there were at least four dozen of them, their expressions conveyed great fear because of what I had just accomplished. Right before their eyes I had killed the mighty Cronn, defeating him in his form of a great beast. Then I slew the dreaded Kho-An-Sa, which most of them considered impossible.

The pain in my body now subsiding, I retrieved the Claws of Sekmet and held my weapons defensively before me. Gazing at the crowd of men around me, I ground my teeth in grim contemplation:

These warriors had taken part in the abuse of my sister, and had laughed unrepentantly as they watched me grieve about it. I could not simply let them go, to report the shame of my family to the northlands, to boast about what they had done. Oh, no, I grimly decided. For the sake of my sister and the honor of my family, all of these men must die.

The first dozen or so I dispatched with a hail of darts as they stood in breathless fear. The others leapt over the dying to confront me, determined to put up a fight. But they were as slow to me as snail to a sparrow, and I wrecked a terrible vengeance upon them. Little did they understand until it far too late: Herukhuti walked among them in flesh.

Using Pan-Kau-Ra-Shen to push them back and Medjay tactics of dodging and faking, I tumbled them against one another, running my long claw through two or three men at a time. Others I knocked senseless with a smashing foot, followed by the stroke of a sharp blade to ensure they would never rise.

But though I clearly outmatched them, moving with speed beyond their abilities, their overwhelming numbers sorely taxed me.

My worse moment came when the bodies piled about me ironically nearly led to my defeat. Tripping on bloody corpses and slippery, oozing gore, I took two blows to my ribs that would have killed an ordinary man. Though I was saved by my hardened bones, I reeled, and the warriors took the opportunity to rush me.

Stumbling backwards, I was shoved against the wall of the ship, but then the advantage became mine.

On safe footing now, my back protected from attack, I proceeded to weave a net of metal about me the likes of which these amazed warriors had never seen. Striking to my left, gouging to my right, I could barely see my own hands before me. Weapons and limbs from the bewildered enemy went flying through the air, as I transformed into a living force of nature: a whirling wind of death and destruction.

The last dozen or so tried to escape, running from me as if I were a Sebau demon. Some leapt overboard, where I cut into them with darts and watched their bodies float away. A few tried begging and screamed for mercy, but the drum beat of justice drowned them out. Just as the chords of injustice had, without a doubt, drowned out the cries of my poor sister.

With a final flash of the Claws of Sekmet, the last of the warriors fell before me. Suddenly there was total silence. I whirled to the left. Then to the right. All of my enemies were now with their ancestors, laying in blood soaked mounds around me. But the work was not yet done, for the time had come for the sacrifice.

Setting about the grisly task put to me by the deity, I proceeded to cut off the heads, hands and sexual organs of the fallen men. The crew of the vessel, watching from the other side of the ship where they all fled during the fighting, stood horrified. I, on the other hand, felt nothing, as

I went on with this grim task of butchery.

Aten was much higher when I piled the body parts into a small boat, placing Kho-An-Sa's head atop the mound, his male organ stuffed into his deceitful mouth. Then I soaked it all in pitch and flammable oils and lowered the small vessel down to the water.

Leaning over the side of the ship, I lit a torch and tossed it upon the pile, then watched as the fire roared to life. Uttering a prayer to Herukhuti, I cut the ropes loose and watched the burning sacrifice float away. As the winds caught the ship and pushed it out to sea, I saw my life for the past three years, flickering in the blue and red flames.

It was then that I finally realized the terrible carnage I had wrought and suddenly I was very tired of killing. Suddenly I longed for only peace.

The deity of justice now satisfied, I sat upon the gory deck with my blades across my lap. Lowering my head, I rested it with Amen for a while, until a familiar voice suddenly rang out.

"Memna-un!"

Opening my eyes, I turned to see Neftiji, Hra-Twa and to my great surprise, Sha-Sah. Overjoyed, they ran forward to embrace me.

"Sha-Sah," I cried, seizing my mate-to-be in my arms. "You saved me, adored one. Thank you for what you did. But what are you doing here?"

"I had to come," she replied. "Hra-Twa came to me. I wanted to be nearby to assist you..."

I looked down at my Anu friend.

"Hra-Twa," I said sternly, "why did you do this?"

"You needed her, did you not?" he responded.

I could only nod my head.

"Yes, yes I did." I replied. Then I considered what had just transpired and turned the women away from the scene behind me. Looking down at Hra-Twa, I shook my head.

"You didn't let them see this, did you?"

"No, Memna-un," the little man said. "We've only just come aboard."

"Thank the ancestors," I said. Turning to my sister, I opened my arms wide, seized her and held her close. The joy I felt after all this time, to have her safe and in my arms was indescribable. But, feeling the swell of her belly as we embraced, I fell to my knees, begging her for forgive"It was not your fault, Memna," she replied. "You were a victim

## SHADES OF MEMNON II

just as I was..."

"Still my sister, I vow never to let you come to harm again. Never..."

I embraced my sister for a moment more before Sha-Sah interrupted us.

"Memna-un, we must leave here," she said gravely. "There are some on shore who saw what happened here this morning. And my brothers..."

"What of your brothers?"

"They have vowed to bring you back to Kamit for justice. I know that you are not responsible for the death of Ra Nefer, for my ka has been with you since you left me. But Ka-Sah and Pa-Sah...they think you betrayed the Medjay. My brothers are..."

"Are already here!" a voice boomed from across the deck.

Looking up, I saw the twins standing there, along with 30 or so Medjay warriors.

"We followed you, my sister," Pa-Sah shouted. "We have come to take Memna-un back. Our orders are to fetch him for trial."

At first great grief overwhelmed me and I could not speak. The thought of fighting, perhaps killing, my Medjay brothers nearly made me nauseous. I would dive from the ship and swim into the open sea before I would allow that. But I knew I could not go back with them.

"My brothers," I said humbly, "this is all a grave mistake. There must be some way to make you believe me."

"The Shekem shall see that you get the justice you deserve," shouted Ka-Sah. "Come along, or we shall be forced to kill you."

I opened my mouth to speak, but Sha-Sah shushed me and stepped forward.

"My siblings," she said, "I told you after it happened that my mate-to-be was not responsible for the crime he is accused of. I have been with him since he left our home..."

Shaking their heads negatively, the twins both grunted. Then the warriors with them spread out and began to surround me.

"Sister stand aside," Ka-Sah ordered threateningly. "Even our blood ties cannot halt the will of Kamit. Memna-un must come with us, alive if possible. But I must tell you that we prefer dead for the betrayal of his Medjay vows."

Looking about for any avenue of escape, I was about to run for the side and plunge into the waves, but Sha-Sah seized my arm.

"Nooo!" she shouted. "Stop! There is a way to show you that he is wrongly accused, but it will only work with the two of you who are my blood. The rest of you will have to trust them."

The warriors stopped in their tracks and turned toward the twins. Ka-Sah and Pa-Sah glanced at each other.

"How are we to do this?" Pa-Sah asked.

"Sit down now and rest your heads with me," Sha-Sah declared. "With the help of those present, I can show you what I observed as I was with my man in spirit."

The twins looked at each other again and nodded.

"We will do this," said Pa-Sah. "But it changes nothing: It is the Shekem's will that he be brought back for trial."

"Please, my brothers," Sha-Sah replied. "Let us just do it."

The three of them then sat down on the deck, linking hands in a small circle. Sha-Sah instructed the rest of us to chant to Auset, the Neter of thoughts and memories.

Neftiji and I, Hra-Twa and the rest of the Medjay gathered into a larger circle around them. Linking hands, we chanted as she bid. For long moments Sha-Sah and the twins remained linked together, their heads lowered, sometimes murmuring.

Several times their bodies shook violently. Then suddenly Ka-Sah gasped, followed soon after by his twin. Tears began to flow from their closed eyes. Then Sha-Sah signaled for the chanting to cease and they looked up.

"You see?" she asked. "Did you see what really happened?"

The twins looked at me, tears running down their faces.

"Yes," said Pa-Sah.

"Indeed," added Ka-Sah. "We see it clearly. Memna-un is innocent. It was a trick of Kho-An-Sa's making."

Then they rose and embraced me.

"We are so sorry, Memna-un..."

"We could not know...the Shekem himself accused you of this..."

The twins beckoned the other warriors aside and they huddled together in discussion. They came back moments later, all bearing a look of great sadness.

"But again, this changes nothing," said Pa-Sah gloomily. "It is the will of the Shekem that you be brought back for trial."

Suddenly I thought of a possible way out.

SHADES OF MEMNON II

"My brethren," I cried, "several of you were at the ritual when I became consecrated to Herukhuti. With your own ears you heard that I belong to him and that my Pa must be found so that the invaders from the north can be finally dealt with."

"Yes?" Ka-Sah replied.

"I will gladly go back to face trial, but first I must find my Pa. Join me on this quest my brothers. Then bring me back to face the will of Kamit."

The twins looked at one another, sly smiles slowly spreading across their faces.

"You know Pa-Sah," said Ka-Sah craftily. "Who knows how long it will take us to find this fugitive Memna-un..."

"I agree, Ka-Sah," replied Pa-Sah. "He is quite slippery. It could take...quite a long time."

Then they turned towards the rest of the warriors.

"What say you, Medjay? You have heard all! Will you follow us on this quest to find the Pa of Memna-un for the sake of Kamit and for Maat?"

There was silence for a moment, then every warrior's weapon sprang high into the air as they shouted their enthusiastic agreement. I embraced each of them in turn, thanking them for risking all to aid me. I had fought alongside most of them and they were my brothers. All expressed their belief that I was not guilty.

Finally I came back to Neftiji and embraced her once again. Both of us looked down at her swollen belly, no doubt thinking the very same thing. Though it was a Kushite tradition never to kill the unborn, I knew that whatever she decided, I would support her. And I knew that one day I would take Aias' head for causing it.

"What now, Memna-un?" Ka-Sah asked.

Standing silent for a moment, I stopped to contemplate our next move. The sailors were still huddled on the far side of the boat, still too fearful to budge. I had to call for the captain several times before a shaky elder finally stepped forward.

"I am the captain of this vessel," he said fearfully. "Are you going to kill us too?"

"No, good captain," I replied reassuringly, "I am not going to kill you. I will be commanding this ship from now on, though."

"Yes, sire," he replied. "To what lands do we sail then?"

"I will tell you when I decide. For now get us away from this port.

# CHAPTER 10: "ALL OF THESE MEN MUST DIE!"

And have the crew clean up this deck."

"Yes, sire."

As the sails unfurled and the winds pushed us from the port of Canaan, I continued to consider our destination. With a price of 50,000 gold oxhides on my head, there was no where under the sway of Kamit where we would be safe. The bounty killers would come, of that I had no doubt. And for the amount upon my head, they would gladly harm my loved ones to get me.

The northern lands at this point were also out of the question, filled as they were with the enemies of my family and people. And if what Kho-An-Sa said was true, we would need an army for any effort to rescue my Pa from this prison at "Mt. Olympus." But with all hands turned against me due to the price upon my head, where was I to get such an army?

Drawn to my whit's end, it was then that I decided to call upon the wisdom of the great serpent. After consulting with Hra-Twa to be sure it was safe, I settled down to rest my head and call upon him. Within moments I had linked with my beloved mentor.

"Ah, Memna-un," Kam-Atef's voice echoed inside my mind, "how do you fare this day?"

Briefly I told the great serpent what had transpired since last we had spoken and apprised him of our present situation.

"Ahh, little one," he answered, "there is only one choice for you at this time. But to make use of it you must again assist another..."

"Who, great serpent," I asked. "Who must I assist?

"One of my serpent brethren," he replied, "once known to your very own Pa. His name is Quct-zal-co-atl and he is in very great peril..."

The great serpent detailed the task before me, then quickly bid farewell so that our communications would remain undetected by evil ones who may be trying to listen. Considering all he had told me, I rose to my feet, calling out to the captain and my companions.

"Where to sire?" the captain asked as they all gathered about me.

I glanced at the faces of Neftiji, Sha-Sah, Hra-Twa and all the Medjay, as they stood awaiting my answer. Then I turned toward the horizon, sweeping my hand towards where Aten sets each day.

"To the west, across the great ocean, good captain," I replied. "We go to the homeland of my Pa. Set sail for fabled Atl-anta!"

# AN EPICOLOGICAL GLOSSARY OF TERMS:

**Aahmes Nefertari** - The greatest hero of ancient *Kamit*. Queen **Aahmes Nefertari** led the coalition from southern *Kamit* that defeated the dreaded **Hyksos** invaders. Though practically ignored by historians today, this queen was made the most honored **Sheps** of *Kamit's* entire history. Temples built in her honor rivaled those of the **Neteru**, and parades were staged in her name until the beginning of the **Christian** era.

**Aat** - *Kamitic:* A region of the **Taut** underworld.

**Agaru** - The sacred island home of the **Anu**, located off the coast of modern day southern India. Small blacks live on islands in this area to this day.

**Allat** - A female deity, popular among South Arabian blacks until the coming of Islam.

**Amen** - *Kamitic:* Meaning "hidden" and "unseen." The most high, creator deity of the *Kamitians* and other **Kushites**. Traditional Africans have always believed in one god working through many aspects of itself. These aspects are called angels in the Judeo-Christian tradition. The Kamitic people called them **Neteru.**

**Amen-Ra** - *Kamitic:* Another name of the most high, with emphasis on the deity's aspect as a creative power - see **Ra**.

**Amorites** - Ancient name for a nomadic, warlike **Shashu** people in the Middle East. They blended with the **Hittites** to become the **Habiru**, forePas of the modern day Hebrews.

**Anetch Hrak** - (A-net ha-rock) -*Kamitic:* Common greeting given to honored elders, priests and royalty in *Kamit*.

**Ancestor Communication** - A **Spiritual Science**- Rituals and psychic abilities developed to ensure that the links between the living and deceased are not severed after death.

**Anu** (Ah-Noo) - The sacred ancestors of the **Kushites**. These small blacks, originating near the **Mountains of the Moon**, once lived all over the Earth. They were related to the modern day forest pygmies of central Africa, whose traditions say they once lived in large cities. **Anu** remains have been found near ancient monuments worldwide, such as Stonehenge, the great Pyramid and in **Olmec** ruins. Highly skilled in the **Spiritual Sciences**, they were the source of legends of pixies, fairies and elves. The only *race* of very small people ever known are of African origin.

**Apademak** -(App-aa-dim-aak) **Kushite** deity of protection. Depicted in lion form, the deity was popular in upper *Kamit* and lower **Kush** from very ancient times until the **Christian** Era.

**Araby** - Ancient name for modern day Arabia, especially South Arabia.

**Atef** -(Aah-teff) - *Kamitic:* Brother/friend, potential Pa.

**Aten** - (Aah-tin) - *Kamitic:* The sun.

**Atl-anta** - (Aah-til-an-taa) -Ancient name for the fabled land across the Atlantic ocean, known first to the **Kushites,** then to the ancient Greeks and others. The Greek writers Pliny and Diodorus stated that western Ethiopia (homeland of the elder **Memnon**) and Atlantis were one and the same. The geographer Marcellus (1 BC) wrote in his **"Ethiopic History,"** that there were islands across the Atlantic where people kept traditions of legendary Atlantis. **Atl-anta** is North, South and especially, Meso-America, which was settled by the mighty **Xiu**.

**Ausar** - (Ohh-sayer) -*Kamitic:* Deity representing the highest aspects of spirituality.

**Auset** - (Aw-set) - *Kamitic:* Deity representing mothering and nurturing.

**Baa en pet** - *Kamitic:* Metal from the sky, a meteor.

**Bektan** - A country located in the modern day Middle East, near Syria. A great trading nation of **Shasu** and **Tamahu** peoples during the Bronze Age, it was destroyed during the **Great World War**.

**Blybos** - A **Canaanite** city famous for its seaport and shipbuilding.

**Basileia** - Ancient homeland of main contingent of the **"People of the Sea,"** located in northern Europe near the Baltic and North Seas.

**Canaan** - Ancient country once located in the modern day Middle East, a **Tamana** settlement.

**Canaanites** - The black people who once ruled in **Canaan**, migrants from **Tamana**.

**Chi** - The life force, **Rau** in **Kamitian**, Kundalini in South India.

**Children of Geb** - *Kamitic:* Human beings alive on the Earth.

**Children of Impotent Revolt**- *Kamitic:* Unchecked emotions, assistants of **Set.**

**Dark Deceased** - *Kamitic:* Unruly human spirits that refuse to rest after death. Confused and in need of light, they stay on to plague the living.

**Desher Sea** - *Kamitic:* The Red Sea.

**Djahy** - (Ja-hee) - A region of the Middle East just south of modern day Israel.

**Eastern Kushite** - Blacks related to modern day South Indians and South Arabians, with brown to jet black skin, curly to straight hair and sharper features than **Western Kushites**. Originally from **Tamana.**

**Five Great Kushite Nations** - The five groups of **Kushites** from **Tamana** who most adhered to the great teachings embodied by the **Spiritual Sciences**. These are the *Kamitians*, **Hal-tam-tians, Xiu, Canaanites** and **Meluhans.**

**Geb** - *Kamitic:* The deity of the material plane, Earth. The world was recognized as conscious by *Kamit* thousands of years before the modern day Gaia theory.

**Great Green** - *Kamitic:* The Mediterranean Sea.

**Great World War** - Around 1200 BC the Mediterranean area became embroiled in devastating warfare. This was due to invasions by a mysterious coalition led by northern **Tamahu** dubbed the **"People of The Sea"** by *Kamit.* They destroyed great nations in Europe, Asia and on the islands in the Mediterranean, before they were finally defeated by a coalition of **Kushites** in **Kamit.** At the same time, in West Asia and India, **Eastern Kushites** were fighting other **Tamahu** who swept down from the Eurasian steppes. This **Great World War**, some historians think, was the source material of the greatest epics in ancient world history, such as **The Iliad**; the Norse **Ragnarok Sagas**; the Philistine tales in the **Old Testament**; the Indian epic **"The Mahabharata;"** the story of **Atlantis** and **"The Ethiopis,"** which starred **Memnon**.

**Habiru** - (Hay-be-roo) - Ancient name for the semi-nomadic tribes of **Tamahu (Hittites)** and **Shashu (Amorites)** who settled in the Middle East just after 2000 BC. They came together in the land of **Canaan,** forming the Hebrews of the **Old Testament**. **"And say, thus saith the Lord God unto Jerusalem; Thy birth and nativity is in the land of Canaan, thy Pa was an Amorite, and thy mother a Hittite." - Old Testament, Ezekiel 16:3.**

**Hal-tam-ti** - Ancient Elam, located in modern day Iran. Settled by various groups from **Tamana**. Linguistic studies indicate domination by the **Xiu**, who also dominated in regions of China and Meso-America.

**Hapi** - (Haa-pee) - *Kamitic:* The river Nile.

**Hatti** - Ancient country once located in modern day Turkey. Originally settled by **Kushites**, it came under the domination of **Tamahu** who adopted the local culture. Sometimes enemy, sometimes ally of the *Kamits,* they were a mighty civilization. They were destroyed by the **People of The Sea** during the **Great World War.**

**Hittites** - The **Tamahu** people of **Hatti**. Some settled in areas of the Middle East, blending with the **Amorites** to become the **Habiru**, fore-Pas of modern day Hebrews.

**Heru** - (Hay-roo) - *Kamitic:* Deity governing heroism, stability and maturity.

**Herukhuti** - (Hay-roo-kaa-hoo-tee) - *Kamitic:* Deity governing justice, warfare and the upholding of natural law.

**Hesperides** - Greek mythology says that islands called **Hespers** or **Hesperides** were located in a fabled land across the Atlantic Ocean and that **Memnon** was raised there. In reality these were the settlements of the **Xiu** people in ancient Mexico. Archeologists today are puzzled by the engineering feats of the **Olmecs (see Xiu)**, who moved thousands of tons of earth and stone to create artificial islands, platforms for temple complexes and giant stone statues. A careful examination will reveal that sophisticated earth moving and stone working was a common technology of **Tamana** migrants worldwide. Direct mention was made by Greek writer Scylaxus of Coriandre, who recorded that Phoenicians traded with Ethiopians on an island across the Atlantic Ocean. Today major **Xiu** settlements are known to have been located on islands in Ancient Mexico.

**Het-Heru** - (Het-hay-roo)- *Kamitic:* Deity governing pleasure, sexuality and imagination.

**House of Life** - *Kamitic:* School, place of learning.

**Hyksos** -(Hick-sos) - A coalition of **Tamahu** and **Shashu** who controlled *Lower Kamit* for a time (1640-1532). They were overthrown by a coalition from Waset (Thebes) of *Kamitic* and **Medjay** warriors led by the great queen, **Aahmes Nefertari**.

**Indu** - Ancient name for the **Eastern Kushites** who lived in **Indus Kush**.

**Indus Kush** - Ancient name for the area stretching from modern day Pakistan throughout northern India. It was once dominated by **Kushites** who fled the area during the time of the **Great World War.** Anthropologists today call their culture the **Indus** civilization. They were migrants from **Tamana**.

**Ifrits** - Demons from Arabic folklore who represented the fearful and destructive forces of the desert.

**Ish-Ra-El** - Ancient Israel of the **Old Testament.**

**Ka** - *Kamitic:* Eternal spirit, the soul.

**Kabba Stone** - Ancient black rock considered sacred by **Islam** today and also revered by ancient goddess religions of Arabia.

**Kam** - *Kamitic:* Meaning dark, black. Mistranslated in biblical texts as "Ham." Black Africans are children of **Kam**, not of a rump of pork.

**Kam-Atef** - Famous creature from *Kamitic* metaphorical legend. His name means "friend of black people."

**Kamit** - Correct name of ancient Egypt, meaning the land of black people (**Kushites**). Part of the **Tamana** cultural/civilization complex, *Kamit* had both **Western** and **Eastern Kushites** in the population, explaining why many monuments do not look like the stereotypical "Negro." **Kamit** created the greatest achievements known to mankind, seeding the world with their knowledge and puzzling the world with **Spiritual Sciences** that have yet to be fully understood.

**Kamitic** - Things of and from *Kamit*.

**Keftui** - (Keff-too-ee) - *Kamitic* - The island nation of ancient Crete in the Mediterranean Sea.

**Khepera** - *Kamitic* - The sacred beetle representing the act of creation.

**K'un Lun** - Legendary regions of ancient China dominated by blacks (**Xiu** and **Shang**) who migrated there from **Tamana**. One of the greatest settlements was that of the **Xiu** in China's Shensi province. Today dozens of pyramids, one as large as *Kamit's* Great Pyramid, can still be found there.

**Kula Yoga** - A **Spiritual Science.** The children of **Tamana** discovered a third great use for sex, which is today called tantra or tantric sex. It is the use of yoga and meditation techniques during intercourse that combine male and female **Rau** for use in healing, psychic phenomena, spiritual cultivation or magic. Today **Kula Yoga** is practiced primarily in Asian and African cultures like South India, Tibet and Ethiopia. (Illustration on following page)

**Kush** - Land to the south of *Kamit*,. Home to the *Kamits* before they settled further north.

**Kushau** - Various groups of black people in different regions of the world, including the *Kamits*. - Children of **Tamana.**

**Kushite** - Things of and from the **Kushau.**

**Kushite Darts** - An amazing weapon of the **Kushites**, these throwing blades were 3 to 5 inches long and made of finely honed bronze. Razor sharp, they were astonishingly accurate weapons in the hands of a trained darter. Kamitic paintings depict them being used for warfare and hunting small game. A favorite weapon of the **Medjay** warriors.

**Lower Kamit** - The northern region of *Kamit* near the Mediterranean. Referred to as "lower" or "down there" because the *Kamitians* and other **Kushites** lived with a southern orientation. The south was considered "up" and north was considered "down" because the **Kushites** came from mid central Africa, near the **Mountains of the Moon** of Uganda.

**Maat** - (Maa-awt) - **Kamitic:** Deity governing the natural order of the universe.

**Makka** - Ancient name for modern day Mecca.

**Medjay** - A **Kushau** warrior people who moved into *Kamit* after helping to expel the **Hyksos**. The **Medjay** were great trackers, served as the police force of *Kamit,* and were legendary martial artists.

**Meluha** - Ancient name of middle to southern India, a **Tamana** settlement.

**Meluhites** - Ancient name for the **Kushites** who still live in South India, migrants from **Tamana.**

**Memnon** - (mem-none) - The most widely known heroic figure in world history. When the Greeks took over *Kamit* they named two statues near Thebes the "Colossi Of **Memnon**." In Greek myths he came to the battle of **Troy** with warriors from **Susa** (Iran) and his own home land. *"To Troy No Hero Came of Nobler Line, Or, If Of Nobler, Memnon, It was thine! - Homer.*

The name "**Memnon**" means immortal in Greek and **Kamitic**, backing traditions that say he was made immortal by the gods: *Kamitic: Mem* **-** cummin (a black seed) ; **na** - to go on, **un** - living. **Greek** - Resolute, always there.

There was a temple in ancient **Hal-tam-ti** (biblical Elam-today's Iran) called "The Temple of **Memnon**" and recent scholarship on Greek myths point to Ancient Meso-America (see **Hesperides, Xiu**) as his homeland. In Asia, Africa and Europe there are many legends of **Memnon**; some indicating that there was more than one. Some people south of **Kamit** claimed relation to **Memnon**, while ancient Greeks claim he went to **Kamit's** Thebes. In reality, **Memnon** represents the worldwide influence of the children of **Tamana**, especially the *Kamits* and the **Xiu**.

**Men Ab** - *Kamitic:* Meaning "still heart." Meditation technique to gain control over emotions and assist spiritual development.

**Middle Atl-anta** - Ancient Meso-America, homeland of the Elder **Memnon**, who hailed from the mysterious **Xiu** peoples, who were originated in **Tamana.**

**Mountains of the Moon** - Ancient mountain range near the traditional homeland of the *Kamitians,* other **Kushites** and the **Anu.** Near modern day Uganda today, it is the sight of fantastic anthropological discoveries indicating that technical civilization began *100,000* year ago in this area.

**Mut** - (Moot) -*Kamitic* : Mother or elder woman. The symbol for Mut was the vulture often worn on the crown of royalty and deities to symbolize the nurturing aspects of government.

**Mycenea** - Ancient name of area known today as southern Greece. In Greek myth, home of the legendary hero Persus and his **Kushite** wife, Andromeda. The Persus/Andromeda myth represents the peaceful coming together of **Kushite** and **Tamahu** peoples in pre-Greek history. **Mycenea** was nearly destroyed by the **People of the Sea.**

**Myrmidon** - Legendary warriors from Greek mythology. Led by Achilles, they fought during the Trojan War.

**Nabata** - Ancient name for a South Arabian region.

**Nabataens** - The people of **Nabata**, migrants from **Tamana.**

**Nekhebet** - (Neck-eh-het) - *Kamitic:* The cool electromagnctic force of the Earth responsible for some psychic phenomena.

**Neter** - *Kamitic*: One of the conscious governing forces; a deity.

**Neterit** -*Kamitic:* The natural forces manifested negatively, evil deities.

**Neters** - *Kamitic:* A group of deities. Never worshipped in the modern sense, the **Neters** were revered as conscious forces of nature, aspects of the creator **Amen** assigned to run the universe. Statues and images were used as reminders of this, as well as focal points for meditation to control **Neter** forces inside human beings. Misunderstood to this day as "idol worship," this **Spiritual Science** is still a common practice of people of **Kushite** descent.

**Neteru** - All of the deities that govern the Earth.

**Nimrod** - Legendary warrior from the Bible and other West Asian lore. He actually represents **Kushau** groups who migrated from north Africa (**Tamana**) into West Asia to form the Elamites, Sumerians, Akkadians, Nabataens and others. *"And Kush Begot Nimrod...He was* *a mighty hunter before the lord"* - **Genesis 10:8, Old Testament.**

**Nome** - *Kamitic:* a city, home district.

**North Atl-anta** - North America.

**Oracle** - A **Spiritual Science** developed to provide insight into the inner workings of a situation, decision or occurrence. True oracles are never fortune telling devices. They provide a means of examining the underlying spiritual structure of a situation, similar to a computer program that analyzes stock market trends. Card games, dice and other games of chance of today are based upon oracles developed by **Kushite** and **Anu** people thousands of years ago.

**Oxhide** - Various metals cast into the easy to carry shape of an oxen's hide.

**Pa** - *Kushite:* father.

**Pan-Kau-Rau-Shen** - *Kamitic:* meaning "defeating enemies with the force of Ra." A **Kushite** martial art. A form of it survives in modern day Greece and is called Pankration.

**Petra** - Ancient name of a city in northwest Arabia.

**Petrans** - The people of **Petra**, including **Kushites (Tamana** settlers) and **Shashu**.

**People of The Sea** - An ancient group led by Germanic people who migrated from **Basileia** in northern Europe to the Mediterranean area. Renowned sailors, pirates and warriors, this coalition initiated the **Great World War**, probably over trade issues, circa 1200 BC.

**Ra** - *Kamitic:* The deity representing the Great Power, the creative life force emanating from the creator **Amen**. Misinterpreted as the "sun god" because the *Kamitians* often used the sun as **Ra's** symbol (see **Aten**). Through their **Spiritual Sciences**, the *Kamites* discovered that all life is sustained by interaction with the energy of the sun, which is a modern day scientific fact.

**Ra Mesh III** - Proper name for Ramesses III, the great king who defeated the **People of the Sea**. **Ra,** meaning the great power behind all life, and **Mesh**, meaning born of, or son of. Literal translation: Son of the Great Power III.

**Rau** - *Kamitic:* The life force, *serpent fire*, **chi** to the Chinese.

**Saba** - Ancient land in South Arabia ruled over by a line of legendary **Kushite** queens, such as the Queen of Sheba (Saba) of the **Old Testament**.

**Sabaeans** - The people of **Saba**, who were **Shashu** and **Kushau** migrants from **Tamana**.

**Sebau** - *Kamitic:* The assistants of **Set**; raging emotions, demons.

**Sebek** - *Kamitic:* Deity governing verbal communication, logic and craftiness.

**Seker** - (Seck-eer) - *Kamitic:* Deity governing death, rebirth and the power of the hidden natural order.

**Sekmet** - *Kamitic:* Deity of war and the destruction of negative influences.

**Serpent Fire** - One **Spiritual Science** was the knowledge and manipulation of the human life force, called the **serpent fire** among the **Kushites**. A metaphor for awakened life energy arching through the human body, gurus and martial artists today say this knowledge can work miracles.

**Set** - *Kamitic:* Also called "Setesh"- the principle of evil and disorder, similar to the Christian Devil.

**Shang** - Ancient group of **Kushites** and Classical Mongoloids (brown skinned Orientals similar to Indonesians) who ruled parts of ancient China from 1500 to 1000 BC. The **Kushites** were **Tamana** migrants, who settled in areas called **K'un Lun**.

**Shashu** - (Shay-shoo) - *Kamitic:* Arabic or Semitic peoples. Originally **Tamahu** migrants who came down from Eurasia around 2000 BC, **Shashu** peoples developed by interbreeding with **Kushites** and adopting their cultures.

**Shekem ur Shekem** - (Sheck-um-err-scheck-um) -*Kamitic:* Means Power Great Power. This was the common designation of *Kamitic* kings, not pharaoh.

**Shemsu - *Kamitic:*** Follower, devotee.

**Sheps** - *Kamitic:* Honored ancestor. One of the **Kushite Spiritual Sciences** is **Ancestor Communication**, misnamed ancestor worship. A person who became exalted in life would be deemed worthy of special communication efforts by the living after thier death.

**Shepsu** - *Kamitic:* Plural- the honored ancestors.

**Sky-boat** - *Kamitic*: In ancient *Kamit* there was a legendary tradition of flying vehicles. They were mentioned in magical tales like "The Stories of Setne Khamwas" and depicted and discussed upon the temple walls of Edfu. It was at Edfu, the traditions say, that the **Neter Heru** established a "foundry of divine iron" and maintained a flying vehicle used in the war with **Set**. Illustrations of this flying vehicle can still be seen on the Edfu temple today.

**Sofik Aabut -** (So-fick  Aah-boot) - *Kamitic:* The female deity of learning. Later called Sophia by the Greeks: Philo (Greek for "love") + Sophia = philosophy.

**South Atl-anta** - South America.

**Spiritual Sciences** - The **Kushite/Anu** technologies of spiritual upliftment, social ordering and natural resource manipulation. These included oracle systems, spirit possession/trance, natural healing, meditative techniques, **Kula Yoga**, the manipulation of earthly and human energies (pyramids, acupuncture) and the coercion of the laws of nature through heightened spirituality combined with hidden knowledge (magic). The **Kushau** and **Anu** shared in a civilization complex that recent anthropology indicates stretches back 100,000 years, originating near the **Mountains of the Moon**. During this time they developed their **Spiritual Sciences**.

**Tamahu** - People of European descent. (*Kamitic:* **Tama** means people,

**hu** means white) Various **Tamahu** peoples dwelled near the Mediterranean Sea, living in relative peace with their **Kushite** neighbors until the **Great World War** circa 1200 BC. At this time nearly all of these civilizations were destroyed by a coalition led by northern **Tamahu** called the **People of the Sea.**

**Tamana** - Ancient region of trading cities and countries located in what is now the Sahara Desert. (*Kamitic:* **Tama** - people, **na** - to go, to travel) The children of **Tamana** are the **Kushau** or **Kushites**, linked by similar languages, spirituality, technology and race. Tremendous engineering feats like stone tunnels hundreds of miles long beneath the north African sands, giant megaliths in Morocco and other north African countries, and well known **Kamitian** and **Kushite** monuments attest to the level of civilization attained by these people. When the Sahara, (which is larger than the land mass of the continental United States), dried up, the people of **Tamana** migrated, giving birth to the major civilizations of the ancient world.

**Ta Neter** - *Kamitic:* Meaning "Land of God." Ancient birthplace of **Kushite** people near the **Mountains of The Moon.**

**Taut** - *Kamitic* - The spiritual world. The place of residence for the dead and the source of all non-material life. In the lower regions of the **Taut** dwell low spiritual forces, in the higher regions dwell the purer.

**Tehuti** - (tey-hoo-tee) *Kamitic:* Deity of wisdom.

**Tem** - *Kamitic:* Bad, negative.

**Tenehu** - Ancient Libyans. These people lived in the region just west of *Kamit*, and were the source of considerable trouble due to their attempts to invade **Kamitic** territory. They formed a partnership with the **People of the Sea** against *Kamit*. The **Tenehu** were a mixed people, with **Tamahu, Shashu** and **Kushites** in the population.

**Trojan War** - The legendary war documented in Greek mythology by Homer in **"The Iliad"** and **"The Odyssey"** and by Arctinus of Miletus in **"The Ethiopis,"** which starred **Memnon**.

**Troy** - An ancient trading city located in modern day Turkey. In Greek mythology it was the home of Priam, whose brother Tithonos was the Pa of the Elder **Memnon**, who came to **Troy's** assistance. In real history **Troy** was a trading center of the ancient world, similar to modern day Hong Kong, where **Kushites, Tamahu** and others lived in peace together. In the mythology the city fell to forces led by Achilles and Agamemnon, whom many historians now believe were a **People of the Sea** coalition.

**Tu** -(too) - *Kamitic:* Good, positive.

**Uachet** - (Oo-aa-chet) - *Kamitic:* The hot electromagnetic force of the Earth, responsible for some psychic phenomena.

**Universal Principles** - The Ancient Kushites' pattern of behavior inspired awe among the ancient Greeks, who called them "Blameless Ethiopians" and referred to them as "the most favored of the gods." This was due to a code of spirituality and ethics that the Kushites propagated to the world. Here is that list, compiled from the traditions of the Kushites themselves and what witnesses such as the Greeks said about them.

## UNIVERSAL PRINCIPLES

1. COVET NO LAND OR RICHES THAT THE SUPREME BEING DOES NOT NATURALLY GRANT YOU.

2. RESPECT THE OPPOSITE SEX AS YOUR EQUAL AND YOUR COMPLIMENT.

3. GIVE UNTO THE WORLD WHAT YOU WOULD HAVE THE WORLD GIVE UNTO YOU.

4. ALWAYS SEEK BALANCE IN ALL THINGS, FOR ONLY IN HARMONY CAN THERE BE GROWTH.

5. HONOR YOUR ANCESTORS, ESPECIALLY THOSE WHO SOUGHT JUSTICE AND BALANCE IN THEIR TIME UPON THE EARTH.

6. SEEK NOT SIMPLY TO DO GOOD, BUT ENCOURAGE OTHERS TO DO GOOD AS WELL.

7. ALWAYS SEEK HIGHER WISDOM IN ALL OF LIFE'S ENDEAVORS.

8. HONOR AND SAFEGUARD THE CHILDREN, WHO HAVE COME TO FORGE THE FUTURE OF THE WORLD.

9. SEEK TO BE PART OF A BROTHERHOOD, SISTERHOOD OR GROUP, FOR WE ACCOMPLISH MORE TOGETHER THAN APART.

10. HAVE NO TOLERANCE FOR EVIL AND INJUSTICE, SO THAT YOU WILL FOREVER BE KNOWN AS BLAMELESS.

**Upper Kamit** - Southern *Kamit.*

**Uraeus** - (you-ray-us) - *Kamitic* - **Uachet** and **Nekhebet** harnessed for psychic attack or protection, represented and focused by the rearing snake worn on the brows of *Kamitic* royalty and deities. The *Kamitic* texts describe the power of the Uraeus as laser-like and instantly fatal.

**Urim and Thummim** - Oracle used by the ancient Hebrews (**Habiru**) as mentioned in the **Old Testament**. (1 Samuel 28:6).

**Western Kushites** - Black people with broader noses, wider lips and kinky hair - stereotypical African.

**Xiu** - (shee-oo) - **Tamana** migrants who left the drying Sahara, settling in ancient China, Iran and Meso-America. The **Xiu** were dominated by **Western Kushites**, linguistically and culturally related to the Manding, a people living today in West Africa. In Iran they built "ziggurats" and left many artifacts, while in Mexico they built pyramids and carved huge stone portraits.

The native Americans Maya called them **"Tul Tul Xiu"** and remember them as teachers. (Tul Tul in Manding means "Supporters or teachers of the High Order.") Today they are called the Olmecs, mother civilization of the Americas and referred to as the "Shi Dynasty" by Chinese anthropologists.

In China they left African physical remains and dozens of pyramids(many still standing) in that country's Shensi province. While artifacts and statues from settlements in Mexico indicate that the **Xiu** had **Kushites** and Orientals among the population, hinting at an empire, or at least trade relations, that may have stretched from China to the Americas.

The **Memnon** tradition and the **Xiu**:

1. The **Xiu** were renowned for their architectural wonders and statues wherever they settled; the legendary character **Memnon** has been affiliated with architectural marvels and statuary world-wide.

2. The **Xiu** had major settlements in both the far east and the far west; the Greeks said **Memnon** lead **Kushites** to **Troy** from the far east and

## SHADES OF MEMNON II

far west.

3. The **Xiu** had settlements upon islands, (like Laventa in Mexico); the legends of **Memnon** say he came from islands called **Hesperides**, located on the far western shores of the Atlantic ocean.

These things strengthen the contention that the **Memnon** tradition originated from the activities of the mighty **Xiu** and lives on to this day due to the awe that the Greeks had for the architecture and statues of the **Xiu's** mighty cousins, the *Kamits*.

# SELECT BIBLIOGRAPHY

AMEN, RA UN NEFER. METU NETER VOLUME 1. KHAMIT CORP. 1990

AMEN, RA UN NEFER. METU NETER VOLUME 2. KHAMIT CORP. 1994

AMEN, RA UN NEFER. AN AFROCENTRIC GUIDE TO A SPIRITUAL UNION. KHAMIT CORP. 1992.

APOLLODORUS. THE LIBRARY OF GREEK MYTHOLOGY. OXFORD, 1997.

BAILEY, JIM. THE GOD KINGS AND THE TITANS. ST. MARTIN'S PRESS, 1974.

BAILEY, JIM. SAILING TO PARADISE: THE DISCOVERY OF THE AMERICAS BY 7000 BC SIMON & SHUSTER, 1994

BEKERIE, AYELE. ETHIOPIC: AN AFRICAN WRITING SYSTEM. THE RED SEA PRESS, INC., 1997.

BEN-JOCHANNAN, YOSEF A.A. AFRICAN ORIGIN OF THE MAJOR WESTERN RELIGIONS. BLACK CLASSIC PRESS, 1991.

BERNAL, MARTIN. BLACK ATHENA. VOLUME I. RUTGERS UNIVERSITY PRESS, 1987.

BERNAL, MARTIN. BLACK ATHENA VOLUME II. RUTGERS UNIVERSITY PRESS, 1991.

BRAGHINE, ALEXANDER. THE SHADOW OF ATLANTIS. ADVENTURES UNLIMITED PRESS, 1997.

BUDGE, E.A. WALLIS. THE GODS OF THE EGYPTIANS: OR STUDIES IN EGYPTIAN MYTHOLOGY. VOL. 1. DOVER PUBLICATIONS INC., 1969.

BUDGE, E.A. WALLIS. AN EGYPTIAN HIEROGLYPHIC DICTIONARY. DOVER PUBLICATIONS INC. 1978.

CHIA, MANTAK. TAOIST SECRETS OF LOVE: CULTIVATING MALE SEXUAL ENERGY. HEALING TAO BOOKS, 1986.

CHIA, MANTAK & MANEEWAN CHIA. HEALING LOVE THROUGH THE TAO: CULTIVATING FEMALE SEXUAL ENERGY. HEALING TAO BOOKS, 1986.

DAVIES, MALCOLM. THE EPIC CYCLE. BRISTOL CLASSICAL PRESS, 1989.

DIOP, CHEIKH ANTA. THE AFRICAN ORIGIN CIVILIZATION. LAWRENCE HILL BOOKS, 1974.

DIOP, CHEIKH ANTA. CIVILIZATION OR BARBARISM. LAWRENCE HILL BOOKS, 1991.

GANTZ, TIMOTHY. EARLY GREEK MYTHS. JOHN HOPKINS UNIVERSITY PRESS, 1993.

GRAVES, ROBERT. THE GREEK MYTHS. PENGUIN BOOKS, 1990.

HANSBERRY, WILLIAM LEO. AFRICA&AFRICANS AS SEEN BY CLASSICAL WRITERS. HOWARD UNIVERSITY PRESS, 1977.

HERODOTUS. THE HISTORIES. PENGUIN CLASSICS TRANSLATION, 1972.

HIGGINS, GODFREY. ANACALYPSIS. 1936. REPRINTED BY A&B BOOK PUBLISHERS, 1992.

KITCHENS, K.A. PHARAOH TRIUMPHANT: THE LIFE AND TIMES OF RAMESSES II. BENBEN PUBLICATIONS, 1982.

KARENGA, MAULANA & JACOB CURRUTHERS. KEMET AND THE AFRICAN WORLDVIEW. UNIVERSITY OF SANKORE PRESS, 1986.

MASSEY, GERALD. A BOOK OF THE BEGINNINGS. A&B BOOKS PUBLISHERS, 1994.

NAGY, GREGORY. THE BEST OF THE ACHAEANS: CONCEPTS OF THE HERO IN ARCHAIC GREEK POETRY. THE JOHN HOPKINS UNIVERSITY PRESS, 1979.

OSTRANDER, SHEILA AND LYNN SCHROEDER. PSYCHIC DISCOVERIES. MARLOWE & COMPANY, 1997.

RASHIDI, RUNOKO. AFRICAN PRESENCE IN EARLY ASIA. JOURNAL OF AFRICAN CIVILIZATIONS LTD., INC, 1995.

REDFORD, DONALD B. EGYPT, CANAAN AND ISRAEL IN ANCIENT TIMES. PRINCETON UNIVERSITY PRESS, 1992.

SAGGS, H.W. F. CIVILIZATION BEFORE GREECE AND ROME. YALE UNIVERSITY PRESS, 1989.

# SHADES OF MEMNON II

SARNO, LOUIS. SONG FROM THE FOREST: MY LIFE AMONG THE BA-BENJELLE' PYGMIES. HOUGHTON MIFFLIN, 1993.

SERTIMA, IVAN VAN. AFRICAN PRESENCE IN EARLY AMERICA. JOURNAL OF AFRICAN CIVILIZATIONS LTD., INC. 1992.

SERTIMA, IVAN VAN. EGYPT: CHILD OF AFRICA. JOURNAL OF AFRICAN CIVILIZATIONS LTD., INC. 1994.

SNOWDEN, FRANK M. JR. BLACKS IN ANTIQUITY. HARVARD UNIVERSITY PRESS, 1970.

TEDLOCK, DENNIS. POPUL VUH: THE MAYAN BOOK OF THE DAWN OF LIFE AND THE GLORIES OF GODS AND KINGS. SIMON & SCHUSTER, 1985.

WICKER, F.D.P. EGYPT AND THE MOUNTAINS OF THE MOON. MERLIN BOOKS, 1990.

WINTERS, CLYDE A. LES FONDATEURS DE LA GREECE VENAIENT D' AFRIQUE EN PASSANT PAR LA CRETE. AFRIQUE HISTOIRE 8, PG 13-18. 1983.

WINTERS, CLYDE A. BLACKS IN EUROPE BEFORE THE EUROPEANS. RETURN TO THE SOURCE, 3, PG 26-33. 1984

WINTERS, CLYDE A. THE PROTO-CULTURE OF THE DRAVIDIANS, MANDING AND SUMERIANS. TAMIL CIVILIZATION, 3, PG 1-9. 1985

WINTERS, CLYDE A. TAMIL, SUMERIAN, MANDING AND THE GENETIC MODEL. INTERNATIONAL JOURNAL OF DRAVIDIAN LINGUISTICS, 18 PG 98-127. 1989.

WINTERS, CLYDE A. THE PROTO-SAHARA. IN THE DRAVIDIAN ENCYCLOPEDIA(VOL. 1 PG 553-556. TRIVANDRUM, INDIA: INTERNATIONAL SCHOOL OF DRAVIDIAN LINGUISTICS. 1991.

*Clyde Ahmed Winters, Brother G and Ra Un Nefer Amen*

*For more information about the history and scholarship of Memnon go to*

WWW.MEMNONLEGEND.COM

SHADES OF MEMNON II

# *MEMNON MUSIC!*

brother___g
@hotmail.com

Printed in the United States
26158LVS00004B/311